MY NAME IS MUSA

PATRICIA RANTISI

Published in 2012 by FeedARead.com Publishing –
Arts Council funded

To Susan and Hilary

PROLOGUE

The piece of paper was slightly scrumpled but the writing was clear. It was in Arabic, written with a black biro pen, '*Ismee Musa.*' That scrappy little note, which we didn't understand the meaning of, would come to change our lives.

PART ONE

ROSA

CHAPTER ONE

1989

It was the tone of Rebecca's letters that finally persuaded me. I had never imagined going to Israel but Rebecca had been persistent. 'You must come…this is a new vibrant country…this is my home now…you'll love it…Why not come during David's Easter holiday, then we can celebrate Passover together…'

David wanted to go to Italy for a holiday like we did for our honeymoon, but I finally won him over. "Darling you'll love visiting all those ancient sites. Israel is full of antiquities."

"But staying with your friend, will we have a chance to go places?"

"Of course we will, silly. You'll enjoy it."

"OK. I'll leave you to do the booking," he sighed, giving me a desultory kiss before leaving for work.

Two months later we arrived in Tel Aviv. Rebecca was waving frantically, pushing her way though a swarm of humanity, shoving, sweating, swearing, shouting, the likes of which I had never seen. The babble of languages seemed to be mostly Russian, with a mixture of Hebrew which I knew a little of.

I hardly recognised Rebecca. She looked different, but then I realised it had been more than ten years. She kissed me on both cheeks, gave David a welcome handshake, then linked arms with me.

"Amos is waiting in the car… Rosa, you don't look a day older!"

I laughed. "You look well Rebecca. It's been a long time."

She took my small cabin bag and guided me through a group of robust Russian matrons. "Rosa, how great is that, all these Russian immigrants escaping from persecution. What a wonderful country this is!"

"Gosh!"

"Phew," David exclaimed, taking off his jacket and wiping his brow. He was weaving his way through the crowd trying to follow us with the luggage. There was a man running towards us looking very much like a professor with his broad receding forehead.

"That's Amos. I told him to wait in the car." Rebecca was obviously put out by the appearance of her husband. Amos looked flustered but smiled and shook hands with us cordially then turned to his wife. "The police wouldn't let me sit in the car. I drove round and round but finally had to go to the car park. We'll have to walk quite a way."

"That's OK," said David.

Finally our bags safely in the boot, Amos drove us out of the airport on to the main highway, bypassing Jerusalem and on to what looked like a brand new road heading north. When we arrived at the community it was gated and guarded with armed soldiers but Amos was waved through with a friendly smile. It was then that I realised our friends were living on an exclusive Jewish settlement.

They gave us a very warm welcome. The house on a hill top was brand new, bungalow style with an open plan reception area and all the latest kitchen equipment. Rebecca had tastefully decorated the walls in cream with aquamarine floor tiles and striped rugs in various shades of blue and green, giving a peaceful atmosphere. And we were certainly enamoured with the beautiful countryside, wide sweeping hills covered in the green of spring with wild flowers growing unhindered, tiny pink wild cyclamens, red anemones, yellow narcissi and miniature bright-eyed pimpernels. We could see from the windows that at the foot of the hill there was a brook, now flowing swiftly and clearly over the rock bed, after all the winter rain.

What an astonishing morning it would turn out to be.

"We're just going for a little walk," David had said to Rebecca early that morning.

"Where?"

"Just down the hill." David pointed through the window.

"What outside our community? You'd better take a gun," she warned, as she reached up to take the rifle which was hanging on a hook by the front door.

"No way. A gun? Whatever for?"

"We never go anywhere without a weapon," Rebecca said.

"You mean we can't go for a little country walk without a gun? The goats aren't going to attack us are they?" David tittered and shrugged his shoulders.

"What nonsense. I'm certainly not going to carry a rifle and I wouldn't know how to use one if I did."

David sounded so indignant and I watched his eyebrows screw up and feared he would get angry, but I decided not to say anything. I just stood there debating with myself whether I should take a jacket but figured it would be warm enough.

"If you decide to come and live in Israel, you will have to learn how to use one."

"You must be joking! How can you live surrounded by guards and barbed -wire fences? And carrying arms, too! Aren't you living in fear all the time? I said. "Your letters were so full of wonderful views; you never mentioned guns, for goodness sake."

I can see Rebecca now. She stood proudly, her shoulders pushed back, her long auburn hair tied loosely over one shoulder, her face serious, unsmiling. She was waving her arms.

"Don't you understand? God gave us this land. It's all written in the Scriptures. We have to live here to stake our claim to it. This is Judea, part of Israel, as God promised us thousands of years ago and one day it will all be ours." She sighed, exasperated, giving her arms a broad sweep which either meant that she was encompassing the whole world or that she was dismissing any responsibility for the safety of her friends. We weren't sure which.

"Anyway, go for your little walk, but don't wander too far away. We will talk more about this later."

"Don't worry, we won't go far," I said, as we walked out of the door feeling small like children who had just been told off.

As we left the gate of the settlement we felt the eyes of Israeli guards watching us.

I quivered with fear realising their guns were trained on us as we took the steep descent into the valley. David slipped his arm around my waist tight against his broad chest. It was just a dirt path so we had to be careful to avoid stones and goat droppings.

"What do those soldiers think they are protecting us from?" I remarked to David who seemed to be more irritated then fearful.

"Goodness knows!" he said. My mind and possibly David's too, was so occupied with many thoughts about the life of our hosts, that we were almost oblivious to the calmness of the hillside.

"Fancy having a rifle hanging by your front door."

"Absolutely ridiculous," agreed David.

Amos and Rebecca had chosen to live here and now were trying to persuade us to leave England to come and join them. Apart from a couple of Arab children playing, everything was so peaceful. We had come to Israel a little apprehensive after watching the violence on television, yet wanting to know if the rosy picture painted by Rebecca was all true.

She had described to us the delightful villas with beautiful furnishings, living in friendly communities with all social and medical benefits...and above all, so cheap, because of government subsidies. It was true that we were struggling to pay the high mortgage for a house near London and we were considering moving but we hadn't even imagined immigrating to Israel. I remember some of my Jewish cousins in London talking about Israel as if it was their own country even though they had never been there! In fact, I remember as a child going with my mother to the local Jewish bakery at the time of the six-day war to find out that Mr. Abrams, the owner, had sent his son to fight with the Israelis. I was too young to understand at the time but I do remember Mum talking to Dad later, questioning why on earth would someone send their son to join a foreign army. I still go to that shop to pick up the sweet honey turnovers and bagels, my usual weekend treat and David continually teases me about my sweet tooth.

"Rosa, how can you stay so slim when you are always eating candied bread and cakes," he'd say. I'd always just laugh.

Rebecca had also stressed in her letters the benefits of a wonderful climate. Hot and dry all summer. Leaving the cold and damp of England was certainly something tempting to think about. We had already spent a couple of days in the settlement and the weather was beautiful. It seemed a fairly tight-knit community though it was a weird feeling that all the residents were immigrants from different parts of the world and each of them had brought their own bit of culture with them. All had some Jewish background and all had to learn Hebrew. To us, fresh from the freedom of England, we sometimes felt nervous as if we were being watched suspiciously.

"Hardly a holiday when you can't relax," I had remarked to David.

 He gripped my arm as I stumbled slightly over a stone. We found a large boulder covered in moss. David took off his jacket and spread it out on the rock. As we sat down, he said, "Aye, you know I like Amos. He's really rather nice but your friend Rebecca! A bit fanatical, isn't she? Personally, I can't wait to go into Israel proper and visit all the sites that we talked about." He reached for his jacket pocket and brought out a little guide booklet, 'Places To Visit In Israel'. We looked at the pictures together but my mind was on other things. I was trying to remember Rebecca when she was younger.

I laughed. "Rebecca was never this religious at school. I can remember her often getting into trouble. She thought she was being smart and wanted to attract a boy called Josh, who had his eyes on someone else. I remember she fought with this other girl, who wasn't even that pretty! Isn't it silly what you get up to at school? She was clever though. She used to help me with my homework and we had some fun times together. She never talked about religion though I do remember her telling me that her grandfather was a Rabbi. Whatever has changed her, I can't imagine!"

"I'm just glad you're not like her!" David hugged me then pulled me up, grabbed his jacket and we continued our walk.

In the valley was a brook, happily bubbling over the stones with the water that looked clear enough to drink. I spied a small basket, lodged between two rocks.

"Look, David, look over there!"

"What on earth?"

"Oh my God! No, it can't be."

We approached the spot carefully and gazed into the basket. There, wrapped in a white knitted shawl was a new-born baby. I looked at David to see his reaction and he seemed to be as dumbstruck as me. His mouth was hanging open but I had clamped my hand over mine to stop myself from screaming. It was so unexpected that I found my heart pounding. Pinned to the shawl was a paper note, in a foreign language, so we couldn't read it. The paper was so flimsy that had there been a breeze it would have been torn away, but the weather was so calm and the atmosphere so peaceful. Just warm sunshine, which by noon we knew would be scorching heat.

"What shall we do? Shall I pick it up?" I couldn't wait to touch this tiny human being. "Rosa, love, leave it. We've been told never to touch anything strange."

"Don't be silly. No-one is going to plant a bomb under a live baby."

Just then the baby stirred and started to cry. It was as if to prove to us that it was alive. It was probably our shadow that had changed the baby's sense of security.

"Well, what are we going to do?" We looked at each other, pausing to work out the options.

"If we leave it, the poor thing might die, if we take it to the Palestinians in the village, the poor mother might die. You know how it is with them. Any mother discovered with an illegitimate baby could be killed by her family. You've heard of honour killings haven't you? But then again, if we take it to the settlement, the Arabs might come after us for stealing a baby..." David was trying to sound logical yet desperately looking for a nearby face that could be identified as the mother.

I picked the infant up, patting it against my shoulder to pacify it. David looked at me and I sensed that unmistakable look of pity. We were so different in our emotions. He was always more cautious and more practical. I remembered the time when we had run over a stray kitten. David stopped the car and calmly lifted the poor creature on to the grass verge, while I was almost hysterical telling him we should take it to the vet. "It's going to die anyway," he had said.

But here was a human baby and in this instance I think he was irritated and embarrassed by my obvious impetuousness.

"It's a boy and obviously new-born. We must take him home. Rebecca and Amos will know what to do," I said.

Our eyes scanned all around but all we could see was some domestic activity in the village. We were near enough to see women, wearing headscarves and long gowns that looked like housecoats, hanging out laundry or refuelling the bread ovens with firewood. A small dog was jumping up at one of the women, while she pushed it down. There were a couple of young boys tending the goats, hitting their rumps with little twigs and laughing. They must have been only four or five years old. We could see girls sweeping with yard brooms made out of sticks tied together and small children running around but we were not near enough to hear their chatter. Amos had told us that rickety vans, serving as mini-buses come at early dawn to take the men folk to work and the children to school in the nearby town. No one was looking in our direction. We hung around for what seemed like a long time, but there were no bushes for anyone to hide and only a few olive trees. Surely someone must be watching nearby to see if anyone would pick up the baby, I thought. I held the baby while David searched all the area but we were afraid to go right into the village. Eventually, I put the baby back down in the basket but he started to howl. I held him against my shoulder, patting him until he calmed down. David grabbed the basket.

"Let's go," I said. "My top feels damp. I think he just peed!"

We trudged slowly up the hill towards the settlement.

"Why do they always build settlements at the top of steep hills?" David grumbled. I worried slightly about the reactions awaiting us. We were stopped at the gate by a guard, who asked lots of questions like: Where have we been? Did we know that it was not advisable to wander in a Palestinian village? Why were we not carrying a gun?

We told him that we were guests of Amos visiting from London.

He pretended to look angry, but seeing the baby, I noticed a slight turn up of his mouth as if he wanted to smile. "And fancy taking a baby into that hostile environment," he said, waving the gun away from us and pressing the button to open the gate.

Amos and Rebecca were indeed astonished.

"What if some of the village men attack us? Perhaps this is all a trick to enter the settlement, look for the baby and then plant bombs," Rebecca's reaction was sceptical to say the least.

David and I gave each other looks, raising our eyebrows and taking deep breaths but not saying anything. Amos looked at his wife. "Well, it looks like we have a new baby on our hands. Look darling, how sweet he is, those dark brown eyes and tiny wee face. Some poor girl must have been desperate. Let's have a look at the note, *'Ismee Musa'*. That's Arabic and it means 'My name is Musa', which in English is Moses. You found him by the brook in this old basket?" I nodded.

"How about that! It's like the story in the Bible. Moses in the bulrushes. He became our leader, leading the Hebrews out of Egypt into the Promised Land." Rebecca spoke in her high pitched, giggly kind of voice, starting to show signs of excitement yet still too nervous to come near. She sniffed the air.

"Yes, I know, he pongs. He needs changing!" I said, challenging Rebecca to hold him. She backed away and instead went to fetch her English Scriptures to read us the story of Moses. She seemed more concerned to educate us in the Bible than the welfare of our little newcomer. David and I had heard about these old stories from school days but probably I could remember the details more than him. Rebecca quickly found the chapter which quite astonished me. She must know her Bible well, I thought.

'The King's daughter came down to the river to bathe...suddenly she noticed the basket in the tall grass...she opened it and saw a baby boy. He was crying and she felt sorry for him. 'This is one of the Hebrew babies', she said. Then his sister asked her, 'Shall I go and call a Hebrew woman to nurse him?' ... so the girl went and brought the baby's own mother....the king's daughter adopted him and said, I pulled him out of the water and so I name him Moses'.

"But this is not a Hebrew baby, he's an Arab," her husband reminded her.

"Yes, he must be if the note is in Arabic," I said. "Is there somewhere where we can buy some clean clothes? The poor thing's got nothing on except a soiled nappy and this shawl. My top's getting wet."

Rebecca hurriedly spread some newspaper on the couch and I laid the baby down. I examined the shawl, showing it to Rebecca but she did not show much interest.

"You know, Rebecca, this shawl is hand knitted which makes me think that he had a caring mother or grandmother. What on earth happened to make someone abandon him?"

"Typical Arabs," she replied.

"I'll take you to the shop to buy some baby formula and other things, Rosa. Perhaps later on David and I can make enquiries in the village." I was glad for Amos's down to earth attitude, so I put the baby back in the basket and told David to keep his eye on him. "We won't be long." I saw David's worried face as we left. "What if…"

I ignored him and went with Amos. The general store was just around the corner. A young girl with a round happy face scrubbed clean of any make-up, and curly blond hair, served us.

"Shalom, Amos," she greeted us, in English but with a broad American accent.

"Shalom, Rach. We have some friends staying with us from the UK. They have a baby and have run out of Pampers and baby milk. We need a bottle too and if you have any baby clothes?"

"O, Hi... er?

"Rosa," I offered my hand.

"Glad to meet you, Rosa. Welcome. Is it a boy? What's his name? Hope you can encourage Rebecca to have one!" She winked at Amos, chattering all the time as I picked up the items we needed, without, thankfully, giving us time to answer her questions as to the baby's name or the circumstances. As we left the shop, Amos whispered to me, explaining that he didn't dare tell the truth about the baby or he would have had to deal with the police.

"I've got enough to think about."

I think he was talking to himself so I did not make any comment.

It was later that day just before sunset that David and Amos walked down the hill armed only with the scrappy piece of paper. I had cleaned up the baby, clothed him and fed him with the formula milk as I cradled him in my arms. He guzzled it down so fast he was almost out of breath and the milk was dripping on my arm. Then I winded him, patting him on the back, until he fell asleep, grabbing my hand with his little finger. I wanted to cry and laugh at the same time. I'm falling in love with this baby! How can anyone think that new-born babies are ugly, even with the wrinkles?

The baby slept peacefully at first while I waited for David and Amos to return. The minutes ticked by and I could see that Rebecca was getting agitated.

"They're a long time," she said. "I hope they're safe. You never know these days." She took up a book and pretended to read but I sensed that she didn't know what else to say. Occasionally she would chat about how happy she was but I wondered if she was trying to convince herself as well as me. She took no interest in the baby.

When the men finally appeared they looked tired and frustrated. "Well?" I said, rocking the baby back and forth trying to stop him crying.

"Wow, that was quite an adventure but without any resolution." David wiped his brow and I noticed that his palms were sweaty. "Darling you'll have the baby all night by the looks of things. Perhaps tomorrow we will get it sorted."

Apparently their knocks on doors brought alarm to some of the villagers but when the people realised they were unarmed, they welcomed them into their little stone houses. However, their enquiries were met with blank stares. Nobody had been near the brook that morning and had not seen or heard of a basket with a baby. Amos was assured that they were telling the truth because of their obvious astonishment and embarrassment.

"I'll tell you what though. Those Palestinian women are so clever. At the door of one home we saw a young woman sitting on a stool doing some needlework. She stood up in surprise as we approached. She had a pretty face, but her head was completely covered with the scarf like most Muslim girls wear …

"They call it hijab, the headscarf," interrupted Amos. David continued: "…and she was wearing a long grey gown to her ankles. Amos tried to explain our mission, showing her the little note from the shawl but she didn't understand."

I was trying to listen to David but it was difficult with a crying baby though I could see how entranced he was with the beautiful handwork and embroidery that he was describing to me. As an art teacher I know how much he appreciates such things. He told me that he asked the girl if he could see some of her embroidery and then her brother invited them in. He described to me how poor they were and he praised them for the handwork. "It was good that Amos knew some Arabic. He translated for me. The girl's eyes lit up but her mother, I think, wanted to take advantage of our money."

"But what about the baby? Did they seem to know anything?" David had become sidetracked, I realised.

"No they didn't know anything. The scrap of paper meant nothing at all. That was obvious." I didn't know what to think.

"I suggest that you and David return to the village in the morning with the baby," said Amos offering us a drink. "Red or white?" We both indicated the red wine.

Amos continued: "You know, Rosa, the mother of this girl had a sorry story. She said that her husband is an invalid and cannot work, her two sons are unemployed and the only income they have is from their needlework. She said her daughter, Fadwa, by name, had been married but had the misfortune to produce two dead babies, so her husband divorced her. Poor people, I felt sorry for them." He poured us some wine as Rebecca called out that dinner was served.

Baby Musa (I was beginning to call him by his name) had finally dozed off, so we sat at the table while Amos continued to recount their adventure telling us of how the Palestinian family insisted on serving them Arabic coffee in the little mini cups. When they were leaving, the rickety bus arrived from town with all the men folk and one young boy shouted at them menacingly, throwing stones. It was Fadwa that stopped him.

"You see I told you they were dangerous. And all this because you wanted to go for your little walk!"

Rebecca had to have the last word but Amos rebuked her under his breath.

CHAPTER TWO

I was awake most of the night. First it was the sound of gunfire, though admittedly in the distance, then it was the baby crying. I had roused myself several times to feed and change Musa, but he was very unsettled. I kept worrying what the morning would bring.

We had been trying for three years to have a baby, but I hadn't become pregnant and I hadn't plucked up the courage to go and see a doctor. David didn't seem too bothered and I couldn't face going through the trauma of special fertility tests and investigations. Rebecca was childless too, and had been married before us, but I didn't like to ask questions and she never enquired about us. I know many couples these days delay having children until they are more settled in their careers, but I was really desperate to have a baby. Although, whenever I went shopping in the supermarket, I met many mothers, younger than I, who looked tired and harassed by noisy toddlers, with runny noses and grubby hands. Poor Mums, I used to think. I don't think I could stand that. I hate messy children!

Yet, here I am with a baby in my arms, loving him but knowing he is not mine, and wishing he was! Even with his drippy nose and dirty nappies! But I had to keep reminding myself that my care of Musa was only temporary. Soon, the baby would be looked after by his own community, and hopefully, by his own family, wouldn't he? Yet the more I cuddled him and soothed him with my small talk, the more I began to feel stirrings of love and an inner joy that I had never known before. Is this the 'motherly instinct' that people talk about? He was such a helpless yet adorable little fellow. But every time I put him down in the basket he would start crying again. I had 'borrowed' one of Rebecca's small cushions to put in the basket to make him more comfortable. Did he have stomach ache? Did the formula not suit him? Did he sense that his mother had abandoned him? I tried to imagine what it must have been like for her. A thousand questions hit me. Did her family not realise she was pregnant? Did her father kill her and bring the baby to the brook? I had heard of 'honour killings'. How could she have delivered the baby by herself?

I picked Musa up once again, put him on my shoulder, patting him gently and walking up and down the length of the small veranda, and whispering "You are such a precious little boy. Where, O where has your Mummy gone?" I started to sing quietly, remembering nursery lullabies:

'Bye baby bunting,

Daddy's gone a' hunting,

Mummy's gone a' milking,

Sister's gone a' silking,

Brother's gone to buy a skin, to wrap the baby bunting in...'

Musa smiled but I knew that new born babies do not smile. It must be wind! Sure enough he gave a loud burp which seemed to settle him for a bit, then he closed his eyes and slept.

Looking over the veranda, the village was enshrouded with a thick mist, like a cloud. My mind was in turmoil. As much as I loved the location and the beautiful country, I just couldn't accept my friend's religious ideology. How can you claim a piece of land for your own people, when it belongs to someone else, just because of a prophesy given thousands of years ago?

I remembered Rebecca at school. She had seemed to be a normal, well-adjusted schoolgirl and was always getting top marks in her exams. Much cleverer than me, I found myself saying. However I do vaguely remember that Rebecca had gone through a very emotional and traumatic time when her parents divorced, which meant that she had to divide her time between her mother and father's two homes. Did that prompt Rebecca to turn to religion or was it when she met Amos? I don't know the answer.

Later, at breakfast, when David was discussing what would be the appropriate time for us to take the baby down to the village, Amos suddenly remembered something important.

"Hang on," he said, "We can't go today. It's Friday the Muslim holiday and all the men will be at home. And tonight is the start of our Sabbath, so you can't go tomorrow either."

"You mean to say that we've got to put up with the bloody bawling of that Arab bastard two more nights," declared Rebecca, as she started to clear the table.

"Wow! Ee! What did you say?! Bloody, bawling bastard is he? You've changed your tune," said Amos. "Yesterday, you were all excited about a new baby and his name of Moses. The poor baby can't help being Arab or a bastard."

"You'd change your tune if you realised he'll probably grow up to be a terrorist."

"What! How can you say that?" I could see that David was finding it hard to curb his tongue. We had to consider that we were invited guests, otherwise I can imagine David getting extremely angry. I knew only too well that he could lose his temper easily but when it came to issues of racial injustices it was righteous anger, I considered. At least David was honest. One good thing, though, was that Amos and David were in agreement, both equally appalled at Rebecca's outburst. Amos with his dark stubbly chin, deep set eyes and receding forehead and David with his rosy, clean-shaven complexion were both standing open-mouthed.

"I'm sorry we seem to have brought you trouble bringing this baby back. But we really couldn't have left him to die by the brook, could we?" I said, trying to be calm.

"Well, it's not your problem or ours. The Arabs would have found him sooner or later, don't you think?"

"So we made a mistake?"

"No, I'm not blaming you. I'm just scared about the consequences."

"Consequences? What consequences? Are you frightened of a little baby? For goodness sake 'Becca. Get your act together!"

"Re…becca, please."

"Rebecca, then!"

"Well, we'll take him down to the village first thing on Sunday," said David. I could tell by the tone of his voice that he wanted to stop any more ill feelings between us and hopefully close the subject. I was amazed and relieved that David had managed to control himself. But baby Musa had other ideas.

He started to scream again and I went to pick him up muttering something to myself about settlers living in fear and paranoia. It was the beginning of a bitter feud between us women which made it difficult for Amos and David because they were becoming good friends and the original contact had been made through Rebecca.

"As soon as I come home from work, we'll go sightseeing in Jerusalem," said Amos, trying to dispel the storm clouds. "Meanwhile why don't you all go in the car with Rebecca to the shopping mall?"

"But what about the baby?" said Rebecca.

"I'll buy one of those baby-slings. Babies love the close contact with their mother."

"How would you know? Anyway, Rosa, you're not his mother."

"Oh, for goodness sake, nobody knows us, you can just tell anyone you meet that we are friends from England with a baby. That's what Amos told the girl at the little store next door."

"Oh did he?"

"Yes, he did."

"I can see you're already getting attached to the little brat!"

"OK, then I'll stay home with him!"

"No, I can't go shopping with David alone, people will wonder…" said Rebecca.

"If I'm going to be an embarrassment for you, you'd better go alone," said David.

In the end, none of us went out. Rebecca went into the kitchen to prepare the evening Sabbath dinner. I could hear her banging the saucepans around and chopping herbs making more sound than was necessary. I'm sure she was deliberately showing her anger and when I offered to help her she shooed me away with her hands. David took a walk around the community, and so I sat on the veranda with Musa on my lap. When Amos came home, the atmosphere in the house was not exactly what you would call cosy or friendly.

That evening, Amos and Rebecca went to pray in the local synagogue, while I stayed home with David to look after the baby. They returned in a better mood so we were able to sit at the Sabbath table without bickering. Even baby Musa slept all through.

"*Shabbat Shalom*" declared Amos at the head of the table, to which we all replied:

"*Shabbat Shalom*"

It was the traditional religious meal, which reminded me of visits to my grandmother as a child. Grandma always presided over the Friday Sabbath meal. She wore her best dress, usually a high neck with lace frills and took particular care to lay the table with a white damask tablecloth and her best china. I remember, the plates having sepia pictures of the city of London in Victorian times and I can still smell the aromas coming from her kitchen of freshly-baked egg-bread and herbs. I was her only grandchild from my mother but my Uncle had three children. We often gathered together for these special times but Grandma died when I was only ten and after that the traditions seemed to die too. Probably, for David, it was the first time he had partaken of a traditional Jewish Sabbath meal. I wonder what Grandma would have said if she had seen me marry a Gentile!

It was Rebecca who lit the candles, shielding her eyes from the light, as is the custom, while Amos, sitting at the head of the table, prayed the prayer:

'Blessed are You, O Lord God Jehovah, King of the universe, who has chosen us from all peoples, and has

raised us above all tongues, and has sanctified us with your commandments...'

As we joined hands and said Amen, I couldn't help but feel that I had become estranged from God and my birth religion. What was David thinking, I wonder. Then Amos took a small loaf of bread, sprinkled salt on it and passed it round so that we each tore a piece off. Finally Rebecca served us the roast chicken with rice, herbs and vegetables. I complemented her on her cooking.

Sunday came and by mid morning David and I were ready to take the little walk down to the village. I had bathed Musa and filled his basket with the clothes and baby milk we had bought, so David carried the basket while I held Musa close to my chest as we made our way down the hill. Although, in one way, I was reluctantly glad to be relieved of the responsibility and the tension by having the baby in the house, yet I couldn't help but feel attached to little Musa and sorry to see him go.

I hummed a little tune as I carefully picked my way along the path.

"I think he knows my voice, David."

David laughed. "Darling, you mustn't get carried away."

"But, look at his face, he loves me cooing and singing to him."

David did not answer except to say: "Careful, love, look where you're going. You don't want to drop him, do you?"

"As if I would!"

However, as soon as we arrived at Fedwa's cottage, we sensed that we were not welcome. It was a big shock. Fedwa met us at the door warning us by signs and broken English that her father had forbidden her to take in the baby. Her eyes were red and damp, so I could tell that she had been crying. "*Mamnur, mamnur*," (in Arabic 'forbidden',) she kept saying. "No babby here, back, back." Her brother appeared and was able to explain that it would not be appropriate as the neighbours would not believe the circumstances and would come to the conclusion that she had delivered a baby out of wedlock. At first we were left standing on the doorstep, then they brought out some stools in the courtyard and served us coffee.

David bought a few items of embroidery like purses and cushion covers to sell in England and then grudgingly, we trudged back up the hill with our bundles.

"Now what?" I said.

"Well, one thing's for sure," said David. "We cannot stay here."

I hugged Musa close to my heart and whispered to him words of love. "Precious little one, you are safe with me."

CHAPTER THREE

I was trembling with apprehension as I carried baby Musa back up the hill. In fact David and I hardly spoke to each other. He was concentrating holding the basket in one hand and putting his arm around my waist or gripping my elbow to steady me with the other.

Amos had already gone to his office in Jerusalem and Rebecca was out. We let ourselves in with the key they had given us and I busied myself changing and feeding the baby.

"Well, what do you suggest?" David asked me.

"We probably should call hotels in Jerusalem. But we will have to tell them that we have a baby."

It was while we were going through the lists of hotels in the telephone directory that Rebecca appeared with her bags of shopping.

"Hi there! I've been buying special food for the Passover this week. You will be staying, won't you?"

"To be honest I doubt it, Rebecca. We've caused you enough trouble already, so we're thinking of staying in

Jerusalem. We need some more days sight-seeing. Then I have to return to London. Back to work after the Easter holiday, you know." David laughed nervously.

"Easter? Why are you living in a Christian country? Oh, I forgot, David, I suppose Israel and the important feast of Passover doesn't mean the same to you as it does to Rosa and I. But it wouldn't make any difference. You know you are still welcome to live here. The important thing is for the female member of the family to be Jewish."

I couldn't help but sense the supercilious undertone of Rebecca's remarks.

At that point, there was a slight whimper from Musa. Rebecca did not miss it.

"Don't tell me! You've brought that baby back here?" She was trying to control her anger but her face had turned crimson and her eyes popping as if ready to explode. "Bloody Hell! What on earth are you thinking of?"

I butted in before she could say more. "The village family refused to take him. They were afraid. Don't

43

worry, Rebecca, we will be out of your hair as soon as we find somewhere in Jerusalem."

"Huh! You think that's easy. Every hotel and hostel will be fully booked for the Passover."

"What about East Jerusalem?" I said.

"What with the Arabs? You wouldn't want to stay there, would you? Besides there will be Christian pilgrims coming for Easter. I'm told hordes of them come from Greece and Cyprus."

"May we use your telephone to try some of these numbers?" David said.

"Go ahead!" Rebecca dismissed us with a wave of her hands. She was always expressing herself or trying to make a point with her hands. She was right. We couldn't find any place either in West or East Jerusalem. What were we to do? We decided to wait until Amos came home from work to see what he advised.

When Amos did arrive home, Rebecca rushed out to him before he had time to even lock the car. "The baby's still here," she shouted.

He came in and smiled at us, as he took off his jacket and straightened out the cushion to sit down. "So, no luck today, eh?"

"No." He made me feel guilty as if I had caused the problem.

"Don't worry. I have friends in Jerusalem who might be able to help and I've heard of an orphanage in Bethlehem. That's only a short distance by car from Jerusalem. I'm sure it won't be a problem."

"OK if you think that's the right thing to do."

He took the telephone and called his friends. "Sorry, they must have gone away but there are bound to be little hostels in the Old City of Jerusalem."

"Well, do you think we should try again in the village?" I said.

"No, no point. David and I went round all the houses and it was obvious that they knew nothing. The baby must have come from the Palestinian town of Ramallah, which is the other side of that hill over there." Amos pointed in the direction of a hill beyond the village. "They must have hoped that someone from the village would find it and take pity."

45

"I just don't understand. How could anyone leave a little helpless baby? Who could have done that? And, anyway, whoever left him must have run away very quickly. He couldn't have been there long."

"Well, what about taking him to the police or the Mayor in Ramallah?" David scratched his ear and thought he had come up with a brilliant solution.

"Sorry, that's near impossible. First of all for the last two years there's been an intifada going on," said Amos.

"What's that?"

"O Rosa, haven't you heard? It's an uprising. The Palestinians say they are fed up with what they call the occupation and are throwing stones at all Israeli vehicles. Besides, the only police force there, are the Israeli army, so they won't be interested in an abandoned Arab baby. By going to Ramallah and saying you've been staying on a settlement, you will be stirring up a load more trouble. We used to go shopping in Ramallah but not nowadays. Nobody in this community would dare venture there."

"How awful. The Arabs aren't usually violent are they? Do they have guns?"

"No they don't have any weapons. The only way they can show their anger is by throwing stones."

My eyes strayed to the back of their door and I wanted to ask why are they so well armed if the Palestinians don't have any, but I decided to keep my mouth shut except to remark, "So it's dangerous to go into the town?"

"I'm afraid so."

We all sat down contemplating and I realised for the first time how a chance encounter had caused us such a big problem. Rebecca, for once, uncharacteristically, decided to say nothing.

"Come on. If you get ready, I'll take you into Jerusalem."

"Thanks Amos."

We packed our bags. I kissed Rebecca on both cheeks, thanking her for her hospitality. I couldn't help but notice that she offered me her cheeks to kiss, but did not kiss mine. I apologised for all the embarrassment and misunderstandings. She was polite in her goodbyes, saying she had enjoyed our visit and hoped we would find somewhere to stay. Enjoyed our visit? She was probably glad to see us go, but I felt sad that while once we had been such good friends, there was bitterness between us. Amos drove us along the main highway to Jerusalem and we were there in less than half an hour. I was surprised that the road was not busy and that there was only one checkpoint which we sailed through without stopping. Amos explained that Jewish settlers have yellow Israeli number plates, unlike the Palestinian cars. As Amos dropped us off at Jaffa Gate he hurriedly shook hands and told us there were lots of small hostels where we would be sure to find somewhere to stay. Of course we had his office phone number to ring if there was a problem. We carried Musa in the carrycot that David had bought as we made our way through the crowds of people going and coming into the Old City.

We passed through a huge stone arch obviously steeped in history. There were Orthodox Jews with their wide brimmed hats trimmed with fur, long black coats with long socks underneath instead of trousers

48

and dark curly ringlets of hair round their glum faces. Often, they had a wife with them trailing a pram and several small children. We saw religious Christian priests of all sorts identifiable by their different hats and coloured robes, and there were Muslim women covering their heads with tight headscarves. In every corner there were Israeli soldiers fully armed.

A couple of small boys, dressed in ragged shorts and what looked like English football tee-shirts, were sitting on the kerb, playing with small rocks. The soldiers were watching them carefully, taunting them in a manner which seemed to me positively provoking them to throw stones. They went over to the boys and scattered the pebbles with the butts of their rifles. It sounded like Arabic and Hebrew curses flying around.

Foreign tourists of all nationalities and religions mingled with the local population. And as if that wasn't enough, a young Arab man was trying to manoeuvre a barrowful of bananas through the crowd, shouting at the top of his voice: *"Yalla, Moz"*...It was as if the whole world had converged into a small open square with various narrow sideroads leading in different directions. I was amused to see everyone scurrying along to find their way like ants on a molehill.

After asking a few passers-by and following a young boy who was leading the way, we came to a narrow alleyway where tucked away in the middle of shops was a small convent hostel run by nuns. The boy held out his hand and David gave him two shekels as a tip. When we registered our names at the desk and showed the receptionist our British passports, she started to ask questions.

"I see you are David and Rosa Craig?"

"Yes."

"Are you Christian pilgrims?"

"No, just tourists," I said.

"And what is the baby's name?"

"Moses," I replied, before David could say anything.

"Why is he not registered in your passport? Was he born here?"

"We intend to register him tomorrow," I said, trying to avoid the last question.

She must have noticed our hesitancy. David was avoiding eye contact and was shuffling his feet.

"Well, where have you been staying up to now? I see in your passport that you entered Ben Gurion Airport six days ago. I can't believe that you gave birth as soon as you arrived. Did you?"

I couldn't answer. At that moment, Musa, who had been sleeping peacefully, woke up and started to cry.

"Why don't you two sit over there while I call Sister Bridget to speak to you? There is no need to worry." She smiled at us, but changed her expression when she spoke on the phone to the Head nun in Italian, while we sat on comfortable chairs in the lobby feeling very much like criminals.

"We have to tell them the truth. You just can't go on pretending Musa belongs to us," whispered David, looking around to make sure no-one was listening.

"I know, I know." I was trying to calm Musa, patting him on his back. Do babies sense when their security is being threatened?

After about ten minutes, a nun arrived in her flowing white robes and starched cap and with a broad smile on her face. We stood up to greet her.

"Well hello there, Mr and Mrs. Craig, welcome to Jerusalem. Please sit down." She spoke perfect English but with an Italian accent. She smiled at the baby in my arms.

"You have a beautiful baby."

"Sister, I need to explain," David said. "We find ourselves in a predicament. This is not really our baby though we have become very attached to him."

Sister sat there listening to every word, while David explained everything.

"So you see, Sister, if you could give us a room for a few nights while we sort ourselves out, we will try to find an orphanage for Moses, perhaps in Bethlehem?"

"I see," she finally said. "But I think we ought to first inform the police, don't you?"

David and I looked at each other.

"No, I really don't think that's necessary. If you don't trust us perhaps one of your sisters would go with us to Bethlehem?" I said.

"Let me think about that," she said. "But meanwhile I will show you to your room. There are lots of little cafes and restaurants in this area if you're hungry." she said, adding, "We will talk more of this tomorrow after breakfast."

"Thank you Sister." I sighed with relief.

We tried to settle into our new surroundings. It was Sunday evening and dusk had come already. Street lights were on and a half moon was shining. We watched as crowds of tourists flocked to the restaurants and sandwich bars.

"It must be Easter today," said David. "There must have been a big procession in Jerusalem. I've seen it on the TV. The Christians here certainly know how to celebrate. Look darling."

It must have been the tail end of the procession as we saw two young men wearing coloured sashes and beating drums and a third one carrying a banner with a religious picture of an empty cross, surrounded by roses and olive branches and Arabic texts.

Following this were a group of English tourists. They were actually dancing in the street, twirling banners which proclaimed: 'Halleluiah. Christ Is Risen.' They were singing songs at the top of their voices.

"Oh David, I don't think I can stand any more noise. I've got a dreadful headache and am quite exhausted. It's been a long day." Musa was still crying as I leaned back on the ample double bed and looked around the room. "At least we have an electric kettle."

"You rest darling while I go and buy some falafel sandwiches. Shall I bring Cola or do you want to make tea?"

"I'll make some tea."

I managed to pull myself together, feed the baby and rock him, so that by the time David returned he was in a peaceful sleep.

CHAPTER FOUR

What were my dreams about? I seem to remember huntsmen with guns and wild animals and running for my life. Anyway, I woke up early with the sound of the muezzin and the call to prayer. For a second I had to remind myself where I was. I should be happy staying in the Holy City, but the mosque which was almost next door made me feel foreign in a strange country. The loud Arabic chanting gave me an unstable feeling.

Why had Rebecca given us such a cold farewell and even Amos, who had seemed more sympathetic, had literally dumped us in Jerusalem? It wasn't exactly our fault that we were landed with a baby 'out of the blue'. If the baby had been abandoned in a Jewish settlement would they have shown a different attitude? The baby was an Arab so in Rebecca's eyes he didn't seem to count. Rebecca did not seem to be racist but it's just that she has been programmed by her Zionist ideology to think that Jews are a superior race and that they have a right to own all this Holy Land.

I swung my legs over the high bed to land my feet on a small rug. The room was spartan and cold in comparison with Rebecca's home. The double bed had white cotton sheets, a thin blanket and an old-fashioned quilt. In one corner was a small wardrobe and above the bed was a religious picture of the Virgin Mary with the baby Jesus on her knee. No doubt, it was a copy of a medieval painting, which to me did not give an impression of a maternal loving relationship. True motherhood should surely show a mother's smile and embracing arms, which I felt was lacking in this picture. The floor had motley brown ceramic tiles which had seen better days. The ceiling was high and the window was a kind of vertical sash, set in wooden frames that badly needed a new coat of paint. Hanging from ceiling to floor were thin cotton curtains in a dull floral pattern in blue and brown. The only redeeming features were an amazing panoramic view of Jerusalem and an electric kettle to make tea.

I shivered from the cool morning air as I picked up baby Musa, noticing he was awake but so quiet. I became rather alarmed as his little nose was blue and his complexion pale. I made sure he was breathing alright, so I held him to me between my breasts and wrapped the blanket around him to warm him up. Quietly, at first, I started talking to him, sobbing, as the tears rolled down my face. "Musa, sweetie, are you missing your Mummy?" I realised I couldn't bear for anything to happen to him now.

David turned over and woke up. He looked at me rubbing his eyes. "What on earth…?   Is he alright?"
I burst out crying and couldn't answer David for a few minutes. He folded the baby and me in his arms until I could control the flood of tears.

"Do you think babies could give up the will to live?" I said. "This poor little soul is missing his mother's voice. She must have talked to him when she was carrying him and now he is in a new environment with voices in a different language."

"Oh Rosa, don't be silly. All that new babies want is warm milk and a cuddle. Darling you are getting too attached and too emotional. Just relax, for goodness sake. Hopefully we can hand him over today and finally enjoy the rest of our holiday."

"But I don't want to hand him over! He isn't just a parcel of clothes or something."

"Be reasonable darling, you can't hang on to him."

"But I want to keep him. We could foster him if need be."

"What! Are you crazy? He's a stranger, a Palestinian, we don't know anything about his parents. Besides, we have to go back to England so we certainly can't take him with us. That's common sense."

David continued to mutter on and on. I got the impression he just wanted to be absolved of any responsibility. I turned my back on him and went to make up a bottle of formula.

We went downstairs to breakfast in an uncomfortable silence and were greeted warmly by the Sisters.

"And how is little Moses today?"

"He seemed so pale and quiet this morning and his nose was bluish. Now he has a bit more colour, what do you think, Sister?" She came over to examine him.

"You know as a nurse, I really think you should see a doctor and have him properly checked. All *bambinos* are thoroughly examined at birth, which he probably didn't have. You don't know anything about his birth, do you?"

"No, nothing at all."

"We can go to a clinic in Jerusalem or we can take him straight away to Bethlehem. My advice is to go straight to Bethlehem but first I need to call them that we are coming."

"Why don't we go to a clinic in Jerusalem, first?"

"Well we could do that, but you will have to pay in an Arab clinic and they will ask a lot of questions about his birth. It might be embarrassing for them to know that you've been staying on a settlement."

"Will they think we stole the baby?"

"They might. Who knows?" Sister gave me a look that worried me.

"Are you Jewish?" She said this with a questioning stare.

"I was born into a Jewish family, so I suppose that makes me a Jew, but I am not religious. My husband is Christian but not what you would call a believer, are you dear?" I said, looking at David.

David butted in, ignoring my question.

"We did our best to persuade the Arabs in the village to take him, Sister, but they didn't want anything to do with the baby. What else could we do?" He threw his napkin down to collect more toast from the breakfast bar. It was, as if, he was trying to convince himself that it was not his problem.

"So why don't we go to an Israeli clinic?"

"No, I think they would just take the baby and goodness knows where he would end up."

"So what do you suggest?" My chest heaved involuntarily and I let out a big sigh.

"I will call my old friend, who is the Matron of a hospital in Bethlehem and ask her advice. I'm sure God has a plan for this little one!"

I thanked her before she strolled away.

We ate our breakfast in complete silence while Musa lay quietly in his carrycot. Other people milled into the dining room and spotting we had a baby came over and cooed over the sleeping Musa. I picked him up and an elderly gentleman looked at the both of us.

"You can see this one takes after his mother!" he said, smiling. "What an adorable baby."

"Thank you," I beamed back, before David could inject anything to the contrary and I could see this made him more annoyed. Yes, I thought, my eyes are definitely darker than David's and my skin colour is more olive. In fact, some of my contempories used to say that maybe I had some middle-eastern blood. I've never looked into my ancestry but maybe there is some truth in it. Sister Bridget sauntered back to us and said that she would take us to Bethlehem that very afternoon, apologising profusely for the wait as she had some business to attend to.

"Meanwhile," she continued, "One of the sisters will look after the baby while you wander around the *suk* of the Old City. Then, after you have found somewhere to eat lunch, you can return here and I will take you to Bethlehem."

"That's so kind of you. We really appreciate your care," I said.

I handed over Musa's feeding bottle and packet of nappies and David and I set off into the labyrinth of narrow streets of old Jerusalem. It was impossible to walk without being physically jostled and pushed by the crowd. There were tourists in shorts and scanty tops to women completely covered in black with only a slit for their eyes; from Arab men wearing black and white chequered kaffiyas to Christian priests in their long robes. And the smells! From the sweet sickly aroma of syrupy pastries to the odour of donkey dung. Little boothed shops crammed side by side were selling everything from raw meat to trinkets, from herbs to olive wood souvenirs. Tee shirts of all sizes and colours were hanging haphazardly on racks above the heads of the people. Some had Arabic or Hebrew inscriptions

62

with pictures of a dove or 'Peace, Shalom, Salaam.' I had to smile at the ones that said: 'My mother-in-law went to Jerusalem and all she bought me was this lousy T shirt.'

All the time the traders were calling out to us to look at their goods or just greeting us in their best English. We stopped at one shop to examine the beautiful wooden carvings of Mary and Joseph or scenes of The Last Supper. They were also selling the Israeli symbol of the Star of David alongside Christian crosses of every size and style. The Arab traders were anxious to show us a variety of goods and before we could even start to admire the craftsmanship we were sat down on stools and handed tiny cups of sweet black Arabic coffee, poured from a copper pot with an elongated spout. Next door we saw a group of old men at the entrance of a small café, smoking arguiles with water bubbling in coloured glass receptacles.

"Look Rosa, surprise, surprise, chocolate Easter eggs in Jerusalem, of all places. These are from England!" David said excitedly.

There were so many interesting things and people to see that for a brief moment I was distracted. A young Palestinian woman dressed in a Western style skirt and blouse was carrying her baby in a wide shawl round her shoulders. She almost bumped into me and said something in Arabic, probably to apologise? It reminded me of Musa and I started to worry.

"David, do you think Musa will be alright?"

"Oh come off it, Rosa, I was trying to forget him for a little while. Stop going on about him for goodness sake!"

"Maybe we should go back?"

David did not need to answer me. I could see that look. Shut up, it said.

He ignored me while bargaining for some small souvenirs. At one point he started to walk away until the shopkeeper lowered the price. Of course, that was what was expected, but some tourists were gullible enough to pay without bargaining. It was quite amazing to watch David in action. I lifted up a delicate embroidered shawl, which did not go unnoticed by the man. I let David barter for me, which pleased him and tempered his anger.

"Fifty dollars," the shopkeeper said. "Look at the colours and hand stitching. Think of all the work."

"No, Twenty-five."

"Forty-five."

"Thirty."

Eventually David paid forty dollars, which I thought was quite a good price but David stated it was still expensive. I knew he was trying to please me though.

For lunch, we found a restaurant that appeared old Eastern with its uneven stone walls and high vaulted ceiling. Some very ancient ornate tapestries were hanging from floor to ceiling. They were so old that the once vibrant colours of red and blue had faded and in some parts there were holes, giving it an authentic feel.

"I bet those wall hangings are antiques and quite valuable. Maybe they go back to the time of the Crusaders," David said. It was just the kind of arty place that he loves.

The waiters were anxious to serve us and we chose a variety of mezee salads; mashed aubergine with sesame sauce, potatoes with peppers and garlic, hummus, cabbage, avocado, parsley with burgul and others, which were all new to our tastebuds. They all had generous lashings of olive oil and were decorated with olives. Although the dishes were delicious, I found it hard to savour my food and my mind kept wandering.

David, damn him, was always more sensible and practical. He was straight and honest and apart from his temper was so untypical of the arty type. Why was I so sentimental and impressionable? I had become more emotional lately. Perhaps it had to do with the sudden death of my mother a year ago followed closely by Dad going to pieces. Why should I be worried about an abandoned infant? Why can't I simply put him out of my mind and enjoy our holiday? We had been so looking forward to our visit and had been saving up for months. Rebecca had sent us such wonderful letters encouraging us to come and offering us hospitality, so we wouldn't have to pay for hotels. She was so excited about her life in Israel and so in love with Amos. Now a little baby had spoiled all our plans, or had he? Maybe I should try harder to forget him, let someone else take care of him. Perhaps Rebecca was secretly longing for a child of her own and seeing Musa had somehow awakened something in her. She never talked about it so I really don't know. It was so uncharacteristic of her to be antagonistic towards me. All I ever wanted was to be a mother.

I had met David at University, though we were both in different departments. He was studying art and I was into science, more specifically biology. Art and science don't go together, do they? We used to meet in the

Cafeteria and somehow were attracted to each other. I suppose we both loved beautiful things, he in pictures and me in people with all the shades of humanity. Maybe I should have been a nurse or a doctor.

David tapped me on the arm. "Penny for your thoughts?"

"Sorry. I was thinking about Rebecca," I lied. "She was happy to see us go, wasn't she? You know what? We should call Amos to tell him that we are OK."

We asked a shopkeeper to use his phone in exchange for a few shekels. Amos picked up on the second ring and was relieved to hear from us and to know we had plans to go to Bethlehem that afternoon. We told him we hoped to put the baby into an orphanage.

Back at the Hostel, Sister Bridget was waiting for us in the foyer. Musa was dressed in a new pale blue baby jump suit lying in his carrycot.

"You do look smart, little man," I said as I picked him up and kissed him on his cheeks. We sat down on the easy chairs.

"Mrs Craig I need to ask you a few more questions before we set off."

"Please Sister, do call me Rosa. What is it you want to know?"

67

"Well first, how do you know the baby's name is Moses?"

"He was wrapped in a little knitted shawl with a scrap of paper pinned to it. The writing is in Arabic but our friend translated it as 'My name is Musa'."

"Ah, Musa. That could be Muslim or Christian. But you don't know his surname?"

"No."

"We'll have to leave that blank for the time being, then." Sister was writing all this down on a form.

"Date of Birth?"

"We found him last Thursday. Do you think he was born that day?"

"Well, did you notice his belly button? Was it healed when you found him?"

"I think so. I only remember it was dry."

"Well, today is Monday. Let's see, he must be at least eight days old now."

Sister looked at the Calendar and calculated four days before we found him, April 10th. That means he was born before we left London.

Sister led us the short distance through narrow cobbled roads until we came to a wider plaza, with stone steps, going in different directions and with many tourist agencies and other business offices. There was a crowd of men waiting their turn to go into a barber's shop with an array of coloured towels hanging on a rack outside to dry in the sun. David carried the carrycot and some of the men whistled. Whether this was at the baby or me in my pink top adorned with large roses, I shall never know. We turned into a narrow side road where many cars were parked, leaving only a small space for pedestrians. At the end was the ancient wall surrounding the Old City. Another archway led to a wide street. This was obviously another exit into the main part of Jerusalem.

"This is called the New Gate," said Sister. "I've arranged for a taxi to be here, to take us to Bethlehem."

I settled the carrycot on my lap as we took off, uncertain of what lay ahead, but feeling vulnerable and nervous. David squeezed my hand, to reassure me while Musa slept.

CHAPTER FIVE

Going into Bethlehem we were stopped at the checkpoint, and had to wait in a queue of cars. A bunch of Israeli soldiers with guns, who didn't look much older than teenagers, were checking each driver for their licence and searching their car boot. The soldier examined our driver's credentials, looked at us and asked for our passports. Within minutes we found ourselves outside the hospital. The rocking motion of the car meant that Musa slept all the way. David and I carried the carrycot between us as we followed Sister Bridget up the wide stone steps.

"This is some building!" I remarked to David.

"Aye, different from your London place."

Indeed it was very different. I work in the administrative department of a London hospital, with its red-brick, old exterior, but here was an impressive façade, built in white stone with a pink tinge, and huge white pillars each side of the main entrance. Immediately, we were ushered into a large waiting room that smelt heavily of disinfectant and looked spotlessly clean. It was crowded with people, mostly women and children sitting on benches. The nurses were scurrying about like rabbits in a field of cabbages. It was an orderly chaos with the noise of infants bawling and mothers screaming to control their wandering toddlers.

Sister Bridget guided us to a private room and told us to wait for the doctor. She left us, no doubt to try and find her friend. We put the cot down on a stool and I picked up the baby to cuddle him, feeling tense and nervous. I'm sure David sensed it too.

"Darling, just relax, for goodness sake!" he said. I didn't need to answer. I just directed daggers at him as we sat down with Musa on my knee. I think he was looking forward to an end to our predicament, whereas I was dreading parting with Musa. It was as if Musa was becoming a part of me, little by little. He was stealing my heart. I must be sensible, I told myself, you have only had him for five days and now you've got to let him go. David tried to steer our conversation on to other things.

"Let's take a bus into Galilee tomorrow. There are lots of Roman antiquities and art galleries in Tiberius. We could even go swimming in the lake. Perhaps we could join a tour group. I will call Amos and see where the best place is to stay."

"We'll see," I said, wanting to swear, but not wanting to cause a scene.

How can he be so insensitive?

It was like time stood still as we waited, but fortunately Musa lay contentedly until the doctor bustled in with one of the Sisters, banging the door making him cry. We both stood up. The doctor was a distinctive looking young man with dense dark hair, and a thick moustache which hung heavy over his thin top lip. His English was perfect as he greeted us with such a charming smile that I immediately felt at ease.

"Hello, Mr. and Mrs. Craig. My name is Doctor Hussein. You're English, I believe? What part of England do you come from?"

"We live in a suburb of London but my parents come from Scotland," said David.

"Well, well, I studied medicine in Scotland, Edinburgh to be exact. What a beautiful city and such friendly people."

"I went to school near Edinburgh."

The doctor chuckled. "I can pick up some of your Scottish accent!"

After much of this chit chat, the doctor finally indicated for me to lie the baby down on the examination couch.

He then proceeded, much to our astonishment, to gently coo to Musa using Arabic words. He did not need to ask any questions. It was obvious that he had been told the baby's history already. He examined him carefully with his stethoscope while I watched. Then he turned to me.

"Mrs. Craig, this baby needs a full medical. We need to do blood tests and other examinations. Usually blood is tested from the umbilical cord at birth but this is not possible now. Do you notice that his colour changes?"

"Yes, doctor, he does sometimes appear to go blue for a while."

"Well, I cannot be sure, but it seems he might have a slight congenital heart defect."

"Oh no! What does that mean?" I said. My trembling voice betrayed my concern.

"Have you heard of a hole in the heart?"

I nodded.

"The dividing wall between the septum of the heart might not be complete. It happens sometimes during the early development of the child. Usually it rights itself without treatment, but it might mean surgery later on. Anyway, you can be sure the baby will be well looked after here until we can place him in an orphanage or with a family. We may even be able to trace his family in Ramallah."

The inevitable had happened. How could I have ever thought that I could keep him? My heart was pounding and my legs felt weak.

I hesitated, then blurted out: "Doctor, would there be any chance of us fostering him?" I could see David wanted to say something to the contrary, but he just screwed up his eyebrows and let out a sigh.

The doctor shook his head. "It is difficult to legally foster a child here and adoption is extremely difficult. Why don't you enjoy the rest of your holiday and go back to England. You could of course sponsor him with small monthly donations to help financially with his care. There is no social security here, you know, not like you have in England."

"This is something we would have to think about," said David diplomatically.

"Of course. Anyway, we will make a note of your address and perhaps we could inform you of Musa's progress. Thank you for your care of him. You have done a very good job, Mrs Craig."

I picked up the packet of Pampers from the cot. "Shall I change him?"

Sister took them from my hand and patted me on the arm. "My dear, please don't worry about him." She handed me a tissue and gave me a look of pure sympathy. The doctor held out his hand to shake ours and the Sister opened the door so we knew it was time to say goodbye. I left thanking the doctor trying to be composed but with tears in my eyes. I didn't even kiss Musa goodbye, but perhaps it was just as well or I might have broken down.

We were told that Sister Bridget had to return promptly to Jerusalem but someone pointed out to us where we could find a service taxi to take us back to the Old City. Service taxis were mini buses which filled up with passengers and were cheaper than private taxis. We were left standing on the side of the main road, bereft of our little bundle. I clung on to David's arm, my legs tensing with cramp one instance and ready to collapse the next.

I could sense that David did not quite know what to say to me, so instead of talking about the baby, he made chatty observations of people passing by. Groups of schoolchildren in uniforms were skipping and laughing, carrying their school satchels. Some were chasing each other but all of them seemed to be in a hurry to get home.   After waiting more than twenty minutes for transport, we began to get impatient. Suddenly, the whole atmosphere became tense with the noise of helicopters flying low over the town. We could see fear in the eyes of people as they started to run blindly in all directions. The shopkeepers behind us were pulling down the blinds and locking up. Some kids were rolling used car tyres into the road and piling them up to block off the street, then setting them alight. The black smoke and the stench of rubber burning were making me gag. By this time my legs crumbled, and I collapsed, sitting on the pavement with my legs under me. David was probably embarrassed seeing his wife on the ground, but he was gentle with me, holding me by my elbow and lifting me up.

The shopkeeper behind us ushered us into his shop before pulling down the blinds. I slumped down on a stool while David stood with his arm around my shoulders. The shopkeeper left a chink of the shutters open so that we could observe what was going on. Speaking in heavily accented English he said:

"*Shuf Keif,* Look what's happening. The Israeli jeeps are forever coming into the city to harass and terrorise us. The young men, they try to block off the roads by burning tyres but this only makes the Israeli army more angry at us." He paused to see our reaction. I shivered wishing I'd brought a jacket even though the weather was warm. I hugged my arms around me while David squeezed my shoulders in a gesture of reassurance.

"We have to fight them to regain our independence," the shopkeeper continued. "They are stealing all our land to build their bloody settlements. We have no freedom and there is no-one to speak out for us, so that's why we are in this intifada."

Yes, the word 'intifada.' Amos had tried to explain to us and now we were seeing it all for ourselves. We could sense the man's anger by the way he was staring at us, his moustache quivering and either drumming his fists on the shop counter or punching the air, making us feel uncomfortable as if we were the cause of the trouble.

"You know what 'intifada' means?"

"Does it mean 'uprising'?" David asked.

"It means 'a shaking off'. We are determined to shake off this military occupation. Why should the Jews from other countries think they have a right to our land. We were here first! Why doesn't the British Government do something? It is their fault we are in this mess! And as for the American idiots or even the United Nations puppets, the Israelis they don't take any notice. They don't listen to anyone!"

I gripped David's hand, petrified. We didn't dare say another word. We certainly didn't dare tell this passionate man that we had been staying in a Jewish settlement. We just nodded our heads in sympathy. Worse was to come. There was a loud burst of gunfire and as we were still looking through the small space under the shutters we couldn't believe our eyes. A few yards away some youths were throwing stones at the Israeli army jeeps which had crashed through the blazing tyre barriers. One of the young soldiers jumped out of his vehicle, aimed his gun at one of the youngsters and shot him in the forehead. He was dead before he could utter a sound, blood pouring from the wound. The other kids ran for their lives. It was like watching a crime movie on the TV. It felt surreal. We were too shocked to say anything, and we groaned with horror.

The other soldiers got out and started shooting randomly in all directions. One threw a gas canister, like a hand grenade, which let off a stinking smoke. We ducked down in case any of the bullets reached the shop windows, but even inside the locked store we could feel our eyes smarting and our throats choking from the tear gas. I was screaming and David was retching like he wanted to vomit. The shopkeeper produced two pieces of a cut onion and told us to put it close to our nose. It made our tears stream more, but helped in taking away the poisonous smell, which was worse than rancid eggs left out in the sun.

It ended as suddenly as it had started. The army revved up their engines and sped out at the speed of racing cars. Were they frightened of small rocks? Or of the consequences of their behaviour? They left such a cloud of dust that our vision was completely obscured. What with the smoke, the dust and our red swollen eyes we could hardly see.

The shutters were lifted slightly and for a few minutes there was complete silence. Then a small group of women appeared surrounding the boy in his pool of life blood. Their wailing began as soon as the mother of the boy picked him up, hugging and cradling him in her arms. His blood was staining her white cotton house-dress. She wasn't wearing a headscarf; instead she was wiping the blood from his face with her long hair and burying the boy's head in her neck. It was the most

79

harrowing scene I had ever seen in my life. The boy could not have been more than fourteen or fifteen. Even the shopkeeper was moved to tears.

David eventually sat down, trembling, and the shopkeeper brought us two cups of sweet tea.

"*Sheif,* You see," he said. "We, Palestinians are made out to be terrorists. All we have are stones. They have all the latest weapons of war."

We had to agree. He unlocked his shop and turned to us.

"Where are you staying?"

"We are staying in a small hostel in East Jerusalem," said David.

"*Taieb!* OK! In a little while when the coast is clear and the gas all gone into the air I will order you a private taxi to Jerusalem. Don't worry," he said, as he waved his arms around as if to clear the air. We wondered how much this would cost, but when the taxi eventually came the shopkeeper gave the driver instructions and paid our fare! We had been afraid of his passionate feelings and now he turned out to be a kind and generous man. We were both touched. We hardly had time to thank him as the taxi sped off at full speed.

CHAPTER SIX

What a relief! The atmosphere of the hostel was calm and peaceful in comparison to the trauma we had experienced just a short time ago. I had to pull myself together since we had to walk along the cobbled streets after the point where the taxi had dropped us off, but I was still feeling shaky.

"That was cold-bloodied murder. How can they get away with it," shouted David. I could see that he was seething with anger and didn't know how to release it.

"Yes, it was murder, but no need to shout at me!" I was leaning on him rather heavily as we walked up the stairs.

"Sorry."

I had not realised that life in the Palestinian territories was such a powder keg. Of course, I figured out that had we listened to Rebecca and not gone on our little country walk we would not have experienced any of this. The Jews on the settlements are surrounded by barbed wire, but it cushions them from the reality of life. Can barbed wire really be seen as a soft cushion?

Sister Bridget listened to our story without interrupting. David did most of the telling. The news was nothing new to her, but she had been worried about us and apologised for having to leave us. I thought why should she be bothered with us at all? We were paying to stay in the Hostel. It was one of the many instances when I realised that people seemed to really care. Perhaps it was their religion or faith as some might say?

We went up to our room feeling physically and emotionally drained. I kicked off my shoes, slumped on the bed and curled up under the quilt, covering my ears to all noises of the street outside. I must have dozed off and was dreaming, because I remembered seeing my mother's face. She was weeping and wailing and tearing her clothes. But she was wearing a headscarf and my mother never wore a headscarf. It was then that I realised she was not my mother but the poor Palestinian woman whose boy had just been shot dead. Her hair was bright red the colour of a scarf but dripping blood. Then I saw a crowd of women looking at a little boy on the ground and a soldier with a gun pointing at my head. I was one of those women and I was screaming. I saw him put his finger on the trigger and heard a shot. It must have been then that I woke up, sweating, throwing the quilt off. I looked around the room disorientated and realised I was alone. David must have gone out. I gathered together Musa's things to give to Sister, except for the shawl and the note pinned to it, which I was careful to pack into our suitcase.

It was now dark and I was feeling peckish. So when David returned from his walk, we went to a small cafe. We ordered chicken and rice, but it reeked of garlic and olive oil and somehow I couldn't stomach it. But I loved the assortment of sweet, crunchy pastries with pistachio nuts, dripping with syrup. They were piled up on a dish in the shape of a pyramid and the waiter told us to help ourselves. As usual, David teased me about my sweet tooth. Unlike me he was savouring the oily garlic.

"I phoned Amos and he is going to book us a place in Tiberius."

"That's great," I said. As we discussed plans, I made a mental effort to try and put the past few days behind, in order to please David. Perhaps, from now on we could have some fun times together. I realised that it was important to enjoy the next few days of our holiday for our relationship to continue well. I had to try and make an effort to make it up to David as I know I've been a bit unreasonable.

I felt his arms envelope me as we lay in bed that night.

"My lovely Rose…but…sometimes prickly," he teased, soothing me with gentle kisses down my body, his soft chest hair tickling me, even his garlicky breath all sweetness. My worries were dissolved in his caresses as I responded to his passion. Eventually I fell asleep feeling loved and comforted.

The next morning we were woken with the Muslim call to prayer from the Muezzin and I instinctively reached over the side of the bed to pick up Musa, quickly realising in that same instant that he was no longer part of us. I hugged my arms around me and suddenly felt bereft, but there was no time to brood or mourn. David was already up and dressed and told me to hurry up in order to catch the bus into Galilee.

"I'll go and pay, while you finish packing. See you downstairs."

In haste, I dressed in my black jeans and plain black top, without thinking.

"You look as if you're going to a funeral," was David's remark as we drank our coffee.

I pulled out my jewellery pouch from my handbag. "OK, I'll put on my red bead necklace and red heart ear-rings, you gave me for our last anniversary."

"That's more like it." He reached over and gave me a coffee kiss!

Amos had arranged for us to stay in a Kibbutz near Tiberius. We took a taxi to the Central bus station and then found ourselves queuing alongside lots of families with numerous children. I couldn't help but notice that all the teenage daughters wore long dark skirts, white blouses and black stockings. The boys wore long trousers which had string-like tassels hanging from their waists and they looked almost feminine with their side ringlets. These were obviously Ultra Orthodox Jews. Their noisy chatter was all in Hebrew. They ignored us and it was obvious that they did not want to sit anywhere near us as they occupied all the back seats. It was a long journey, but the motorway was smooth and the time passed quickly. We watched the green hillsides with avenues of eucalyptus trees and orchards of oranges and limes merge into the coastline, with the sea lapping on the pebbled beach close to the road. Finally we turned off into the city of Tiberius, buzzing with modern Israelis strolling along the promenades in scanty shorts and bikini tops. What a contrast to the occupants of our bus!

The Kibbutz hotel was close by the lake of Galilee and after registering and settling our bags in the room, we decided to take a late afternoon walk. The water was clear and calm and shimmering with the reflection from the string of lights hung along the shore. I was fascinated by the little fishing boats, which were unpacking their cargo of fish on the dock. Nearby we went into a restaurant displaying large posters of various fish dishes.

"What would you like, darling," said David without looking up from the menu, hardly noticing an American couple who were pulling out chairs to sit down beside us.

"Do you mind if we share your table?"

"Please feel free," David said.

"I recommend St. Peter's fish," said the man, pointing out the item on the menu. "French fries and salad go nice with it. My name's Max, by the way, my wife here is Cassia."

We introduced ourselves and without telling them I was Jewish they somehow, by the way they were talking to us, surmised that anyway.

"Aren't you as excited as I am, Rosa, being in Israel?" Cassia said, as we sat eating ice-cream, after an enormous dinner of fish and chips. The fish was cooked with its head and spine, so we had to fillet it carefully. She wiped her mouth and most of the bright-red lipstick came off on the paper napkin. She paused, her face glowing with obvious excitement, and looked at me.

"Are you and David happy living in London?"

"Why? Yes."

I was a bit surprised at the open way Cassia was talking to me as if she had known me all my life.

"But here it's so beautiful and calm, don't you think? Aren't you tired of the road congestion, the stresses and the pollution? Besides, here you would be amongst your own people. Think of that! Jews from all over the world living together in their own land. Don't you think it's marvellous what the Israelis have accomplished in just a few years?"

"I suppose so. I guess the pioneers must have worked hard against all odds."

"Yes they certainly did," Cassia continued. "They've established a homeland for Jews. My grandparents perished in the Holocaust, but my father was saved by some kind American friends when he was a small child and that's how I was born in the USA. My husband has a similar story and that's really how we came together. Our parents were friends from way back."

"So, why do you want to leave America now?"

"Max and I decided we wanted to learn more about our religion and be with our own people. Besides, we hope to start a family, so what better place than for them to have a good start in life here and learn Hebrew. We plan to return to the States after this trip to settle up our business, but then we will come to live somewhere in Israel. You know we can still keep our American passports, but also have Israeli passports."

"Sounds great, but I don't understand why you can't be Jews in America?" I said.

"I can see you are not convinced. Of course we can still be Jews anywhere but this is a special country for Jewish people, don't you think? Do you have children?"

"Not yet, but we hope to, don't we David?" I looked at him and he knew what I was thinking. I had to admit to myself that my thoughts were constantly in Bethlehem worrying about little Musa and missing his sweet face, but I was reluctant to share my thoughts with this talkative stranger.

89

At this point, Max and David decided to wander off to watch the boats, but Cassia continued: "Imagine, on our return from the US we'll become Israeli nationals."

"Tell me, how is it that you can become Israeli citizens right away?" I said. "Don't you have to go through a course first or a trial period? I'm thinking, of course, of any foreign immigrants wanting to live in England. It takes years for them to get asylum and even after many years living in the UK without legal documentation they can still get deported."

"Ah, but here it's different. Israel encourages Jews to live here. That's the wonderful thing. We just have to show that we are from Jewish lineage and being second generation Holocaust survivors we get a special welcome. We will even get allocated a new house on a settlement."

"You mean any Jew by religion or by race?"

"Well, is there a difference? There are many Israelis who are Jews but atheists!

Just think of it, Jews have been persecuted all down the ages and in every country of the world. Isn't it time for them to have a country they can call their own?" Cassia was continually playing with her loop earrings, accentuating her long neck, but gazing at me with such an eager expression, it was impossible to ignore her questions.

"Sounds like Utopia, but in reality it doesn't always work out like that, does it? Are you sure you are going to be safe living here."

"The Israeli army are the best in the world."

"Don't I know it. We have just experienced their brutality."

Cassia took off her large sunglasses. Her eyebrows shot up.

"What do you mean?"

"We saw a soldier kill an innocent boy in Bethlehem in cold blood, only yesterday. I shall never forget that sight as long as I live." I proceeded to tell her how the army had invaded the city terrorising the children and how we had almost died from the effects of the tear gas.

"What on earth were you doing in Bethlehem? Jews don't normally go there."

"That's another long story. I can't tell you now. But those soldiers were not much older than the boy they killed. It was horrible."

Cassia sat for a time trying to digest it all. I could see she was thinking of a way to justify the actions of the army.

"But think about it, Rosa, in 1967 the Israeli army were not yet twenty years old and they defeated the armies of Egypt, Jordan and….." she paused… "and Syria. And all in six days! Meanwhile, as Americans, we were defeated in Vietnam!"

"True, but they wouldn't have been able to win the war without American weapons and money and now I just wonder who they will fight next."

Cassia sat with her sunburnt arms folded, choosing to ignore the slight sarcasm in my responses. In my view her oversized sunglasses were more like rose-tinted spectacles. I had experienced another side of Israel that she obviously knew nothing about.

"Come on, let's join the men," she said.

David and Max looked as if they were enjoying themselves walking along the quayside and talking mostly about sports as I gathered from David afterwards. They were laughing and joking, as Max lit one cigarette after another. I couldn't help but compare Cassia with Rebecca and wondered if all Israeli women were more fanatical than the men. Rebecca had been brash in her defence of Israel and almost racist in her attitude towards the Palestinians. I felt Cassia was different being more open and friendly. Yes, I could easily be friends with Cassia.

Max was a heavy set man sporting a short wiry grey beard and moustache, fond of his drink as well as his cigarettes. I could imagine him in an English pub. Cassia was a tall, well built woman but not at all the type that I would have paired up with Max. She was not exactly attractive with short, light brown hair but she had a distinctive nose and that long neck with those large dangling earrings.

Later that evening, they came to join us at the bar and Cassia started chatting again.

"Forgive me Rosa, I have been doing all the talking. Tell me about your family and your job."

I couldn't help liking her as long as she didn't pigeon hole me about becoming an Israeli citizen. It's a beautiful country but to become part of it was the last thing on my mind. Why would I want to live in a country where everyone is armed?

"David and I have been married a few years and we both have good jobs. My mother died of cancer just last year. She was only ill for three months. As I am an only child, my father is alone now."

"Oh, I'm so sorry, it must have been a terrible shock." Cassia said.

"Dad is so angry at God, but fortunately he has many friends. He is Jewish but has never been religious. I'm not religious either, but I do believe in God. However, he was the one who encouraged me to come to Israel." I paused briefly then I continued: "David's parents are from Scotland and he comes from a big family. They have a lovely large house and we usually go every year to celebrate Christmas with them."

She gave me a quizzical look. "Christmas? I thought you said you were Jewish?"

"I am, but in Britain everyone celebrates Christmas and David's parents are Christians."

She raised her eyebrows in surprise and I wondered if I had said the right thing.

"I see," she said. "But surely the British Jews celebrate Hanukah around the time of Christmas?"

"Yes, they do. Before I married David my parents always celebrated Hanukah, but since my Mum died he has neglected his Jewish traditions."

"Anyway, I sense that you are still grieving so I would hate to upset you. I actually really like you Rosa."

How refreshing, I thought, that Americans are so much more open than we British.

Max approached me holding out his arm as the band started to play loud dance music. "May I have the pleasure?"

I took his arm but barely came up to his shoulder. He twirled me around dizzily and I found myself really enjoying the fun, except for one instance when his hand wandered to my backside. "You're very attractive, you know," he said. I gave him such a look and slapped his hand away. Meanwhile, David was dancing with Cassia. She was the taller one in that duo. I watched them and realised that David seemed to be flirting with her.

"Did I tell you the joke about the hippopotamus falling in love...?" said Max, as we sat down again.

We laughed at some of Max's jokes, but some were off colour and always Cassia glared at him and tried to change the subject. It was a great evening, though we were getting a bit tipsy, as Max kept plying us with more drinks and he was paying for it all! He was definitely well over the limit as he swayed on his feet and started to use foul language. I couldn't help but stay with the picture in my mind of David dancing with his head too close to Cassia's breasts. When the music stopped I grabbed David, excused ourselves and left.

The next day, we decided to take a tour bus and visit Christian holy sites in Capernaum and Nazareth. David was anxious to see these places and report to his parents in Scotland. It was while we were sitting on the grass in Capernaum enjoying a picnic of humus sandwiches and drinking Cola, that we heard the sound of a fleet of airplanes flying low and making a thunderous noise. Everyone was looking up into the sky. David turned to a lady standing nearby.

"What on earth…?"

"Don't worry," she said. "It's just manoeuvres!"

There were at least three or four large bombers circling round and diving. "It's enough to wake the dead," I shouted above the din.

"What kind of country is this? I can't wait to go home," said David. "Israel is certainly a military country. Everyone has to do military service and security is what they most care about to the point of paranoia."

"Yes, I wonder if Cassia has thought about that aspect. She talked of having a family, but even daughters have to join the army."

"Aye, I'm sure she doesn't realise what it means to belong to this society. We have jet passenger planes flying over London but they don't make a big racket. Not like these bombers do."

Nazareth was quite different from Tiberius yet full of history. Even the language was different, Arabic instead of Hebrew. There was so much to see, but the old market and the Arab traders reminded us of the old City of Jerusalem. And that again inevitably reminded me of my baby. Yes, in my heart, he was still my baby.

Finally, after two more days we had to depart south for Ben Gurion Airport but not before we had exchanged addresses with Max and Cassia at breakfast in the hotel. I got the impression that Cassia had not given up in trying to convert me to her opinion. She seemed to be convinced that it was important for every Jew to consider Aliya, in other words to make Israel your home.

"I do hope we will meet again, Rosa. We must definitely keep in touch. And think about all I've told you." She gave me a warm hug and kissed me on both cheeks.

"Bye. I'll certainly think about it. Who knows, we may meet again in Jerusalem."

"I do hope so." she said.

It occurred to me later, that her motive for being in Jerusalem was very different from mine. I still couldn't bring myself to telling her about Musa because it felt too personal and raw, but if we stay friends then maybe I will tell her.

We arrived in London to grey skies and pouring rain. My father met us and thankfully seemed a little more cheerful. We were glad to be home and as we sat drinking coffee we related to Dad some of our adventures. However, we decided to keep the story of Musa to ourselves for the time being. I was afraid Dad would think us foolish to have cared for a stranger's baby for five days. He went home happy with the little silver and olive wood souvenirs we gave him. Then we started to attack our pile of mail and I wondered if there would ever be a letter from Bethlehem.

CHAPTER SEVEN

Almost six months later and our holiday in Israel seemed a distant dream. David went back to school after the summer talking incessantly about his new art project for his students. It involved putting layers of coloured paper on top of one another giving a 3-D effect of a framed picture or something. He always has some new ideas and a way of enthusing excitement. I pretended to be excited but I don't share his talent. On the contrary, life for me working in the records department of the hospital, keeping track of patients' files, once interesting, suddenly became boring and mundane.

Musa's dark eyes regularly invaded my dreams, but every time I mentioned him to David, he only murmured, "You must try and forget him. I'm sure he is well looked after in Bethlehem. Who knows, they may have even traced his family."

"I don't think so," I said. "He is probably just lying in a cot in a room full of other babies with nobody picking him up for hugs or any care."

"Och! For God's sake, don't be so sentimental." David stressed his Scottish accent when he wanted to annoy me.

It was a Saturday morning and I decided it was probably better not to discuss the subject of Musa. I brushed my hair more vigorously cringing with frustration. As a child, my battles with my mother were mostly over my long curly hair. It used to get so full of tangles that I would cry when she pulled the brush through it.

"What are you doing today, darling." I could see David's face in the mirror. 'Darling' didn't really match his aggravated mood.

"I thought I would go and see how Dad is," I said.

"OK then, I'm off to the library. I'll probably not be back for lunch."

I phoned Dad as soon as David had gone, worrying a little as to how I could improve our relationship. Ever since returning from Israel I felt David had become more distant. I couldn't really put a finger on it, but there was not the intimacy as before. He often came home late making excuses and we just never seemed to go out together any more.

I picked up the phone. "Hi, Dad, how are you?"

100

"Not too bad, thanks love. It's a nice day so I thought I would do some gardening."

"How about if I took you out for lunch? I've got something important to tell you."

"What? You're …you're not expecting are you?" he said excitedly.

"Sorry Dad, no not that. I'll catch the next bus and be with you in just over half an hour."

I found Dad in a real pickle. Dirty dishes stacked up in the sink. Newspapers, bills, letters, magazines all in dusty piles on every available chair so that I had to remove a bundle before I could sit down. Even Dad himself, was wearing a shirt with what looked like tomato juice spilled down the front. Or was it red wine?

"Dad, how can you live like this? You must get a cleaning woman. And for goodness sake go and change your shirt!"

Dad laughed. "It wasn't long ago that I was telling you to do that, young lady. Now I'm the messy one!"

"Dad, you know very well that I'm tidy like Mum was." I punched him on his shoulders, affectionately.

He grunted, then we both laughed as I went to tackle the dishes and make some coffee while he went upstairs to change.

Later, we sat in a corner of the local Italian restaurant and Dad sat on the edge of his chair eagerly waiting for my news.

"Well?" he said after we had given our order of pasta and salads with garlic bread.

"Do you remember my school friend Rebecca?"

"Vaguely love. Was that the one who used to come home and help you with your maths problems? Was she the one with pigtails?"

"She's changed a lot since then and now she is very religious. We stayed with her and her husband, Amos, in Israel. They live on one of those settlements."

"Yes, you've already told me about that. You weren't too happy staying on a so-called settlement, were you?" He leaned over the table whispering, as if it was a taboo subject, his brow furrowing.

"No, that's true Dad. Anyway, one morning we felt a little claustrophobic so we went for a short walk near an Arab village and what do you think…?" I paused. "We found an abandoned baby, lying in a basket by a small brook..."

I held my breath waiting for Dad's reaction. He took out a white grubby handkerchief from a pocket and wiped the sweat from his almost bald head. His large humped nose was red and his cheeks flushed. His dark eyes were looking kindly into mine.

"Go on…"

"We asked everyone in the village, and in fact, David went from door to door with Amos. No-one around laid claim to him. Dad, I looked after him for five days. Think of it, me looking after a baby for five whole days. Oh Dad if you could have seen him. He had the sweetest little face and big dark eyes, you can imagine. I can't stop thinking about him."

He took my hand and squeezed it. It had the exact effect of squeezing tears from my eyes.

"An Arab baby?"

"Yes, his name is Moses."

"How do you know? Anyway, Moses was a Jew."

"Yes, but there was a note in Arabic which said his name is Musa and that is Arabic for Moses."

"So, where is he now?"

"We left him in a hospital in Bethlehem." Dad took the handkerchief back out of his pocket and dabbed subconsciously at the corner of his eyes and gently smiled at me.

"And Rebecca. What was her reaction?"

"At first she was excited at the name of Moses. She was only interested in the biblical connection, though. She didn't want anything to do with the baby. In fact we had a big quarrel, I'm afraid. Amos was more accommodating and helped me buy all the baby clothes and feeding bottles."

"It sounds like you were a mother for a short while. Why on earth have you kept all this from me until now?"

"Because David didn't want me to tell anyone. He keeps telling me to try and forget. But I can't forget him, Dad."

"Rosa, love, I'm glad you've finally told me. Now I understand why you've been so moody!"

"Has it shown that much?"

"I can tell by the colour of clothes you wear. You never used to wear so much black. Not that I see you that often, but I thought you were just broody like a hen fluffing her feathers!" He flapped his arms and started to cackle so that people in the restaurant turned their heads.

"Dad you are so funny!" We both laughed out loud. I was glad that he didn't tell me to forget it all. Later, he mentioned to me in a round about sort of way, that I

104

should seek medical help to investigate reasons for my infertility. I told him that I had already seen the Doctor and was waiting for an appointment at the hospital.

"These things take months to arrange," I said.

Before I left him to go home, I suddenly had a thought.

"Dad, why don't you and I go to a Shabbat service?"

He looked at me quizzically. "Since when are you interested in going to the synagogue?"

"Well you and Mum used to take me sometimes when I was little, remember?"

"Yes, I do remember. Your Mum used to keep up all those old traditions, didn't she?   She was very strict not only about not eating ordinary bread during Passover, but getting rid of anything that had a hint of flour or yeast in the house. She used to clean out all the cupboards. I used to avoid being at home during those days of spring cleaning. Remember, how she got cross with you for bringing home a chocolate wafer bar from school?"

"Yes, she made me go to bed without supper."

"She took you to the synagogue and made you say sorry to God." He sighed. "I still miss her, you know."

I hugged him, "I know you do, Dad. I do, too."

"If you like we could go next Friday evening to the synagogue in North London. It's not far from here."

"Good. I'll ring you next week. Don't forget what I told you about getting a cleaner in."

However, when I got home David was brandishing two tickets for a West End show for the following Friday. "I thought we could go out for dinner before the show."

"Great," I said, trying to sound really excited. I could not, however, deceive David.

"Don't you want to go?" he said.

"Of course, I do. It will be lovely to have an evening out together. It's just that Dad and I were going somewhere, but that can be postponed."

Poor David. He was trying so hard and there I go messing things up.

We did have a wonderful evening out and our relationship was on a high again.

So it was another week before I kept my promise to Dad and went with him to the Synagogue. We were given a warm welcome and everyone was friendly. But I felt out of place. All the women were dressed in their best and some even wore hats. I had put on a navy skirt and jacket, with a white blouse, but it was very plain in comparison. They were excited to hear that I had just come back from Israel and told us how they were trying to raise money for all sorts of projects there, which they considered belonged to them. Judaism has many colours and divisions, but all keep the festivals applying them to modern life. I was glad to discover this was a liberal synagogue with a lady Rabbi. It was a very loosely structured liturgy, partly in Hebrew, but mostly in English. We sang some songs from the psalms and then the preaching was comparing the Biblical leader of Moses to the present day leaders of Israel! The Rabbi prayed that *'El Malei Rachamin, God full of compassion who heals the broken-hearted ...bring peace to all your children...'* Then the prayer at the end went something like this: *'He is the Lord our God, and that we are Israel, His people....With great joy Moses and the children of Israel answered You in song...Who is like You, Lord among all the gods...'*

I was heartened by the prayer for peace but why was I continually being reminded of Moses?

"Tell me Dad, why do I get so uptight every time I hear the name of Moses."

"Rosa, love, I understand, but I don't know how to comfort you. I guess time will heal as time is healing me for losing your dear mother."

As we said goodbye we held each other close.

Two weeks later and within a few days of each other, there were two letters from Jerusalem. I was so excited. One was a brief note from Sister Bridget informing us that she had visited baby Musa in Bethlehem and assuring us that he was being well looked after.

"There you are, Rosa, I told you not to worry," said David with a triumphal grin.

The second letter was from the Doctor at the hospital in Bethlehem but the postmark was Jerusalem. Perhaps Sister Bridget had taken the letter to mail, as Bethlehem post would be erratic with all the troubles?

It began:

Dear Mr. and Mrs. Craig,

Since you requested that I keep you informed about baby Musa, I thought to tell you that he is still under observation at the hospital. We thought it best to keep him under constant care of a doctor in case he has any severe cyanotic attacks. Occasionally we have to give him oxygen, but on the whole he is making the normal progress of any young baby.

However, what he really needs is cardiac surgery. This is not a complicated operation and has been carried out countless times on babies with his condition and with great success. He would be able to live a completely normal life afterwards. Now the problem is we would need to transfer him to an Israeli hospital and this would cost a lot of money. Moreover, he has no family to be with him or to help with costs. The Israeli government are probably not going to take him in as a social case without knowing who his guardians are.

I don't know whether you are thinking of visiting Israel again in the near future? Dare I suggest that Musa would have a greater chance in a London hospital? Otherwise, of course, we will have to appeal to the Catholic charities here to fund his operation and make someone his temporary guardian.

My best wishes to you both.

Yours sincerely,

Dr. A. Hussein.

David and I looked at each other and didn't know what to say, but for me it came as a kind of lifeline of hope. No problem is insurmountable.

CHAPTER EIGHT

When the letter from Bethlehem arrived, I could tell from David's expression that he was not only confused, but trying to reject the whole idea of having anything to do with baby Musa. In fact, I think he was annoyed at having to bring back the memories of our time in Israel. I did not want to jump to any rash decision, though I knew what my heart was telling me.

"Just going to make some coffee," I said.

"Well, I can't stop. I shall be late for work," David replied curtly.

"We have to talk."

"Not now, I have to go. Bye."

"It's early yet. We need to talk about the letter." I tried to stand in front of the door to block his exit, but he pushed past me.

"I'll call you in my lunch hour."

I glanced at the clock. The postman had arrived early. Just after eight and plenty of time, but David was deliberately avoiding the issue.

As I boarded the bus to go to work I was trying to think straight. My job in a general hospital was being responsible for keeping track of patients' files, records and appointments. Although I had no direct contact with the medical staff or patients, at least I had a list of surgeons who worked there. I decided to make enquiries as to who would be a suitable cardio-thoracic surgeon especially one who had experience of operating on the hearts of babies. There were several possible names, but how could I make enquiries without disclosing my reasons?

Then there was the question of money. We were already in debt from having to borrow money for the down payment on our house, which provided we were careful, hopefully, would be paid off next year. We couldn't possibly afford to pay for a private operation for Musa. Would the National Health help a foreign foundling baby? And would the Brits allow him into the country for a start?

I was going crazy and I needed to talk to someone desperately. I was friendly with all my work colleagues but apart from coffee gossip, there was really not one person who I could confide in. During the lunch break I found myself wandering past the cafeteria into the Chapel. It was just a small room with rows of maroon colour padded chairs. Sitting down, I felt myself relax in an unmistakable atmosphere of peace. Obviously it

112

was used by many faiths, but centrally there was a simple wooden cross on a small table, covered by a white lace cloth with the background of a painted glass window. The rays of the sun were streaming through onto a crystal blue lake and emerald green hills. There was a man standing in a boat by the lakeside. It looked like a painting of the Lake of Galilee and I was reminded of our stay near Tiberius. The colours from the stained glass were breathtakingly beautiful, dancing around the walls like rainbow trout. Trying hard to control myself, tears started to cloud my vision and bowing my head automatically, my hair fell around my face so that I did not notice the quiet footsteps of a man beside me. I could not see his face immediately as the colours from the window were giving him a kind of unworldly appearance. Was this an angel? I shivered. I pretended to be praying, my head bowed and my hands clasped in my lap. What were the prayers my mother taught me? There were some words from a psalm I remember. '*O HaShem* teach me Thy way'…it was a cry from my heart; 'Oh God, please show me what to do.'

"Would you like to talk to someone about it?" said the man.

"Oh, I'm OK thanks."

"Well I'm around if you need me." He walked to the back of the room.

Then I thought, there's no harm in telling this stranger.

"Are you a Father?"

He laughed a gentle laugh. "I'm not a Catholic priest if that's what you mean, but I am a father of two lovely children and I am a Vicar of sorts. My name is Kevin and I have been chaplain of this hospital for the past three years." He held out his hand and indicated a couple of chairs. "Would you like to sit over here?"

"I'm Rosa," I said as we sat in a corner of the room away from the window.

"Glad to meet you Rosa." His blue eyes smiled, though I couldn't help noticing a small scar on his right cheek which was accentuated by the creases of his smile.

"That beautiful window reminded me," I began. "You see my husband and I were in Israel six months ago and…" I hesitated.

"How lovely. I've always wanted to go to Israel on a pilgrimage, but do go on," he said.

"I have a problem. First of all I'm not a Christian. Actually, I'm Jewish (why did I tell him that, it's not important). The thing is, my husband and I were

114

staying with some Jewish friends and one morning when we went for a little walk we found an abandoned baby, a Palestinian baby boy. It's a long story, but just to tell you that I looked after that baby for almost a week and just before returning to London we left him in a Bethlehem hospital. Now, we have had a letter from the doctor asking if it would be possible to bring him to London for a heart operation. You see, he has a congenital heart defect. The problem is, how can I bring him into this country, and how can we possibly afford his medical expenses?" I paused.

"I see..." he said, running his hands through his sandy hair.

"There are other problems too. I just love this baby and would like to foster or even adopt him, but my husband is not altogether with me." I looked at my watch. "Oh goodness, I have to go back to work in two minutes."

Kevin smiled kindly. "So sorry you have to rush, but let me think through your problem. I can't promise, but I may be able to help. Where do you work?"

"In the administration department, just close to the entrance of Out-patients. I shouldn't have troubled you with all of this, but thanks for listening. You understand I want to keep this secret for the time being."

"Of course. Let me give you my mobile number. We must talk again," he said as we shook hands and he handed me his business card.

My office phone was ringing when I got back.

"I've just had an extraordinary stroke of luck," David sounded really excited.

"What?"

"The school are letting me have an old shed in the school grounds for free. I have to renovate it and put in heating but I can use it any time as my own studio. Isn't that marvellous, darling."

"Sounds great!" I said. Obviously, David and I were on different wave lengths. While he was working out how much it would cost to set up an artist's studio, I was worrying about how to pay for Musa's operation. That's so typical, I thought, just thinking of his own needs.

"I might be late home," he continued.

"Why?"

"I need to inspect the shed more carefully and see what I need."

"But what about the letter from the doctor in Bethlehem? How shall we answer?"

"We'll talk about it tonight."

"You said you'd talk on the phone."

"Darling I have to go. Bye."

Patience is not one of my virtues and as I prepared dinner that evening I kept reminding myself, patience, patience, patience. Eventually at 7pm, long after school had closed, David made an appearance, looking very pleased with himself. I must keep calm and not start an argument, I thought, so I went to turn the oven back on and had my back to him.

"I've always wanted my own studio." He was practically singing as he described to me how wonderful it would be to spend his weekends and spare time painting pictures in his workshop. "I might even get models in from time to time."

I immediately had visions of young girls in the nude being invited to his private little studio and suddenly I felt threatened.

"Wow," I said, laughing nervously, but cringing at the thought. "Going in for painting nudes now, are we?"

"Don't be so silly, darling." He put his arms round my waist and swung me round in a kind of dance, kissing my neck and sweeping me off my feet. Sometimes, I felt overpowered.

"Jealous are you," he mocked, laughing out loud. I had to laugh with him.

At least, I thought, he was in a good mood to talk about more serious matters.

But not yet. Perhaps reading my thoughts, he said, "Darling, we should celebrate. Just let your hair down for once. Do we have any champagne?"

It was a joke between us as my hair was always down! I pulled it over my face.

"Is that how you like it?"

David chuckled. "Even better if you took your top off and lie on the couch over there, while I go and get my sketch pad."

I clenched my fists and gave him a pretend box. That seemed to turn him on as he took me in his arms and kissed my hair. "Where's your mouth, silly!"

It was easy to pretend to be light-hearted, but what I really wanted was a serious conversation.

The next day around noon, Kevin came to my office, much to the surprise of my colleagues, who must have noticed his clerical dog-collar. He asked me to join him in the Chapel after work.

"I didn't know you were religious," said Dawn, who was a young temporary secretary, working with me.

118

She was always trying out new hairstyles and changing her boyfriends with the same regularity.

"I'm not religious, but Kevin and I have a little problem to sort out."

"Kevin? You know the Vicar, then? What kind of problem would that be?"

I felt like telling her to mind her own business, but decided not to cause friction.

"You will know about it soon enough."

"Oo-ee how soon would that be, I wonder?" She threw her head back, flicking the stray ends and separating the strands of her blond hair with one finger while the other hand was on the typewriter.

Out of frustration, I ignored her, picked up a pile of patients' files and left the office. This would not normally be my job, but I was glad for the opportunity to walk around the hospital. The files were for the children's ward so I took the lift up to the top floor. I was pleasantly surprised. I had imagined a place of bawling infants and impatient nurses. Instead, the walls were decorated with pictures of nursery rhymes and funny Mickey Mouse cartoons, and the atmosphere cheerful. Some of the children were sitting up in their cots playing with cuddly toys. Some little ones were sitting in a circle on tiny chairs with a couple of adults, playing with a choo-choo train putting in various plastic animals as it raced across the floor. One little boy of about two was sitting hugging a purple stuffed dinosaur in one arm with a drip attached to his other arm, strapped to a board. I left the files in the office and spoke to one of the nurses, who was carrying a baby to the theatre, mother in tow, looking very anxious. "What a cheerful ward you have here."

She looked at me with a half smile. "Well, we have our happy times, but also our sad times too."

I could see that the baby, obviously only a few months old was already sleeping, probably anaesthetised. I tried to imagine Musa in the same situation.

I decided to wait until all my colleagues had gone home, before handing over the keys to another staff member and then I made my way to the Chapel. It was already dusk, so the colours of the window were muted. "Hi Rosa, I may have some good news," said Kevin with a beaming smile, waiting for me just inside the entrance.

"There is a surgeon who specialises in heart surgery for infants. His name is Doctor Kahn. If you like, I will make an appointment for you at his office."

"Thank you so much. I appreciate your help."

"I also have some ideas as to how we can raise some money for your baby's operation. We can discuss these notions. What d'you think?"

He had some marvellous ideas about raising funds. I had expected a negative approach or at least discouragement. I thought others would tell me how foolish I was to even consider caring about a foreign orphan child. But here was Kevin as enthusiastic as a small boy with a new bike! Now my next problem would be to convince David.

CHAPTER NINE

It was several days until the weekend but at last there was an opportunity when David was ready to listen. We were in the kitchen after breakfast. David put down his newspaper and got up to wash the dishes. He stood at the sink, humming a current pop tune and rolling his sleeves up.

"David you still haven't discussed with me about answering the letter from Bethlehem. Anyway, I have been making enquiries. Kevin, the hospital chaplain is going to help us."

David turned round, the soap suds up to his elbows. "What? Kevin? First you go to a synagogue with your Dad then you discuss our personal matters with a Christian priest? Are you getting religious or something?"

I studied his face and it was one of amusement. At least he's not angry, I thought.

"No, of course not. But we still have to reply to that letter."

"For goodness sake, Rosa it's not our problem. Why is this so important? It's six months since we were in Israel, so let them sort it out. They must think we're rich people. Just write to the doctor and tell him to contact those Catholic charities he talked about."

I might have known David would want to wash his hands of the whole business, but this time I was going to put my foot down. "Darling, I really care about that child. You know very well I do. You won't even let me talk to you about him."

"You mean you want to bring him to England?"

"Yes, I do." I paused. "I'm sure when you see the baby again you will not want to part with him, either. Please don't keep putting me off."

"Och! You are the limit!" David wiped his hands and stormed off into the sitting room, taking the newspaper with him. I followed him.

"You know, I've never forgotten dear little Musa and I truly believe now that maybe God must have had a hand in us finding him. David I love him." I put the emphasis on the word Love. "I held that baby for five days. He became part of me."

"God? You believe that crap? My wife is getting religious!"

"Yes. I do believe in God, though I'm not sure why or how. I'll never forget Sister Bridget telling us that God had a special plan for Musa."

"I've never seen you so serious. Look, darling, we have to be practical. There is no way we could bring that child to England and be responsible for his medical care. You're talking nonsense. You're dreaming. Tell you what, if it will make you happy, I will write a cheque and send it to the hospital in Bethlehem to help a little with costs."

I threw up my hands and gritted my teeth.

"David, David, just listen to me for once. Kevin's idea is brilliant. He said finding a surgeon would be no problem. In fact he has recommended a specialist to me. As for funds, he said that in less than three months time it will be Christmas and it would make a great story for the media. They would even appeal for funds."

I held my breath expecting David to blow his top. And he did just that. He raised his bushy eyebrows and opened his mouth with incredulous horror. "What! Media you said? Journalists at the door? TV cameras? You mean telling the newspapers about him? I can just see the headlines: 'SAVE A BETHLEHEM ORPHAN BABY FOR CHRISTMAS'. You want the world to know we're bringing a foreign baby into our home?"

He was shouting, while I watched, quietly confident that he would come round.

"Why not?"

"Are you out of your mind?"

"No. It's not madness, but love."

"Anyway he wasn't born in Bethlehem."

"David, we don't have to tell them where he was born. We don't know anyway. He'll be a Christmas baby. The public will love it. A Christmas present of a baby from Bethlehem! Your parents might be excited about the idea. I know my Dad is."

"You've told your Dad?"

"Yes, about Musa but not about Kevin's idea."

"I can't believe all I'm hearing. Where is the reserved, private person I married? Now you are shouting our news to the world?"

"You're the one who's shouting."

He was staring at me with a deflated look and I could see he realised by the quiet tone of my voice that I was not about to give up. He skulked away back to the kitchen while I sunk down in a sitting room chair. Ten minutes later he came back, carrying two mugs of coffee. I felt I was winning. We sat drinking our coffee without saying a word, and then he put his mug down clumsily. I noticed his hand was shaking slightly. He didn't want to admit defeat.

"How do you know my Mum and Dad will like the idea? Have you spoken to them, too?"

"No, but your Mum is a real poppet. I'm sure she will listen."

"Go ahead and talk to them, then. See what their reaction is. Personally, I wish we'd never found that wretched baby."

"David, how can you say that?" I tried to keep my voice low and calm. I knew it was the only way to bring him round to my way of thinking.

"This is not how I imagined our family to be."

"That may be but whatever it takes, I want to help Musa even if it means he has to return to his own country. Anyway, when we first found him you thought like me and you grew fond of him too. Remember how you told the nuns we were both attached to him?"

"Rosa, did I hear you say you would be willing to let him go back to his own country?" David had completely ignored my question.

"Yes." I probably didn't sound very convincing, but if that is what it takes…. "Why don't you talk to your parents first? Maybe we could go for a weekend up to

126

Edinburgh. It's so difficult to explain everything on the phone."

"Och, oh alright then. We could go at the end of this month if that's convenient with them".

In the end, David phoned and made arrangements. His family were delighted, as always, to look forward to our visit. Meanwhile, I wrote a short letter to Doctor Hussein in Bethlehem to say that we were trying to get some funds together and would let him know the outcome. We would, I realised, also need a letter from the surgeon to the British Consulate in Jerusalem to obtain a visa for Musa.

I had an appointment for an examination at the fertility clinic and since it was at the same hospital where I worked it was easy to get the time off I needed. The results of the tests came back positive. There was absolutely no reason at all why I couldn't conceive in the normal way and certainly no need for any subsequent treatment. They suggested that David go for tests but when I told him, he brushed it off.

"There's certainly nothing wrong with me. You can see I'm perfectly healthy."

We decided to go up to Edinburgh by train. It was the end of September and already there was a chill in the air. The trees along the route were showing their glorious coats of crimson, russet and gold hues, which made me feel confident. Indeed, my mood was one of joyful anticipation. I felt sure that David's parents would have a more sympathetic attitude. His older sister, Morag, met us at the station. Being married with three children made her busty and round, which made me feel very thin in comparison.

"Rosa, how are you? What a lovely surprise to have you with us this weekend." She gave me a wonderful bear hug and a huge kiss. She gave David a hug too followed by all the family. David's parents were semi-retired from business, but seemed to be involved in all sorts of village activities. Their house was an old-fashioned large cottage in a country village, only a few miles from Edinburgh. The garden had spacious trimmed lawns and a few apple and pear trees. The leaves were hanging on, but turning yellow and there were a few apples on the high branches.

David's Mum had masses of white curly hair, topped up on her head framing her rosy cheeks. She was bustling around in the kitchen.

"Can I help?" I said, taking an apron from the peg behind the door.

"Thanks, pet. You could put these things on the table. I've got a beef pie in the oven, and by the way, you're not fussy about food are you, because we have cauliflower cheese with it?"

"No, Mum. I eat anything. It smells good."

Then looking me in the eye, she said: "Are you alright? You look a bit peekish."

"I'm fine. I guess I need some colour in my cheeks. This country air will do me good."

After the evening meal, we sat round the fire and David and I related all our adventures in Israel. The large cheerful log fire made me realise that the climate in Scotland was so much cooler than London. I sat watching the glow and sparks, creating pictures. They were joyful scenes, people dancing to sensuous rhythms.

Of course we had told them the main events of our stay with friends and had sent them picture postcards of Jerusalem and Tiberius, but we had not told them about baby Musa. I could sense that David wanted to bring up the subject first.

"You know, Rosa, is very keen to bring the wee baby to England. She even wants to keep him, but I've tried to discourage her. After all, he's not really our problem

129

any more, is he? The doctor in Bethlehem mentioned Catholic charities, but Rosa has got it into her head that because she looked after Musa, she feels responsible. What do you think Mum?"

"David, don't you care! Let us hear what Rosa has to say," Morag butted in.

"Well, I fell in love with that baby. I was like a mother to him for five whole days. I want to do anything possible to bring him to London for an operation and we will see after that what happens."

David's mother patted me on my knee, smiling sympathetically, but his father shifted in his seat and got up to rake the fire and put another log on. He had his back to us. "Tell me Rosa, this baby, Palestinian, you say? Is he...coloured?"

I was surprised that an educated man like David's father should be prejudiced.

I laughed nervously, putting my hand to my mouth. "No, he's just Middle-Eastern. In fact, not much darker than I am." He turned round and patted me on my arm. "Don't get me wrong, pet, I'm not against any colour, it's just to have an idea of what he looks like. Didn't you take a camera with you?"

David spoke up. "Yes, Dad, we did take a camera but I used it for pictures of sites. It just never occurred to us to take a picture of Musa."

"That's a shame. He sounds adorable," said Morag.

"I'm sure he's a wee poppet, my dear," said Mum. "I can see you really care."

David's father got up. "Well, anyone for drinks? Brandy? Scotch?" We had already drunk wine with dinner. I declined, but David went for a 'wee dram.' I think his parents felt they had been put on the spot.

Morag had to go home. She hugged me, whispering: "I do hope it all works out for you."

I helped his mother clear up the kitchen. "Why didn't you tell us all this before, Rosa pet? I can see you've been bottling this matter up for months and obviously this wee boy means a lot to you."

"David thought it would all blow over and that I would forget him. But you know I cuddled him for five days, Mum. He's such a darling child. You can't just forget something like that ever happened."

"Of course, I understand. I've been a mother too you know and all my daughters are mothers. We still hope that one day you and David…."

131

"It's not that we don't want a child. It just hasn't happened yet," I said.

"Anyway, I'm with you, all the way. David will come round, I'm sure."

It was her quiet reassurance that helped me to relax that night. I felt the tension just dissolving from my body and somehow felt more confident about the whole matter.

The next morning, I saw David and his father talking. "That whole publicity stunt sounds a bit far fetched to me. We don't want to cause undue attention to our family." I heard David's father say.

"I'm not too happy about that either but we have to find money from somewhere," David said.

I butted in. "There's no harm in trying. I'm sure people will love the idea of a Christmas baby."

"I will see how I can help you both," his father said, after we had said goodbye to his mother and got in the car for the drive back to the train station.

Back in London, the first thing I did was to make an appointment to see a heart surgeon. After a few days, I took the morning off to find his private surgery. Dr. Khan was a small dapper man with a neat moustache. I guessed by his features, Indian in origin. We sat in his office and I showed him the letter from Bethlehem and told him all about how we found the baby. He put on his glasses, studying the letter carefully, while I studied his certificates on the wall.

"Mrs Craig, this is all very interesting and if he is allowed to come to the UK I am willing to help. Tell me a bit more about him. When you were looking after him, did he go blue and quiet?"

"Yes, he did sometimes, but not all the time."

"I need to know a lot more about the exact medical problem so I suggest that I get in touch with Dr Hussein to ask for Musa's records. I will make a copy of this letter and I see there is a Fax number, so I will fax him right away," he said. "I will be in touch, Mrs. Craig."

I thanked him and returned home.

Meanwhile, I had found out the number of the British Consulate in Jerusalem, from telephone enquiries. When I dialled the number they put me through to the British Consul immediately and I tried to explain my request about granting a visa for a Palestinian baby to come to Britain for heart surgery.

"Mrs. Craig, this is not going to be simple. In fact, more complicated than you imagined. You would need permission for the child to leave the country and he would need a proper identity and an official guardian."

"Oh dear! I hadn't realised it would be so difficult."

"You will need to come to Jerusalem, Mrs. Craig, and we will see what can be done."

Events were moving faster than I had anticipated. I was ready to explode with excitement but asking myself, 'What have you let yourself in for?'

I went back to the hospital and found Kevin in the chapel so I was able to update him on the situation. He was as excited as I was. "I wish I could come with you," he said.

I dreaded telling David that I had to go back to Jerusalem and as expected he was apprehensive.

"Is it really necessary to travel?"

"Yes, I can't do all the paperwork from here."

"But you can't go alone. You know I can't take time off from school right now. What about taking your Dad with you?"

"No, I don't think that's a good idea. He won't want to come anyway, unless it's a tour and I won't have time to take him around. He might be willing to help with my expenses though."

"Darling won't you be afraid with all that's going on? The situation is getting worse according to the news. You were really afraid in Bethlehem, remember?"

"How could I ever forget? But Sister Bridget will be a great help, I'm sure."

"I'm just worried about you freaking out!"

"Don't worry," I said, trying to look confident though inside I was trembling equally with anxiety and excitement.

Within the next two weeks I had a ticket to fly to BenGurion Airport. Kevin had suggested I take a widow lady from his church to accompany me, because she had been on Holy Land trips several times, but in the end she couldn't arrange to come.

David came to the airport to see me off. I could see he was worried about my safety, but I tried to appear strong in front of him at least. However, as I went through the barrier, waving goodbye, I panicked. How was I going to cope?

CHAPTER TEN

Mid October and it was still summer in Israel. I emerged from the plane sweating with the heat, shedding my top winter jacket and went through security and immigration as if I was sleep-walking, wheeling my suitcase through the exit and expecting a familiar face to wake me up. There was no one to meet me. It suddenly hit me why I was here and seeing all the other passengers being greeted made me realise how alone I was. For a moment I panicked, looking around nervously. I was not used to travelling by myself. I hailed a taxi to the Old City of Jerusalem and found everything the same. The Palestinian peasant women were sitting on the steps outside the Damascus Gate selling their little bits of produce; huge tomatoes and radishes. A handful of children were running after me, holding gaudy bracelets and fake gold necklaces to sell. A young man, wearing a grubby tee-shirt tried to relieve me of my suitcase but I hung on to it, dragging it over the rough concrete path until I reached the Hostel.

Sister Bridget was expecting me and suddenly seeing a familiar face, it was as if I woke up. I fell into her arms.

"Even before your letter arrived I had this feeling that you would be back!" she said as she hugged me.

"Well, here I am," I announced. I felt like an eager teenager, waiting for exam results.

"Tomorrow morning early, I will take you to see little Moses, or is it Musa? He has grown, you know."

"I can't wait," I said.

Sister Bridget had put me in a different room with a single bed. The oriental atmosphere was still there. The Arabic music, the rhythmic prayer chants *'Allahu Akbar'*, the noisy quarrelling of local families crowded into tiny rooms, including crying babies, plus the distant cracking of gunfire. But it was all the smells of the bazaars, perfumed incense and spicy, barbecued meat that brought all the memories flooding back. My heart was thumping with nervous excitement.

At breakfast the next day, Sister came to me looking perturbed.

"I'm afraid I have some bad news."

"No, not Musa, surely?" She put her hand on my arm.

"No, but there was a lot of trouble in Bethlehem last night. I heard on the radio that one soldier has been killed and three Palestinians dead. One of them was only a small child. So now there is a curfew. Goodness

137

knows how long. Maybe it's only for one day, but we cannot go and see Musa today. The road to Bethlehem has been completely blocked off. I'm so sorry."

"Oh, no!"

My heart sank. Not only was I disappointed in not seeing my baby but worried that David would hear the news and be concerned for me.

"My husband will be worried. I must phone him." I stifled a groan, putting my hands to my mouth. Sister patted my shoulder.

"Don't let him worry too much. Anyway, you can move about in Jerusalem so I suggest you go to the British Consulate. You need to register your name since you are not with a party of tourists. And at the same time you can tell them about Musa. You did bring a paper from the heart surgeon, didn't you?"

"Yes, I have the letter with me."

She gave me directions to the Consulate, so that is what I did. Security was tight, as I had imagined it would be. The first thing I noticed was a large English garden with well watered lawn and flower beds. Considering the scarcity of water in Jerusalem, this would be a luxury. With my British passport, there was no problem entering, but I had to be checked out by a guard and go through a turnstile. I noticed there was a queue of people, mostly Palestinians. As we sat in the waiting room, I asked the woman next to me why so many people were filling in forms. She said they wanted visas to go to the UK, because of all the daily troubles. I had a long time to wait.

Finally, a man with greying hair took me into a small room to interview me. He was dressed in a light smart suit and spoke with an impeccable Oxford accent for a Palestinian.

"My name is Mr. Khoury and I am the Pro-Consul." He shook my hand warmly, his mannerisms genteel, but when I explained the whole situation as to how we found baby Musa and why he needed to go to London for an operation, he stiffened. He said he did not seem hopeful that a visa would be easily granted.

"Mrs. Craig, your husband did not come with you?" he asked, frowning.

"No, he's a school teacher so he couldn't get time off."

"I am puzzled, Mrs. Craig. Didn't you consider that you should have involved the police in Ramallah from the very beginning? Where exactly were you when you found the baby?"

I was beginning to feel uncomfortable, my hands sweating.

"We were near a village not far from Ramallah. I don't know the name of it."

He ran his hands through his thinning hair, as if he doubted all I had told him. Then he leaned forward with his hands clasped on the table, staring at me.

"But where exactly were you staying? What were you doing in an Arab village? Why did you keep your discovery secret from the Authorities?"

I was beginning to feel like a criminal. "Have I committed a crime, Mr Khoury?"

"No, of course not, but I need to have more details." I found his tone cold, verging on hostile.

"Does the child have a birth certificate?"

"Well, he has been in a Bethlehem hospital for the past six months, so I presume they have made him a birth certificate by now."

Mr Khoury was furiously scribbling some notes down in Arabic.

"You see our friends told us it would be too dangerous to go to Ramallah to contact the police because of all the troubles."

"Who were the friends you were staying with?"

"Amos and Rebecca Steiner."

"Do you have their telephone number?"

"Amos works in Jerusalem. I have his number but I would rather you didn't involve them," I said, thinking that Amos would consider me foolish coming all the way back to Jerusalem to claim the baby. However, I felt that Amos would know his way around this city, if I needed more instructions.

"I'm sorry, but I need to talk to Mr. Steiner as a witness."

My knees trembled with nervousness but there was no other way but to go along with all the questioning. I was beginning to wish David was with me.

"Let me talk to Amos first," I said. "He doesn't know I'm here."

"Go ahead," he said, pushing the telephone towards me. "I'll just go and get some forms."

I found Amos right away. He was happy to hear my voice but surprised to know that I was in Jerusalem.

"Amos, I'm sorry to pounce this on you out of the blue, but I need your help." I explained the reason and said the Consul wanted to speak to him.

"Look," he said, "I'll ask for a couple of hours off and come to the Consulate myself. See you in about half an hour if you can stay that long?"

"I'm not going anywhere. I'll be waiting for you." I breathed a sigh of relief. I felt that Amos would be sympathetic and confirm my story. Mr. Khoury directed me back to the waiting room.

Amos arrived later than he had anticipated and looking rather flustered. He greeted me with a bristly kiss. "Good to see you Rosa, sorry I'm late. The traffic you know."

He looked the same as ever with his stubbly chin. Why doesn't he either grow a beard or shave? I thought, but chided myself. He apologised for not answering my letter of thanks but I told him I didn't really expect a reply.

"That baby stole your heart from the very beginning, didn't he?"

I smiled. "Yes, he did, but of course I didn't know he had a heart problem then. It was only after the doctor in Bethlehem told me. I must confess, Amos, I've never stopped thinking about him. By the way, tell me, how is Rebecca?"

"Rebecca is fine…"

We were interrupted by the arrival of Mr. Khoury. "Mr. Steiner, I believe?" We stood up and they shook hands firmly.

We were led back into the small room and Amos was bombarded with the same questions. He was calm and deliberate in his answers. I got the impression that Mr. Khoury's attitude was more favourable with Amos. Sort of man to man thing, I suppose.

"Mr. Khoury, I was the one who persuaded Mrs. Craig not to go to the Authorities in Ramallah. You understand we were on a settlement. It would not have been safe under the present tension. But I realised quickly that she and her husband had become very fond of the baby. We did not think that we were breaking any laws. And we did our best to persuade the villagers to take the child. They didn't want anything to do with it."

"What village was that?"

"They call it A'yn Qenya."

"Yes, I know that place," Mr. Khoury said. "Well now, I hope you will be able to help Mrs. Craig in accomplishing everything that needs to be done before I could consider granting a visa for baby Musa. Here is

143

what you need to do. Good luck," he said, pushing a list in front of us.

We thanked him and said goodbye. We walked back to the waiting room to study the list:

1. *Contact a lawyer to make out papers in order to make Mrs. Craig legal guardian (temporary).*

2. *Apply for a travel document from the Israeli Ministry of Interior, taking with you:*

3. *a) Doctor's recommendations from Bethlehem.*
   b) Letter from the London surgeon.
   c) Note you found on the baby.
   d) His birth certificate.
   e) A clear full face photograph.

4. *Bank account details of Mr. and Mrs. Craig, or a guarantee from a sponsor of full financial support.*

5. *Airline ticket booking.*

6. *If satisfactory, a visitor's visa will be granted for six months which could be renewed in the UK.*

"Gosh!" I said. "I have a lot of work to do."

"I will help you," said Amos. "I need to go back to the office now but I will be in touch. I know a lawyer who might be able to help. For now, let me give you a lift back to the Old City."

"You have saved my life and Musa's too. Can I invite you to have lunch with me somewhere? There are lots of nice restaurants in the Old City. You're not afraid of going into the Old City are you?"

"No, of course not. I often come here. But today, I have to go back to work. I don't know what Rebecca will say when I tell her you're here!"

I wanted to know so much more, so we just sat in the car and chatted for a while.

"Tell me how Rebecca is doing. We were interrupted before."

"Rebecca has not been well but she is so much better now. I don't think she told you that she had an early miscarriage about a year ago, but now we are hoping that this time all will go well."

"She's pregnant?"

"Yes," he said, smiling broadly.

"How many months?"

"Four." He started the car and we drove out of the car-park.

"That's great! Congratulations!"

"I'm trying to persuade her to live in Jerusalem where she can make more friends and have a better social life. You know, I went to live in the settlement purely for economic reasons. Rebecca is more religious, as you realised, no?"

"Yes. She has changed a lot since the Rebecca I knew at school and I'm really sorry our friendship soured rather."

"She's sorry, too. She thought she would be able to persuade you to her way of thinking about Israel."

"I'm afraid I could never come to live here. There seems to be so much injustice."

"I understand how you feel but I'm happy here. The insurance company I work for brings me into contact with Arabs and Jews so I have to be open-minded."

It was only a ten minute drive but the traffic became more and more congested as we approached the Old City. There was a pall of thick black smoke coming from the south. "That's in the direction of Bethlehem," said Amos.

"Oh God! When will it ever be safe enough for me to go there?"

146

He dropped me off at the Damascus Gate and promised he would be in touch to offer any help whenever I needed him. There was a sandwich cafe selling spicy lamb meat on skewers, so I sat at a small table outside and watched the passers–by, eating my late lunch before returning to the Hostel. It was another two days before I could finally go to Bethlehem. That morning, in anticipation of tears of joy, I had been careful to apply my usual amber eye shadow, but not any mascara.

Baby Musa was tucked away in a ward full of children, but I recognised him by his bright eyes immediately. He struggled to stand on his feet holding on to the bars of his cot and reached an arm through. He smiled at me!

"My darling child!" I picked him up and hugged him and he responded. Did he recognise my face or my voice? He had grown, of course. His hair was dark and wavy, his eyelashes curled like a girl's and his chubby face had bright ruddy cheeks. I was overcome with longing to hold on to this vulnerable little boy and as I hugged him closely, the tears streamed down my face.

CHAPTER ELEVEN

The nurses pottered about smiling to themselves as they saw me hugging and smothering my baby with kisses. He gurgled in response and actually chuckled when I tickled him on his tummy. He was dressed in a pale blue cotton jump suit with buttons at the waist and a motif of Pooh Bear. I held him to my chest and felt his soft cheek touch mine, so my tears wet his face. I saw his lower lip tremble as if he was going to cry, but he brightened up when I wiped away my tears. I bounced him up and down on my lap and he smiled.

"You are going to live with me," I whispered in his ear. "Very soon, we are going to go in a big aeroplane all the way to London."

Dr. Hussein came in, smiling. "Reunited are we?" He laughed as he saw my tear-stained face.

"Thank you for all your care, doctor. He looks well, doesn't he?"

"Yes, he's one tough little guy, aren't you, Musa?" he cooed. "*Keifak mobsut?*"

I realised then, that Musa had only been listening to Arabic so he would understand that the doctor was enquiring if he was happy. He understood more than me! But soon it would be all English and he would forget the Arabic. The doctor beckoned to the nurse and she came and took him back to his cot. I went with the doctor to his office.

"I have all the documents you need, Mrs. Craig, so I hope it works out for his surgery and everything. But you have to convince the British Consulate that all the financial side of things will be covered." He handed me a file of medical records from the last six months.

"Thank you Doctor, the London hospital is finding sponsors for him." I wasn't quite sure whether he would approve of the media for a 'Christmas baby' so I decided not to mention that.

"Matron wants to have a little chat with you, so I will leave you now," he said.

The Matron was Sister Bridget's friend and from our conversation it was obvious that she had taken a personal interest in Musa from the very beginning.

"Hello, Mrs Craig. We meet at last. I've heard so much about you," she held out her two hands like a double greeting. She was tall and dressed in a navy uniform dress with a nurse's cap, and not as a nun as I had expected. She handed me a birth certificate in the name of Musa Awad with unknown parentage. It was in Arabic but with an English translation.

"Matron, I see you have given him a surname?"

"Yes," she said. "Though of course we don't really know his father's name and we don't know if he is Christian or Muslim, but this is a Christian surname and I have to tell you that we also have a baptismal certificate."

"Oh, why?"

"You see, when he was very unwell, we decided to baptise him as a Christian. This will also be helpful in getting a visa. And, later, if you do think of adopting him it will be easier. For Muslims, adoption is against their religion, you know. I hope you agree with all of this?"

"Oh, of course, especially if this helps," I said. She showed me the baptismal certificate with the heading of the name of the hospital 'The Holy Family Hospital of Bethlehem' and a small logo scene of the Nativity. It, too, was in Arabic and English.

"You don't mind about this? Sister Bridget told me you are Jewish?"

"I don't mind at all. Anything that will help him to get a visa and be accepted in an English hospital."

"God bless you," she said. "We will be seeing more of you in the coming days. Let me know of any concerns, won't you?"

"Thank you, Matron. We don't know what the future holds for this little one, but I will do my best to care for him."

"I'm sure you will. You know all the Staff of this hospital are anxious to hear of his progress." With that, she walked with me to the main entrance and waved me goodbye.

When I returned to Jerusalem, there was a message from Amos to say he had made an appointment with a lawyer the following day and to meet him at the Damascus Gate at three in the afternoon. By now, I had become quite familiar with the Old City, though it was easy to get lost in the maze of streets with the countless traders trying to sell their goods and the tourists looking for bargains. The narrow alleyways were thick with people of all sizes and colours plus boys with their barrows, transporting goods and pushing people out of their way. Then there was the noise; the prayers chants from the Mosque, the blaring loudspeakers of Arabic pop music, the occasional hymns from bands of Christian pilgrims and above everything the traders trying to shout out their wares. The foreign atmosphere was becoming familiar. I remember how frightened and nervous I had been with David. Although, I wished him with me at the Consulate, now without him, I was becoming fearless and bold. He would be surprised to see me like this. I was falling in love with the Old City of Jerusalem!

But, there was one day, I shall not easily forget. Israeli jeeps stormed in, ignoring the laws about motor vehicles, looking for Palestinians suspected of hiding arms or planning some kind of resistance activity. I was inside a shop looking at an assortment of baby clothes, admiring the pretty frilly dresses for little girls but rather plain outfits for boys. Suddenly, I saw a crowd of tourists pushing their way into the shop and looking frightened. One young American woman was screaming, which only raised the atmosphere of fear. The shopkeeper was trying to shut the doors but the entrance was blocked with the chaotic crowd. Then I saw the soldiers blindfold a young man, tie up his hands behind his back and force him into their car, beating him up first with the butt of their guns. It struck terror into the passers-by, who were running in all directions, as soon as the jeep had passed. There were long gowns, pyjamas, and shirts hanging up on hangers at the entrance to the shop, but with all the people pushing some had been knocked down and trampled on. I helped the shopkeeper tidy up and spotted two little boys steal small articles while his back was turned. I shouted at them and another man ran after them. The shopkeeper sat me down as I was shivering from head to toe and gave me a cup of strong Arabic coffee. It reminded me how terrified I had been in Bethlehem with David, but at least this time, there was no shooting. I observed that while the Palestinians were calmly continuing with their shopping, the tourists were still huddled together. Moments like these made me feel very unsettled.

Two elderly Palestinian women, wearing worn embroidered dresses, were squatting on the ground by the Damascus Gate. They were selling bunches of herbs; thyme, parsley, rosemary and other leaves which I did not recognise. Arrayed on the pavement were bunches of what looked like spinach, cauliflower leaves and dandelion greens. I learned later that Palestinians use a lot of what we would call weeds, as a nutritious food in salads and stews. With the throng of people pushing their way through the stone archway and trying to hold on to bags of shopping and errant children's hands, I accidentally brushed past their basket and tipped up their goods. At the bottom of the basket they had a dirty looking handkerchief tied up with a few coins. I bent down, apologising for my clumsiness, trying to put things straight. One of them started to shout in Arabic, looking very angry. I naturally thought she was telling me off. The other woman pulled her headscarf over her eyes, as if she did not want to confront me eye to eye.

"I'm so very sorry." I hoped the look on my face would explain my regret and confusion.

"They are not angry with you," a young man standing nearby translated. "It's just that they have lost their home to the bulldozers. The Israelis destroy many Palestinian homes."

"How terrible! Why?"

"That's what they do, no building permit, probably, but that's just an excuse." He wiped his sweaty brow with a corner of his keffiyeh, and looked at me. "Do you need a guide?"

"Thank you, no. I know the way." I guess he was looking for some pocket money, but I was beginning to understand more of the personal tragedies of these people. I had only tipped over a basket but they had had their whole lives turned upside-down, probably to make room for a Jewish settlement.

I phoned David again to tell him the latest developments.

"Darling, are you alright? I've been worried about you."

I think he was amazed that I was coping mostly on my own, but glad that Amos was also helping.

"I'm fine." I did not mention any of the little scares. "Amos is helping me by finding a lawyer and Sister Bridget gives me advice on all sorts of things."

"What about money?"

David, the most important document I need right now is a guarantee of sponsorship or a bank statement to show there are enough funds to take care of all the medical and legal costs. Please get in touch with Kevin right away. Or could we borrow a few thousand from your Dad?"

"Och! I'll see what I can do. Give me the fax number of the hostel. I will try to work something out. By the way Rosa, have you been in touch with Max and Cassia? They might be helpful in getting around."

"Yes, I intend to do that today. I will let you know. Anyway, thanks darling for standing by me. I love you." I threw him kisses down the phone. "I'll be in touch very soon."

The next day was the interview with the lawyer. I was relieved that Amos was with me. The lawyer's cheeks were covered in purple spidery veins and his face furrowed as if he was permanently angry. He reached forward over his desk with his spectacles perched on the end of his bulbous nose. He seemed too old, I thought, to be still working.

"Mrs. Craig, you are Jewish, am I correct?"

"Yes, sir."

"May I ask why you are interested in caring for an Arab baby?"

"I was staying with my Jewish friends, Amos here, and his wife, and we found the baby abandoned outside the settlement, and I have taken an interest in him ever since."

"Are you sure he is Arab?"

"Yes, his name was written in Arabic." I showed him the scrap of paper, which I kept in my wallet. I was surprised that he could read Arabic.

"I see," he said scribbling something down in Hebrew. "You are aware, I suppose, that had he been Jewish you would be granted an Israeli passport for him straight away, which would make his travel much easier. As it is, it is going to be very difficult for me to make you a guardian for an unknown child."

"Yes, I understand."

"However, Mr. Steiner is a friend and I will do my best."

"Thank you," was all I could say.

He promised he would be in touch when he had made out a legal document to say that I could accompany the baby to London and be his temporary guardian, until some permanent solution could be worked out. Amos was pleased, but I still had a niggling feeling that things were going to be difficult. Surely there must be a hitch somewhere?

"How long do you think all these legal procedures are going to take?" I said to Amos, as we sat in the car.

"Don't worry Rosa, I will get after him. I will tell him that Musa's operation is urgent, so as not to delay. I know most lawyers take their time to settle problems. It's all a matter of finance, you know. We will have to pay him generously."

"You mean like a bribe?"

"You can look at it how you like," he said, smiling in a sly kind of way that I understood.

"This is getting so complicated..."

Amos dropped me off at the Damascus Gate and I returned to the Hostel feeling quite exhausted by the day's events and worrying about the finance.

Max and Cassia had sent us a note many weeks ago to tell us that they had returned from the USA and were now living in a suburb of Jerusalem. I had said to David that suburb probably means settlement in which case I wasn't prepared to go to a settlement because I don't believe in their ideology. Once was enough. However, as I had spare time on my hands, I thought I could call them at least. There was no mistaking Cassia's broad American accent when she answered.

"Hi Cassia, it's Rosa."

"Rosa, what a surprise!"

"What do you think? I'm back in Jerusalem!"

"Are you claiming Aliya this time?"

I knew what she meant. As a Jew it would be easy for me to claim Israeli citizenship. "No. I'm just here for a short while," I laughed. Same old Cassia, I thought, still trying to get me to move.

"We must get together. Can you meet me for dinner tomorrow? There is a restaurant near the King David."

"That would be lovely. What time?"

"Shall we say seven?"

When I turned up at the place in West Jerusalem, I was the one who was surprised. She was alone.

"Rosa, so good to see you. You're looking wonderful," she enthused. I noticed that her makeup and appearance was much more subdued.

"Great to see you too, Cassia. Where's Max?"

"Sit down, I'll tell you all about it." We ordered a simple meal as the waiter poured out some wine and she poured out her troubles.

"I feel I can talk to you about anything. Max and I have always had our differences. We thought we could make a new start by coming to live in Israel away from critical relatives and tempting dodgy business deals. We were prepared to start afresh here, thinking we would be amongst Jewish like-minded people. But unfortunately, Max has become disillusioned with Israel and was missing his friends and business colleagues too much, so he has returned to America. I want to stay here, so I really don't know if our marriage will survive."

159

"I'm so sorry," I said. "So what are you going to do?"

"It seems I have to decide between our marriage and this country. I don't know what to do."

"Don't rush into any decision yet. I could see from when we first met that your relationship with Max was shaky, but I think you should take time to think the matter over."

"You're right, of course. I guess our parents, being friends, kind of threw us together, but I have realised that we are not really compatible."

"That's a shame. You spoke of raising a family in Israel."

"I know. Anyway, tell me how is it that you are alone, Rosa?" Cassia looked at me with such concern that I had to explain that David hadn't left me, but that he was busy teaching.

"Do you, remember, Cassia, that I told you we were in Bethlehem, but couldn't tell you the reason?"

"Yes, go on." She leaned forward, tugging on her long ear-rings, while I took a deep breath. I told her the reason for my visit and the background to the reason. She listened carefully while I related the story and she seemed genuinely sympathetic.

"What an exciting experience. That's wonderful …like a fairy tale. I can hardly believe it. And you want to take care of that poor orphan child?"

"Yes, I just love him."

"I can see that. You look so happy!"

"David and I have been trying for a baby for a few years but nothing has happened, so I am overjoyed," I whispered.

"I'm so glad for you. How can I help?"

I shook my head, laughing, but before we parted, she took out her cheque book and wrote me a large cheque in dollars. "That's to go towards the baby's ticket, or whatever. Best of luck to you both."

I let out a gasp of astonishment as I got up from the table and embraced her. "Cassia, I don't know how to thank you. Please do keep in touch and if you are ever in England, we would love to welcome you."

"I will visit you when you have your baby," she said.

I couldn't help but notice a tear forming in her eye as we said goodbye. I thought how circumstances can change in just a few months. Poor Cassia. She had seemed so excited when we met the first time. She had talked about having a family, but now it looked as if her marriage was crumbling. Here I am about to

161

embark on becoming a mother and for Cassia this aspect is no longer a hope.

It was another two weeks before all the documents were finalised. I had spent every day travelling between the lawyer, the Ministry of Interior and the British Consulate, not counting the constant little trips to Bethlehem. The money spent on taxis alone was frightening. Sometimes, there were lengthy curfews in Bethlehem which meant I couldn't visit. I had become familiar with Jerusalem; its multitude of political problems, and differences of religious opinions. On the one hand I had met Israelis, like Rebecca and Amos, and Cassia who were proud of their country's achievements. I had also talked with some Israeli soldiers at Damascus Gate, who although bored with their job were ready to die for their country. On the other hand, I met plenty of Palestinians. Like the taxi drivers, the shopkeepers, the hostel staff and many others I had conversed with, who were proud to be Palestinians and committed to resisting the Israeli occupation at all costs. As a Jew, I would be expected to side with the Israelis, but I found my sympathies more and more with the Palestinian people, who felt they were being portrayed unjustly by the West and betrayed by the British and Americans. I tried to be non-political but it was almost impossible. The situation itself was hostile and at times volatile.

The Ministry of Interior was within walking distance, but I had to be there early in the morning to obtain a number. Crowds of people were always waiting outside and twice I was turned away only to have to come even earlier the next day. I was informed that some Palestinians from the villages had been camping out all night trying to get 'family reunion', that is a certificate to reunite families separated by the occupation. Many families had had their applications turned down by the Israelis, not just once, but time and time again.

Anyway, now at last, I could collect Musa from the hospital and return to London. Almost a month had passed in Jerusalem and now I was ecstatic, desperate to take my baby home. A decision had been made in London to send a nurse to accompany me. She arrived two days before we were to travel so I was able to get to know her. Kathy was a mature, sensible and experienced nurse, so I was greatly relieved that she would take charge during the flight back. Sister Bridget had managed to find her a room in the hostel. I took her out for a meal the first evening and as we sat sipping wine, we chatted.

"I've been to Jerusalem before," Kathy said. "My husband and I came years ago before we had children with a church pilgrimage. There was much less turmoil then. We had a great time. I am a widow now. My two grown-up sons were both worried about me coming this time."

"I can understand that. My husband is also worried because of the conflict. But Sister Bridget has been such an encouragement. She is so sweet."

I passed her the plate of stuffed vine leaves and the pitta bread. "These are delicious, try them."

She took a bite and smiled. "Umm, they are. Now, Rosa, tell me all about this baby. I want to know how you found him."

I never tired of telling the same story over and over, but at the same time I occasionally panicked when I thought about what might happen when we get to London. Was it all going to be worth it, or was I really crazy, as some people may think.

Finally the day arrived. Sister Bridget, Kathy and I all went together in a taxi to collect Musa and found him ready in his carrycot (was it the same one that

David and I had bought?). The Matron handed him over and wished us blessings. "You will let us know how he gets on, won't you."

"Of course, thank you for everything. I won't forget you."

Once again, I found myself on the brink of tears as I said goodbye to Matron and all the staff.

Musa had his own travel document with his own little photo. Naturally we were held up at security at the airport, but I expected that. Even with all the legal documents, the airport authorities were suspicious and we were thoroughly searched. They even took away the carrycot to X-ray it. We were told to unzip our suitcases and take out all the contents while they went over everything with a hand-held device even though the luggage had already gone through the big machines. They did not even trust the tin of baby milk! Eventually one of the security staff accompanied us to the aircraft. We were the last to board. The British stewards were fussing around us as if they had never seen a baby before. Kathy had already arranged with the airline about the possible need for oxygen, so they were fully prepared for such an emergency, which fortunately was not needed. Kathy took over the baby's care. I was able to relax and for the first time in days I slept soundly, while Musa slept quietly most of the way.

As the plane descended my thoughts were inevitably with David. Is he going to accept the baby? At Heathrow, we exited Immigration and Customs without a problem, but on emerging we were met with a barrage of flashing bulbs from photographers. I felt like a celebrity as they took countless pictures of me with baby Musa. A fuzzy tipped microphone was thrust into my face while I was walking, carrying Musa. Kathy was behind me wheeling the trolley with the luggage and carry-cot.

"Mrs. Craig, what will happen to the baby after his surgery?"

"I don't know."

"Mrs. Craig, will you be thinking of adoption?"

"I don't know."

I could see David, but before I had the chance to greet him properly, microphones were thrust into his face too.

"Mr. Craig, what do you think of all this. What is going to happen?"

"Please leave us for now..." He took my arm. "This way darling..."

166

"Gentlemen, we have a sick baby who needs to go to hospital immediately," Kathy said, finally persuading the photographers to move away so she and Musa could get into the waiting ambulance while David and I followed in the car.

Next morning, still in bed, David brought me up a cup of tea and presented me with half a dozen tabloid newspapers. It was mid November but Christmas had come to London early. *'Bethlehem Baby Arrives for Christmas'* and *'Orphan Baby Arrives from Bethlehem'* were the headlines.

I gasped. My hand went to my mouth in horror. "Oh no, David, this is too much! My face is plastered on the front page."

"Well, you asked for it!" I couldn't quite make out whether he was just amused or disgusted and that worried me.

CHAPTER TWELVE

David and I made our way to the hospital and found Musa sitting in a high chair being fed with baby food. When he saw me, he started kicking his little legs and reaching out, smiling. I was so ecstatic to think that he recognised me.

They were going to do more tests for about a week before his surgery, but they wanted me to stay with him. All the other babies in the ward had their mothers or grandmothers with them as a matter of hospital policy to help in the recovery. Of course, this meant more time off from work.

"I'll have to give in my notice at work, David dear. They were generous in allowing me a month, but now I shall be looking after Musa full-time."

He clicked his tongue. "But how shall we manage without your salary?"

"We'll cope somehow. Anyway, I'm here now, so please bring me some things from home for tonight until I can pick up stuff tomorrow." I gave him a list and he reluctantly left me to go back to work.

Florence was one of the grannies looking after her little grandson. She was large with skin the colour and shine of black treacle and was always full of smiles. She would often loll in a big armchair, chatting or napping or going for walks outside.

"Keep an eye on Sam for me lovey, jus'out for a fag."

Sam had had some bowel surgery as far as I could gather and was very poorly, but was the most adorable two year old. She told me the child's mother was suffering from depression, so she was literally left holding the baby. She didn't know who the father was. I didn't let on that Musa had no mother or father. Musa is going to get better, I told myself, however the prognosis for Sam wasn't so certain.

On the day of the surgery, David was working, so I sat with Kevin in the corridor near the operating theatre. I was so grateful to Kevin as he had taken an interest ever since that day we met in the Chapel. We chatted about my time in Jerusalem and drank strong coffee together from a vending machine. Occasionally Kevin bowed his head and I realised he was praying. I paced the floor anxiously, and spent time gazing through the window watching the ambulances and cars come and go. After about three hours, a group of green gowned nurses and doctors wheeled baby Musa past me in his cot. I caught a quick glance of his pale face and tiny tubes emanating from his chest attached to a monitor. My heart stopped. The doctor pulled down his face mask.

"Hello! Are you the mother of Musa?"

"Yes," I said, without hesitation.

"Well, you will be pleased to know that everything went well with the surgery. He should soon make a full recovery."

"Oh, thank you so much, doctor." Kevin was by my side and I hugged him for joy. "There you are Rosa, God does answer prayer," he said.

"Yes, I believe He does." Then I called David to tell him the good news.

I was amazed how quickly children can recover from operations. The tiny 'hole' in Musa's heart had been stitched up and his recovery was almost instant. For the first two days, a nurse was by his side monitoring the machine which registered his vital signs and then my baby was sitting up eating, gurgling and crying like any normal infant. I had become friendly with some of the other mothers and grannies who were going through far more difficult domestic experiences like having to get in baby-sitters for children at home or changing places with fathers at odd hours. Sometimes

David would drop by and sit with Musa, but he never stayed long. I got the impression that he was embarrassed. Kevin too, would often stop by on his hospital rounds so I had the opportunity to ask him about his scar. He told me that as a teenager he was in a gang of boys. There was a fight and he got slashed on his cheek. It was after this that he turned to God.

One sunny morning, the doctors were doing their rounds followed by a group of student doctors.

"Good morning, Mrs Craig," said Dr. Kahn. "I've been telling the students about your baby coming all the way from Bethlehem. He has made a remarkable recovery and all the tests are positive. So the good news is that you can take him home."

"That's wonderful to hear. Thank you doctor."

He picked up Musa's chart and notes to show the students, firing questions about congenital heart defects.

I was astonished that I could actually take my baby home so soon. They said the district nurse had been contacted and she would be paying me regular home visits.

When David came to collect me, he told me the newspapers had been calling and two photographers were outside the hospital waiting to take pictures of Musa being discharged. I was not surprised.

Suddenly my whole lifestyle was transformed. Now I was a fulltime mother. It was seven months since we first met Musa in such an astonishing way, so it was almost like going through the months of pregnancy without having to buy maternity clothes and without the pain of childbirth. (Though I reckoned I had been on an emotional and sometimes painful rollercoaster.) By the time we came home David had a few surprises lined up. He had prepared the spare bedroom into a nursery, even putting some of his students' paintings on the walls. He had also bought a cot, some baby clothes and a beautiful wind mobile of coloured butterflies. But the biggest surprise was that his sister Morag had come down from Scotland and arranged a baby welcome party for the following weekend. My Dad, too, was as excited as if we had already adopted the baby.

"David, darling, it looks like you're happy with the situation?"

"You've already made me bankrupt Rosa, what's another little project going to do to our bank account?!"

"Does that mean you want to go ahead and adopt?"

172

His answer was not in words, but it was the way he made love to me that night. In a way, I was a little surprised, but also deliriously happy.

The appeal of the London newspapers had raised several thousand pounds, but they still wanted more pictures at Christmas! I agreed on condition that only pictures of the baby would be published.

The welcome home party was a huge success. Several of my work colleagues came and other friends, but Kevin had sent his apologies. Two of the young girls from the office, who I didn't really know because they had started work after I left, turned up. They appeared at the door with parcels wrapped in Christmas paper. Morag had hung balloons on the door and coloured streamers from the ceiling in the hall.

"Is this the home of the Christmas baby?"

"Yes, indeed, come in. Come and see baby Musa. David, some drinks here, please. Help yourself to all the snacks!" I was rushing about enjoying being hostess to so many people, even strangers, but touched by their interest. I picked up Musa, alternately carrying him and sitting him on my lap. I didn't want to let go of him. Morag was handing out the cakes she made, the sausage rolls, cheese puffs, ham, chicken, salads and sticky pastries. David was happy to serve everyone with drinks until we were all a bit merrier than we should have been. Dawn, the temporary secretary, who I felt disliked me, came, probably out of curiosity. She handed me a small parcel saying: "Shall I leave the receipt with you-erm- just in case, like?"

"If you like, but thank you." I didn't immediately get her meaning at the time, but then it dawned on me (like her name!) that she wanted the gift back if Musa did not stay with us! I thought what a cheek to imply that my baby isn't here to stay.

Musa was confused at first, but giggled with delight at all the smiling faces drooling over him. "What a beautiful baby. Where did you find him?" many people were exclaiming.

"Don't excite him too much. He's just had a heart operation, remember," said Kathy, who had often popped in unofficially. Suddenly, Musa started to bawl. It was too much for him and I had to calm him down and take him upstairs.

The visitors had left behind a room full of gifts, including a baby bath, a playpen and a stroller. I was overawed. What if after all this I am not allowed to keep the baby? What if he has to return to his own country? My mind was churning out all sorts of possibilities. What if David won't co-operate when it actually comes to signing the adoption papers? Why is he being so bloody nice to me? Why am I always thinking sceptical thoughts?

"I don't deserve all this kindness. Am I doing the right thing? Do you think everything will work out?" I squeaked to Morag. She hugged me so tight, I could almost feel my ribs crack.

"Och, Rosa, of course you deserve it. He's such a bonny wee lad. Everything will work out pet. David loves you and will support you, I'm sure. But you must look after yourself and put some more flesh on," she laughed.

Inevitably, Morag had to return to her family in Scotland but as she was much older, she had become almost a mother to me. I appreciated that enormously.

"Just call me anytime, Rosa. You know my wee kids are big now, so I can always come down for a few days if you need me to."

"Thanks a lot." I waved her goodbye as David drove her to the train station.

For the first time, I found myself alone. Musa was crying and needing attention. I pulled myself up straight and determined to be the best mother ever. It was strange being left in the house to get on with things on my own. I changed Musa and settled him down for another nap while I sat at the kitchen table with my cup of tea. The doorbell rang and the district nurse arrived. Barbara was a new nurse and except for the difference in uniform she reminded me of Sister Bridget, the same round face and bright rosy cheeks without makeup. She examined the baby's chest with her stethoscope, and then looked at his feet, without disturbing him too much. He half woke up, fluttered his eyelashes and smiled, then went straight back to sleep again. "He's having a happy dream," Barbara said. It had never crossed my mind that babies have dreams.

"Are you thinking of keeping him, Mrs. Craig?"
"Yes. My husband and I want to adopt him, how do we go about it? Coffee?"
"Thanks no. I've had too many cups already," Barbara laughed. "I'm glad you're thinking of adoption." She took off her apron, and sat down. "Since Musa is a foreign baby you will have to get in touch with the International Adoption Agency. Then the Social Services will come and interview you and investigate all your home and family circumstances."

"People tell us that it will take up to three years to adopt a foreign child, but since we don't have to go abroad to pick one, what do you think Nurse?"

"I don't think it will take that long as he is already with you." She poked about in her bag to look for a booklet.

"Here," she said. "This is the number you need to ring for the preliminary interview. This is the first step. How long is the child's visa for in his passport?"

"He has a travel document, *Laisse Passe* they call it, because the Palestinians in Jerusalem don't have passports." I took it out of my handbag. "Look, six months."

I showed it to her where the British Consulate had stamped it.

"Six months is not enough time to finalise an adoption, you will need to apply first for foster care."

"But I have a document from a Jerusalem lawyer to make me a temporary guardian."

I found the document and showed her.

Barbara smiled. "Mrs. Craig, I doubt if that has any legal value in this country." She paused and looked at it again. The letter heading was in Hebrew but the wording in English: *'This is to certify...'*

"In fact," she said, "you'd better apply immediately for foster care, otherwise the authorities might take the baby away. I don't want to frighten you, as I know how attached you have become to Musa, but we have to be realistic and go along with the law. Here is the number you must ring. Best of luck," she said, as she put on her jacket, gathered up her bag and left, leaving me feeling as fragile as the autumn leaves which were being blown about by the high winds.

"I'll pop by tomorrow," she shouted, as she walked down the path.

I had another cup of tea to collect my thoughts before I picked up the phone.

I called David first but he was in a class and wasn't free to talk. So I plucked up courage and rang the Social Services, then the International Adoption Agency. In the first instance, it was some time before a senior person could speak to me. I explained everything.

"Ah, Mrs Craig, I read all about your baby in the paper. I will send my colleague round to see you, let me see…er…er.. we are so busy, what about two weeks tomorrow?"

"Can't you come sooner?"

"Sorry, there is no hurry, you know. Don't worry. I'm sure it is not an urgent matter."

"But, I was told…" I sighed. He had put the phone down. I wanted to scream. Why are they not taking me seriously? Next, I called the International Adoption Agency. They seemed to be more professional and said they would send a lady tomorrow for a preliminary interview and to give me all the forms to fill in. I felt reassured. I tried calling David again but no answer. How am I going to deal with all of this on my own?

The lady from the Adoption Agency arrived at the same time as Nurse Barbara, but she did not stay long. She merely introduced herself and left me a bundle of forms and booklets to read. She told me to call her when I had studied everything with my husband. I could see it was going to take me hours. When is David going to find the time to sit down with me to study everything? The forms were extremely detailed and complicated.

However, the first thing needed was a Home Study conducted by social services. This involved detailed health reports from our doctors, physical, mental, psychological, as well as any genetic tendencies in the family history. Questions like medical history of our parents, their marital stability, number of siblings, etc. etc. Then there were questions to do with finance, how much money do we have in the bank? Are we savers or spendthrifts? Do we have a mortgage? Do we have any dependant relatives? Clubs? Hobbies? General interests and political involvement? What were our views on a multi-cultural society with different religions? David and I poured over the seemingly endless list of questions, answering them as best we could. I could see that David was indignant about his private world being violated, especially when an inspector came to look round the house, taking notes and asking about insurance policies.

Our lifestyle had completely changed and I think David was having second thoughts, though he did not say so. He just continually complained about the invasion of our privacy. Although it was a stressful experience, to me it was worth every minute.

"You don't know how much trouble you're causing your Mummy and Daddy", I said to Musa as I soaped him in the bath and then rubbed his dark curls. "You've got your Mummy's curly hair and she loves you soooo much!" He giggled as I stood him on my lap. He was steadily gaining weight and looking so healthy. It was such a joy to look after him, even when he woke in the night and even when he was grouchy. David usually turned over and groaned when I had to get up in the middle of the night.

Christmas was spent in Scotland, as usual. It was perfect; sparkling lights on the tree inside, to match the sparkle of frosty trees outside, glowing log fires, turkey dinners with punchy wine and above all the sharing of gifts and loving hugs. Musa was, of course, the centre of attention and how he loved it. He made friends easily and since there were so many baby sitters, I could enjoy going for walks with David. Surprisingly, David was co-operating in every way, even changing Musa's nappies, and playing with him on his knee, which he had never done at home.

"Rosa dear, I'm so happy for you and David." David's mother was chatting to me in the kitchen as I helped her. She toned down her voice. "But, pet, I know David can be moody. Am I right in sensing that he's not as enthusiastic as you about adoption?"

"Yes, you may be right, Mum. It frightens me sometimes. Right now though, in front of all the family, he is showing himself the father that I would like him to be."

She tried to hug me but her hands were too floury from baking. "I do pray that it will work out," she said.

Just then, Morag's children came bustling in with Musa in the stroller. "Nanna, we can smell goodies." They snatched up some hot mince pies, while I laughingly shooed them out of the kitchen.

We returned to London on a high.

Then spring came to London and eventually in April we had a letter to attend Court to go before a panel to finalise the adoption. David and I breathed a sigh of relief when we were given the Certificate of Eligibility. Musa became Musa Benjamin (after my father) Craig.

CHAPTER THIRTEEN
1994

"Shall I read you a bedtime story?"

"Yes, please, Mummy."

I began: *'Billy and Bobby Bear were twins. Billy was always busy doing gardening, cleaning the house or making crumpets with honey to sell to the neighbours. Bobby was the opposite. He never wanted to get out of bed; he was too lazy to do any work and only went to the market when he had to. But he was very keen to eat his brother's honey crumpets. One day, Billy asked his brother to go with him on a bus to another town as there was no more honey in the market. But Bobby wouldn't get up and Billy had to go on his own. So Bobby slept all day and got very, very hungry...*

I looked at Musa who was fast asleep before I had finished reading. I kissed his dark tousled head, determining to take him to the barbers before his fifth birthday in two weeks time. Five years old and time to register him to start his primary education proper in September. He had been going to nursery school for the last two years, while I had found myself a new job working part time as a dental assistant.

Five years of pure joy, watching him grow up. Pure joy? No, there were many teething problems not only for Musa's literal teething pains, but also for me. Yes, we had watched him discover his fingers, watched him crawl and hide and disobey, watched him proudly take his first steps and discover the freedom of adventure, heard him utter first Dadda (Why did David have to be the first?) then Mum-mum-mum-mummy. He loved to 'steal' anything lying about and hide it under the chairs, so I would have to make up the game of hide and seek with new rules. And how he laughed if I pretended not to be able to find it. His favourite word was 'Look,' while mine was 'Don't.'

"Musa, you don't eat jam with your fingers. What a mess!"

"Musa, don't pull Jessie's pigtails. Look, now you've made her cry! You must say 'Sorry'." Jessie was his new little friend from next door.

"Musa, don't put your grubby hands through your hair. Oh no, you've been playing with nasty little worms again!"

If it wasn't 'Look Mummy' it was 'Why?'

"Why do dogs do their dirties on the street? Why don't they have doggie toilets?"

184

"I don't know, darling. It would be much better if there were doggie toilets!" I laughed at all the funny things children say, but was glad to see Musa had such an inquisitive mind.

"Why do I have to have my curls cut off? Jessie has her hair long."

"She is a girl."

"But old Mr. Williams has long hair."

"Any more questions?" It was getting a bit tedious and I was trying to mash the potatoes for dinner.

"Can I have another chocolate biscuit?"

"No. We will be eating dinner in a few minutes."

"Just one, Mummy," as he stealthily grabbed another biscuit before I put the tin away. "Why isn't Daddy home yet?"

The last question rattled me and it was a question I asked myself many times. Why is David so late these days? He always mumbled his apologies, saying he had been working in his studio. That was another thing. He had taken me one day to see his new 'studio'. From the outside it looked like an old abandoned shed but inside I was taken by surprise. He had furnished it. There was a cupboard to keep all his paints in and a large easel with all the paraphernalia of a professional artist. I was impressed.

"This is beautiful, David, but how did you manage to paint the walls, put in heating, buy a couch and all these other things?"

"Darling, I've been doing it gradually. I borrowed some money, too."

"From where?"

"You know. I'll give it back when I've sold some of my paintings."

"You mean…?"

"Yes, don't worry I'll soon pay it back."

I could not believe it. The money that was left from the fund set up to pay for Musa's operation had been put into savings for his higher education.

"David that's not borrowing, that's stealing!"

I was livid and almost felt like striking him. How could he?

"David how can I ever trust you?" I had always said that for all David's faults, at least he was honest.

"Och, Rosa, don't go on so. I told you I'll pay it back."

"You'd better. Why didn't you discuss it with me?" We are joint account holders of that fund."

"Well, have a look at my work. He picked up a rather abstract looking painting. Do you fancy one of these for our sitting room?"

I looked at the canvases lined up around the walls. The colours were vibrant but the shapes? I couldn't quite make out what they were supposed to be, lots of squiggles, flowers with faces, female forms with prominent breasts. I picked up one of the paintings, turning it round and sideways. At first I couldn't make out which way up it was supposed to be. There was a vague landscape mingling with the sky, so that there was no definite horizon. In the foreground was a crude nude figure, wearing only a scarf to shade her face, but the whole picture was blurred and fuzzy.

"Do you fancy yourself as a new Picasso or something? What kind of art is this? I've never studied like you but d'you think people are going to buy these? They're positively....." I screwed up my face.

"Positively what?"

"Positively primitive, ugly..." I knew I had gone too far. He laughed, but it was an angry laugh, his face going crimson.

"You don't understand anything. This is contemporary art. This is art for these post-modern times," he shouted. He took hold of my sleeve and gave me a push towards the door. I shook free from his grip and punched him hard on his arm, shouting back. "How dare you. You steal Musa's money then you throw me out like a beggar woman."

"Don't you ever come to my studio again. Go home to your beloved boy. That's all you think of and all you have time for these days!"

"He's yours too," I blurted out, but David had the final word.

"He's not mine, nor ever will be."

Back home, I went directly next door to collect Musa who was playing happily with Jessie and then at my house collapsed into a chair in a flood of tears. If David didn't want to acknowledge Musa why did he go along with me so agreeably with the adoption? Was it to get the money for his studio? Is he really so selfish? Somehow I couldn't believe it. That was not the David that I had married. Maybe I had been neglecting David and not showing any interest in his activities. Maybe he was jealous of the child taking his place. Musa sat by me, put his arms around my neck and wiped my tears with his hand. He didn't understand why I was crying.

"Cheer up, Mummy." He put his hand deep into his pocket and gave me a grubby sweet. I had to smile.

David didn't come home that night nor the following one, but he turned up the third day which was a Friday. Where he had been staying I had no idea and I didn't even want to ask. I certainly didn't think he had been sleeping on his couch. It would be too cold at night. What was the couch for anyway? Young models I presume? We did not speak for a whole day but I did his laundry and cooked him a meal with a heavy heart. Musa, however, clung to him.

"Where've you been Daddy? Look what Mummy bought me, dinky cars!"

David stooped down to him. "Look what I've bought you." He handed him a big colouring book and a box of wax crayons. He tried to show him how to use the colours, but it was obvious that Musa was more interested in racing his little cars around. I'm sure David felt snubbed which didn't help the atmosphere.

My Dad had been going fairly regularly to the synagogue which surprised me at first until I realised that he was dating a widow. Clara was rather loud and outspoken and 'over the top' in her taste of clothes, too. The total opposite of how my mother had been and I couldn't understand why Dad was attracted to her. However, I figured if he was happy why should I complain? She seemed to be well off in her own right so she wasn't after his money. In any case, my Dad wasn't exactly rich.

Sometimes, I would take Musa along to the Sabbath meetings on a Saturday morning. He enjoyed being in the children's class and liked his teacher.

"What did you learn today?" I asked him.

"Oh Mummy, Mrs. Freedman told us a Bible story."

"What about?"

"About a little baby in a basket by a river. A princess found him and called him Moses."

"That's a lovely story," I said. "Did you know that your name means Moses?"

"No." His big black eyes opened wide at this information. "But, Mummy, Auntie Clara said my name should be Moshe not Musa."

"Did she then?"

"Yes, she said that a famous soldier was called Moshe."

I tackled her. "Why did you tell my little boy his name is Moshe, not Musa?"

"Rosa dear," she said, stroking my arm, "your father told me that Musa comes from Israel, so his name should be in Hebrew. Moshe is a great name. Moshe Dayan helped us win the six-day war!" She took me aside and whispered, "Rosa, I hope you don't mind, but I took your little boy to the toilet and couldn't help but notice that he has not been circumcised. How have you neglected this?"

I opened my mouth aghast and looked her in the eye, angrily: "Well, it's none of your bloody business!" How dare she, I thought. Why did Musa let her take him to the toilet instead of coming to me? She must have done it purposely to examine him. I was disgusted. Dad told me later that she had complained to him how his daughter had been so rude to her.

Later that evening, when I took Musa upstairs and I was washing his hair in the bath, I asked him:

"When Aunt Clara took you to the toilet, did she …like…touch you?"

"Yes, Mummy, she pulled my willie," he whispered, blushing with embarrassment.

I was ready to explode, my face crimson. Was this a case of sexual abuse, or was it to make sure I was carrying out the strict religious observance for Jews? I did not have a brother but I remember attending the circumcision ceremony of my uncle's son when I was a child and I know that all Jewish boy babies are circumcised at eight days after birth. My memories of the *Brit Milah* are that of a Rabbi chanting prayers, but the children were not allowed to witness at the actual operation. When my mother explained why the baby was crying, I thought how cruel! Obviously Clara had thought Musa was a Jew. After Musa was tucked up in bed I went downstairs to phone Dad.

"Hi Dad, how are you?"

"Fine thanks love. How are you and how is my lovely boy?"

"We're OK but Dad, I know you will be shocked by what happened today. Your friend Clara took Musa to the toilet to examine him. She thought he was Jewish and told me off for not having him circumcised. I am speechless, Dad. How dare she?"

"No! That was totally out of order. I can see, love, that you're upset. Let me deal with her."

"Thanks a lot."

It was not long after this that I heard Dad had broken up with Clara.

While Dad had broken up, David and I had patched up, at least for the sake of peace in the house, though the loving intimacy was still absent. He was still often late coming home but I thought it best not to complain anymore. If he liked to spend more hours painting than being with his family…

"Mummy, why are you so sad?" I was standing over the kitchen sink, trying to wash the dishes, but quietly weeping.

"Darling, I'm just tired, that's all. Let's go and have a little game together. What do you want to play?"

"Shall we play that card game where you have to spot things?"

"Oh, the one with pictures of jungle animals?"

"Yes!" He jumped to scramble amongst his box of toys to bring out the pack of cards. It was easy for Musa to count the leopard's spots and the tiger's stripes. It was fun and momentarily I cheered up.

After Musa had gone to bed, I was sitting watching television, when I heard the front door. David poked his head round the door. "Sorry I'm late."

"I'm weary of hearing you say, *'Sorry I'm late,'*" in a squeaky sarcastic tone, mimicking his voice. He shrugged his shoulders. "Anyway, there's food in the oven. It might still be warm, if you're lucky."

The TV programme was a documentary about the Israeli/Palestinian conflict and I was completely riveted by it. It told of the frustration of lack of international support and awareness of human rights and the total disregard of the Israeli government to calls for an end to the occupation.

David came in with a plate of food and sat down to eat it on his knee. "I heated it in the microwave." I looked at him with an expression that said 'so what'!

"Why, on earth are you watching that? We see enough violence going on. Dramas these days are nothing but violence and sex!"

"This is not a drama. This is real life. I can't help it, but I just feel drawn to Middle-eastern affairs."

"I don't understand you. There are so many other things going on in *this* country. What about that terrible Chinook helicopter disaster? All those top security men killed in Scotland. That was a tragedy and…closer to home. I do wish you'd put Israel behind you."

I knew it was no good having an argument, so I switched to another channel, which was a detective-murder tale. "Does this programme suit you better?"

David snorted with a half-hearted hollow laugh. "Silly you, always so serious." He put down his plate and sidled up to me, attempting to put his arm around me, but I did not feel amorous. "I'm going upstairs," I told him.

I knew that David would never understand my interest in politics. But then I'm not enamoured by his art. We were so different. I felt that keeping up with current news was important for Musa's sake. Also, I was continually being reminded by my Jewish friends that Israel is part of my heritage even though I don't believe in the Zionist policies. Kevin would understand. He had shown an interest in Musa's progress ever since we first met and especially since the heart operation. Only yesterday he had sent me a little magazine. Inside was an advert of a Christian pilgrimage trip to Israel/Palestine with all the details of where they would stay and the trips involved, the leader being Kevin himself. He had told me that he had been on a pilgrimage and now it seems he was leading tours himself. In a way I was surprised that he would be so courageous as to take a bunch of tourists during this time of conflict. I was envious. I yearned to get on a plane immediately to be amongst those lovely warm people again, to experience their simple joys in the midst of sorrows and their resilience and hope when there was no freedom. Looking back on my month in

Jerusalem I had discovered myself a different person! I realised that David and I have opposite goals and dreams in life. But just as I expected him to understand me meant that I needed to take more interest in him.

I called Kevin the next day.

"Oh Rosa, good to hear you, how are you?"

"I'm fine thanks. Kevin, I'm surprised to see you are taking another tour to the Holy Land. Are many people interested?"

"Yes, amazingly, though some people are understandably afraid. I try to reassure them that we won't be going to dangerous places."

I held the telephone close to my ear. Why was my heart doing flip-flops at hearing Kevin's dulcet voice? Rosa, pull yourself together. Kevin is a married man and a Christian priest. No, I told myself. You are not in love with Kevin, only in love with what he represents.

I knew, practically speaking, that it was out of the question to travel again now. What with being in debt and Musa being too small, besides the fact that David was being so un-cooperative, it was impossible.

CHAPTER FOURTEEN
1996

We had been debating how and when to tell Musa about his beginnings and our adoption of him. David believed we should sit down on purpose, but I said we should wait until Musa becomes aware and asks questions. Our discussion was never resolved. He was now seven years old and we knew that he was discovering about the facts of life from his friends at school. We need not have worried. As it happened, it all came out naturally.

Jessie, our neighbour's little girl who was the same age as Musa, knocked on our back door one Saturday morning, her long chestnut hair loose around her shoulders and her hazel eyes bright with excitement. We were having breakfast at the kitchen table just the two of us, as usual.

"Musa, Musa, you must come round. Our cat had three kittens in the night. They're so cute, but still blind. Come and see!"

"Can I go, Mummy?"

"Of course, darling, but finish your milk first."

It was not long before Musa was back home again excitably giggling.

"Mummy, those poor little kittens can't see, but the mother cat is feeding them from her…" He was embarrassed to say the word 'breasts' even though he knew it. "Jessie says that she was born in the middle of the night from her Mummy's tummy. Did I come from your tummy too, Mummy?"

I was prepared for such a question though it was not as I had anticipated.

"Musa, come with me and I'll tell you all about it."

I took him into the living room where I had my desk. There was one small drawer that I had locked. I found the key and unlocked it. There were all the documents to do with Musa's adoption including his birth certificate, but first I showed him the white knitted shawl and the Arabic note I had laminated to preserve. Musa stood silent, mystified.

"You see this beautiful shawl?" He nodded. "Well, Mummy found you wrapped up in this by a little stream of water in Palestine. I fell in love with you straight away. You were the most beautiful baby I had ever seen, but you didn't actually come from my tummy."

I could see his lips trembling and his little podgy hands rolled up into a ball. He didn't know whether to cry or be angry. I gently put my arms around him and held him close.

He looked at me and frowned. "You mean you're not my real Mummy?"

My heart was torn. "No, darling, I don't know what happened to your real Mummy, but I love you more than anything else in the world."

He pushed me away and sat down on the settee, releasing the tears that had been building up. He was quiet for a few seconds then he looked into my face.

"And Daddy? Is he my real Daddy?" I shook my head.

"He doesn't love me, does he?"

"He may not be your real Daddy but I'm sure he loves you."

"Where are my real Mummy and Daddy?"

"I don't know, darling. We just found you, a little baby on your own."

"Why can't I remember?"

"Babies don't remember anything, but I remember everything about that day."

David ambled down the stairs in the middle of this drama. He had obviously heard the last comments and I waited for him to add something to reassure our little boy that we loved him like our own, but was let down. He should have gone to Musa and touched him at least, but instead he walked away into the kitchen. I watched him through the open door. He took two pieces of bread and popped them in the toaster, then filled up the kettle. He seemed completely cold to the emotional scene unfolding before his eyes. He had turned his back on us. At this point I realised I was on my own. I went to sit beside Musa, putting my arm around his shoulder.

"Remember that Bible story you heard at the Sabbath meeting? D'you remember I told you that Moses is the same name as Musa?"

"Yes." He looked up at me with his tear-stained face. My heart went out to him.

"Well it was like that, we found you in a basket by a small river and this note was pinned to the shawl. Look, it says: 'My name is Musa', only it's in a different language, Arabic, so you can't read it."

He looked at the scrap of paper and thought for a moment, rubbed his fist over his face, then brightened up.

"You see Daddy and I were on holiday. We were staying with some Jewish friends. We went for a country walk and discovered this baby." I ruffled his curls and kissed him on his forehead. "It was near an Arab village but nobody from the village knew who you belonged to. So then we took you to Bethlehem. After a few months, I went back for you and brought you to England. So you were born a Palestinian, but now we have adopted you, so you became British."

"Wow that's a long story Mummy, but you were like the Princess in the Bible story!"

"Well, yes, I suppose I was."

"But Mummy you're much prettier than Princess Diana!"

That was the nicest thing he could ever say to me. We hugged each other and somehow I knew everything was going to turn out alright.

He clambered onto my lap, put his arms round my neck and we sat for a while just savouring the moment.

"Can I still call you Mummy?"

"Of course, darling."

"Does Grandpa Ben know? Is he my real grandpa?"

"He's like a real grandpa and he loves you too." Then I asked: "What would you like to do today? Would you like to go to the zoo?"

"Oo! Yes, could Grandpa come with us?"

"OK, that's a good idea." So that is what we did. I knew it was no good asking David to join us, but Musa asked him anyway. His reply as expected was negative, saying he had a lot of exam papers to mark. At least, I thought, it was something different to spending time in his studio. I realised, of course, too late, that I should have asked David myself and let him have a say in our decision making. This was another case of his being resentful that I was yet again planning all family activities. But why was he so dismissive.

Dad took us in the car. Musa's questions were endless and I was often at a loss to know how to find the answers, but it was such a happy day out, both for Musa and his Grandpa Ben.

"Grandpa, why do tigers have to eat meat when big elephants only eat leaves?"

"Mummy did those lion cubs come out of their mother's tummies, like the cat next door? Can a baby monkey be looked after by another monkey's Mummy?"

There were lion cubs struggling to get their teeth into pumpkins and playing with them like balls, and there were small monkeys swinging from branches and scratching each others backs which made Musa giggle.

Meerkats standing like the sentries at Buckingham Palace, and gorillas thumping their chests and glowering at us angrily. So many fascinating animals. Dad treated us to lunch in one of the cafeterias and Musa was so excited. With many other things to occupy his mind, I think his thoughts were momentarily distracted, but I could still sense that he was unsettled. He clung to me much more than usual.

Later that evening, we were relaxing with a glass of wine when David said to me: "Why didn't you wait until we could talk about the adoption together?"

"That's what I had planned, but somehow it didn't work out that way. He asked me straight if I he had come from 'Mummy's tummy'. What could I have said?"

"You could have said that we will both tell him a bedtime story about how he was born."

"Bedtime stories are fiction and anyway David you're never around at bedtime. Why didn't you join in with my little talk to Musa this morning? You went into the kitchen and totally ignored him. You could, at least have put an arm on his shoulder."

"For goodness sake, Rosa, you know what I'm like first thing in the morning. I needed my coffee."

204

"And that's more important than reassuring Musa that you love him?"

David was getting angry. He stood up and leaned on the mantelpiece with his back to the gas fire.

"I'm sick of being told what to do. I buy him little presents. What more do you want? I shall never be a father to him and right now I don't even feel I'm your husband. That boy is destroying us, Rosa. Don't you see that?" He stormed out of the room to the kitchen to fill up his glass. I followed him but just stood in the doorway.

"Why did you go along with the adoption then?"

"Maybe it was a big mistake. I just wanted to please you as you were so keen, but you know it's never been the same between you and me since that boy came."

"Is everything you do just to please me?" He didn't answer.

"I'm sorry you feel that way." The thought of going to bed with him in a bad mood, made me change my tactics, so after a pause, I tried to speak normally. "How about another family holiday this summer? All of us could go. Cassia has been urging us to go back to Jerusalem and invited us to stay with her. How about it?"

205

"You go with the boy. I have to prepare for an exhibition that I'm hoping to have in the autumn."

"The boy has a name," I shouted. It pained me that he always referred to Musa as 'the boy'. "Maybe I *will* take him to Jerusalem."

"Hold on. Do you really want to go? Is it safe? What about all those suicide bombings we hear about?"

"Well, I'll see what Cassia says. She believes it's safe where she lives and she can drive us up to the Galilee, via the Jordan valley. By the way, did I tell you that in Cassia's last letter she told me that she and Max are now divorced."

"That doesn't surprise me."

Sunday morning and Musa was up with the lark anxious to tell his little friend that his Mummy was like a princess and had found him as a baby in a basket. He pulled me out of bed, while David just went back to sleep again, groaning, "Today is Sunday. Can't you let me have a bit of peace!?"

Musa scampered downstairs and I put the radio on for news. It was bad news again in the Middle East. For every suicide bombing, with the resulting deaths of innocent bystanders, the Israelis were acting revenge by bombing many Palestinian homes and killing hundreds of people. It was war. Talks of peace were just that, talks and more talks. I must be crazy to entertain the thought of taking my little boy into that situation.

Crazy or not, I knew we had to go. One day when Musa was grown up, I was sure he would want to look for his real family and even if that didn't work out, I knew I had to expose him to the geography and the politics of that land. The Holy Land, as everyone called it. My Jewish acquaintances were always saying 'Next year in Jerusalem'. It had become a greeting like *Shalom*. We sat down to breakfast. I had boiled an egg for Musa and lined up strips of buttered toast. He loved that, pretending to march the soldiers up and down before drowning them in the yolk!

"Mummy, can I go and tell Jessie what you told me?"

"Darling, it's Sunday today. I think they go to church sometimes. I'd better ring them up first."

Jane, Jessie's mother, was expecting another baby. I was almost envious. I picked up the telephone in the hall.

"Hi, Jane, how are you?"

"Oh hello Rosa, I'm fine, thanks."

"Are you busy today? Musa wants to come over. He has something to tell Jessie." I had told her about the adoption, but not all the details.

"Actually, we're going to church in about an hour. How about Musa coming to Sunday School with Jessie?"

"That sounds like a great idea," I said. Musa couldn't wait. He was out of the house before I could stop him and I had to run after him with his coat.

When they returned from church, Jane rang to ask if Musa could stay for lunch so I agreed. At last, David made an appearance and made himself some coffee. He suggested we go out for a meal saying he had something important to tell me.

He did not speak until we were settled into a corner table at the pub and ordered our meal. I chit-chatted aimlessly while David gave non committal answers.

It was a Carvery, so we took our plates and helped ourselves to roast beef and vegetables. I was chatting about the neighbours and told David that Jane was expecting another baby. I could see that he was not listening, but poking at his food and turning over the slices of meat with his fork as if he was distracted. Then he pushed his plate away and screwed up his napkin, before I could finish eating. He looked around at the other people in the pub, went to the bar to fetch another glass of beer and sat down facing me, leaning his head close to mine.

"I sometimes feel I don't have a family any more. You have to admit that we are drifting apart."

"Well, don't all couples go through sticky patches in their marriage? But you don't understand me at all."

"I do my best to understand your needs but I've made my mind up. I'm moving out," he said, watching my face. I could see that he was willing me not to make a terrible show of emotion in a public restaurant.

"What... Why...Where to... There's someone else?" The words tumbled out but I kept a straight face.

"Yes," he said, simply. He paused to wait for signs that I would break down, but I was too shocked to take it in.

"You will be happy to know that I've cleared all my debts. I sold enough paintings to pay back the money."

"Where are you going?"

"I've moved out of my studio and am renting a room in a house. The lady of the house was one of my models and she's a good friend."

"Your lover?"

He gave me a 'yes' with his eyes and waited for my response, but I was shocked into silence. Did he expect me to rage at him in front of everyone?

"I'm sorry, Rosa. I will collect all my stuff over the next week. I will, of course, provide for you and the boy."

Still no reply. I was lost for words. 'The boy,' there it was again.

Finally I squeaked, "I thought you loved me David." I attempted to take hold of his arm, but accidentally knocked over the beer which spilled all over the table, soiling the cloth.

"Ow…Damn!"

"You stupid…!" He got up to pay the bill and walked out. I followed him.

We drove home in silence, but on reaching the front door, I finally found my voice. "Why didn't you say something last night when we were discussing Musa? I suppose you wanted me to make a fool of myself in front of all those people at the pub."

"No, I'm the fool, Rosa." He stomped up the stairs. After about twenty minutes, I heard him leave and caught a glimpse of a small suitcase. Then I heard the car drive away.

I sat down in the kitchen, drinking coffee. I thought about last night, never imagining that he already had it on his mind to leave me. I wanted to stir up some romanticism and had worn my honeymoon negligee purposely. I had clung to him in bed, needing him and coaxing him by rubbing my leg against his thigh and kissing him on his neck. "I love you," I had whispered into his ear. We made love briefly but without any passion and immediately afterwards he turned his back on me.

I picked up the phone and decided to talk to Morag. It was only when I heard her voice that I finally broke down in tears.

"Morag?" I bawled. "David's left me."

"What?... Sweetie, how could he?" I could hear her gasp.

"There's someone else."

"Oh you poor dear." She paused, waiting for me to calm down. "David is a stupid fool. I love my brother, but sometimes he just doesn't use his head. Rosa, no-one else would have put up with his moods, like you've done. He was a spoiled brat, as a child the only boy with three older sisters. I wish I could come down to see you but I have to go into hospital in a few days time."

"Why? What's the matter?"

"Pet, this is not the time to discuss my troubles. You have enough to cope with at the moment."

"No, tell me."

"It's one of my breasts. They are taking a biopsy. It may be cancer."

"Oh, my dear, I am so, so sorry."

"Well, I'm sorry for you. Shall I tell Mother about David? She will be upset."

"Do whatever you think."

"Well, don't worry about me. I have the family around me."

"What can I do?"

"Just try and let David know about me, that's all. I will be in touch. By the way, how is wee Musa?"

"He's just fine. I've told him about the adoption."

"How did he take that?"

"It took him a while to understand, but he has accepted it quite well. I told him it was like the story of Moses in the Bible."

"That's good pet, but I can't believe that David's left you. I truly think he will soon realise his folly. You will always have a family in Scotland, you know, whatever happens."

"Thank you Morag. That means a lot to me."

It was a contrast when Musa came skipping into the house, so happy and full of beans. I dried my eyes and tried to put on a brave face.

"Mummy, it was great at Sunday School, there are lots of children from our school there." He was chattering away, the words tumbling out faster than I could take them in. It was something about Jesus, but I wasn't really listening. Finally he said: "Mummy, I wish I was a Christian."

I laughed at first, then realised he was looking at me seriously. I went to my desk again and found his baptismal certificate and showed it to him. It read:

'Musa Awad was today baptised in the Holy Family Hospital Chapel in Bethlehem. In the name of The Father, the Son, and the Holy Spirit. Amen' Date: May 20th 1989.

"What does it mean?"

"It means that you *are* a Christian. They gave you the name of Awad before we adopted you and your name changed to Craig."

213

"But I thought we were Jewish?"

"I am Jewish, you are Christian but we both believe in the same God." This is too confusing I thought. How can I explain everything to a seven year old? I told him the whole story of his time in Bethlehem and then coming to London. He already knew about the heart operation, because he still had to go for annual check-ups.

Eventually he said: "Mummy can we go to Bethlehem? That's where Jesus was born."

"Yes, I said. "We will try and go in the summer holiday."

"Whoopee, whoopee," he shouted, jumping and dancing around.

It was the confirmation I needed. I would find out about buying tickets tomorrow, and David be damned if I care!

CHAPTER FIFTEEN

School broke up mid July and within a week, Musa and I were on our way to Heathrow Airport. Dad took us in the car on a bright Sunday morning. I had obtained a British passport for Musa, the only problem being where it stated: 'Place of birth'. I explained that although he was born in Palestine, I did not want that to appear on his passport, in case there were difficulties travelling to Israel. Musa most probably was born in Ramallah, which strictly speaking is Palestine, but since the Israelis do not recognise Palestine as a country and we had to travel to Israel, I was at a loss to know what to write on the form. Eventually, the man at the Home Office reluctantly wrote 'Unknown (Adopted)'.

Musa was so excited, I couldn't hold him down. How many more days, then how many more hours, was his constant nagging chant. He could talk of nothing else to his school friends and especially Jessie whom he went to church with every Sunday. I, on the other hand, kept wondering nervously if I had done the right thing. Now, totally ignored by David, even though he often sneaked into the house unannounced, I often wanted to scream and many times cried into my pillow at night. I tried to remain cheerful in front of Musa and now embarking on another journey to the Holy Land I thought, perhaps might help me to recover the smiles in my life.

Although the flight was only just over four and a half hours, it seemed an eternity to Musa. I made up little packages, each containing a surprise, sometimes, sweets, sometimes a puzzle, or a word game or a story book. I told him that at each half hour I would give him a new parcel to unwrap. That kept him busy! Cassia was meeting us so I was able to give a West Jerusalem address on the Immigration forms which I thought would help, but on landing in Israel we had to go through security. The questions were endless and Musa was getting agitated.

"Mrs. Craig, what is the purpose of your visit?

"To renew acquaintance with old friends."

"Business contacts?"

"No, not at all, just pure holiday."

"Mrs Craig, where was Musa born? There is no place of birth on his passport." The female officer was scanning the computer with one eye but looking at me aggressively with the other.

"I don't know," I said.

"I think you *do* know. He has an Arabic name and you took him from here in 1989, didn't you, Mrs. Craig?"

I felt, once again, like someone caught red handed. I had to think quickly, without showing concern on my face. "True, but I really do not know where he was born and I adopted him six years ago."

"Why are you bringing the boy to Israel?"

"He wants to visit the holy places." I said, getting irritated by all these irrelevant questions and with Musa trying to pull me away.

"Please collect your luggage and come with me."

Our suitcase had already been taken off the carrousel and most of the other passengers had gone. I picked it up, with one of the guards close to my side and eyeing me intensely.

My knees felt weak as I wheeled it with one hand and held on to Musa's hand firmly with the other. He wriggled his hand free. "You're hurting me," he complained.

We were taken to a small bare room where another security female officer told me to place my bag on a bench and unzip it. She put on nylon gloves and took out everything, piece by piece, examining it with a

217

hand-held machine. I had wrapped up some presents for Cassia in fancy paper and they made me undo the wrapping. They even looked inside our shoes. I had to repack everything again and we were kept waiting for more than an hour. It was humiliating and all because of a little boy of seven years old. I'm sure it was nothing but harassment. I suppose the worry on my face made Musa a little frightened, but I quietly reassured him and fortunately he stayed silent, clutching my hand.

"Is someone meeting you?"

"Yes, my friend Cassia Cohen, who lives in West Jerusalem."

"You can go now," the security officer said with a bored expression. There was no apology and when we approached the exit there was a big banner in English: Welcome to Israel!

I literally fell into Cassia's arms, relieved. Musa was clinging to me, his eyes getting bigger with all the sights and languages around him. When I apologised for keeping Cassia waiting, explaining the delay, she understood.

"The Israelis know everything. You can't keep anything secret from them. They are also experts when it comes to computers," she said.

She gingerly took hold of Musa's hand, while I manoeuvred the baggage into her car.

"So you are Musa. I've heard so much about you. You are one lucky boy."

"Auntie, is this Jerusalem?"

"No, this is Tel Aviv, but soon we will be in Jerusalem. And you can forget the 'Auntie' bit. Just call me Cassia"

I was surprised, but pleased that he was talking so readily with Cassia, but then Musa gets along with everybody. I wasn't sure whether that was such a good thing. As a child I was always being warned of making friends with strangers.

Cassia's apartment was on the third floor of a big complex in an attractive suburb of Jerusalem with leisure parks and trees all around. The steep hills were covered in more apartment complexes built in hexagon shapes to look like bee hives. Each 'beehive' had a wide balcony overlooking the ones below. I could see some families gathered around a barbeque. There was a big supermarket nearby, as well as various other stores, but everywhere was quiet. It was such a contrast to the bustling, noisy Old City that I had become familiar with. The only noise was the purr of the air conditioning. Musa had no sooner eaten half of his supper than he was asleep in his chair. I took him to bed. Cassia and I sat on the veranda, chatting, until the drone of the mosquitoes sent us inside.

"Musa has been so excited for weeks and last night he didn't sleep at all," I said.

"He's a lovely boy, Rosa, and you're looking so well."

"Thank you. And how are you, Cassia? You're looking so much happier."

"Yes, I'm well settled now. Max would never have settled here, you know. He missed his friends and family too much and we really didn't match as a couple. In a way, I was glad he agreed to the divorce... but I have a new friend, Jacob."

"Oh, my!" I was surprised but pleased. "I'm glad for you."

"Yes, Jacob has asked me to marry him, but it is too soon. I need to get to know him better. He is also divorced and much older."

"Do you have a job?"

"Only part-time in an office. I seem to spend a lot of time in Hebrew classes. You can't get a proper job here until you are fluent in Hebrew."

I slipped a light jacket over my shoulders as it was getting a bit cool and waited for a lull in Cassia's chatting.

"I don't think I've told you that David has left me." I hadn't really planned to say anything but somehow it just came out. I was still hurting, yet still trying to deny the fact. Cassia was facing me, with only a small wicker table between, listening, her face showing real surprise. She was not wearing her usual hoop ear-rings, but they were a long string of chains with coloured stones. They jingled slightly as she moved.

"Rosa, I don't believe it. He seemed so much in love with you."

"I can't believe it myself. It is two months now since he moved out, but he keeps coming back to the house with one excuse or another. Can you believe that he had the nerve to get involved with one of his models. You know he's an artist and has been having models to his studio."

"Oh, I'm so...oo sorry. But coming back now and then means he hasn't left you for good. I suppose he has his own keys and just walks in, does he?"

"Yes. I don't want to change the locks because he still picks up his mail and he pays some of the bills. He hasn't left a forwarding address, you see. But he just ignores me, collects whatever he needs from the cupboard or bookshelf and lets himself out again. At least he doesn't leave any laundry."

"Maybe he's a little jealous of Musa?"

"Perhaps. I confess I have been protective and perhaps too possessive of Musa. David resented that and said he didn't feel he belonged any more." I did not know what else to say and was feeling rather emotional. "You know Musa is such a comfort to me."

She got up to get me a drink and decided it was best to change the subject. We continued talking until late, even though my eyes were getting heavy. I wanted to know how she felt about the political situation.

"Cassia, are you still in love with Israel?"

"What shall I say? I love it here and I've made a lot of good friends, but many times I don't agree with the Government policies. I really thought it would be wonderful living in an all Jewish community, but it's not like that at all. There are always quarrels, especially between the religious and secular Jews. I'm certainly not anti-Arab like some of my neighbours here. They think the Arabs are uncivilized almost and that we should find a way of expelling them. Mind you those are extreme ideas."

"Why do you think the Jews hate Arabs and the Arabs hate Jews? Aren't we all human beings?"

"The problem is mostly about land, Rosa, you see. The Jews say that God gave them this land. It says so in the Bible."

I was reminded that Rebecca had said exactly the same thing. I even remember her exact words to David: 'God gave us this land. It's all written in the Scriptures…'

Cassia went on: "You know, though, the ironic thing is that Israel has a majority of secular Jews, many of whom don't even believe in God."

"Yes and the Palestinians have been here for hundreds of years. Why should Jews from other countries think they have a right to throw them out? Oh, I do wish the international community could get their act together. Three years ago there was a peace deal but no sign of anything happening on the ground."

"You're right. So far, all the so-called Peace talks have come to nothing." She got up again to fill up my glass, but I stopped her.

"I think I'll call it a day. Thanks again for having us."

"The pleasure is all mine. Thanks again for the gifts."

Next morning, Musa was up early and surveying the scene from the veranda.

"Phew, it's so hot here", he said, as I joined him. Cassia made us American pancakes with maple syrup for breakfast.

"Yummy, Mummy, yummy Mummy," said Musa in a sing-song voice. We were all laughing when Jacob arrived. He greeted Cassia with a peck on her cheek which seemed so formal. He was a tad shorter than Cassia and seemed more quiet and serious, quite a contrast, to her ex-husband Max who was so large and boisterous. After coffee, we went for a ride in Jacob's car. He was pointing out landmarks in the New Jerusalem, but apart from the Hebrew signs and the garb of the Orthodox Jews, it didn't look too different from London. By the eager look on his face, Musa was taking everything in.

"Cassia, how can those Jews wear long black coats and fur hats in this hot weather? They look so funny with their curly ringlets. Phew! It's never this hot in London, is it Mummy?"

"Musa, these are very religious Jews. They wear black because they are sorry for the destruction of the temple two thousand years ago. Like some people wear black when a relative dies."

"Oh, but that was such a long time ago. Why are they still sorry?"

"I don't know Musa. I guess it's just part of their uniform."

"I have to wear school uniform. It's boring, navy blue and white."

"Do you enjoy school?" Jacob injected.

"Yes, mostly, but not all of the time." He turned to me.

"Mummy, when can we go to Bethlehem?"

"Bethlehem? Why do you want to go there? That's a no go area," Jacob said, before I could answer.

"Is it, Mummy?" he said, frowning, pleading me with his eyes.

"Darling, we will go to Bethlehem very soon." I explained to Jacob that that is where Musa was as a baby and I brought him to England for heart surgery. Obviously, Cassia had not filled in the background before we arrived. He looked at Cassia by his side and

225

half turned to me, open mouthed. I suppose he was shocked to realise that Musa was Palestinian, not Jewish. Cassia looked embarrassed at this turn of events, because I could see that she didn't know how to explain, but Musa piped up:

"My name is really Moses and my Mummy found me like the story in the Bible," he giggled, waiting for Jacob's reaction.

"Oh," he said dismissively.

I knew that Jaffa Gate was the point where the New Jerusalem met the Old City, so they dropped us off there and we arranged to meet Cassia later that day.

Immediately the sights and smells invaded my whole being with familiar memories. Vivid memories of Amos dumping David and I at this point with a new baby. As we walked through the huge stone archway I hugged Musa, telling him how I had carried him through there in a carrycot as a small baby. He looked up at me in wonderment, pulling my face down for a kiss.

"Mummy, are you sorry you found me? Why are you sad?" He wasn't sure what my tears meant.

"Oh no, darling. Of course not. I love you heaps and heaps. Finding you was the best day of my life. These are happy tears." I said, kissing him on his cheeks. "And I'm going to show you many exciting places."

We walked down the steps into the labyrinth of narrow streets where the Arab traders and foreign tourists were jostling for space.

Musa was fascinated at all the little shops displaying their wares outside. "Look Mummy, wooden donkeys…look at that man wearing a funny hat…look that man wants to show me his T-shirts… Mummy those orange cakes look smashing! Can you smell them?"

"Yes, darling." The sounds and smells of Old Jerusalem brought back so many happy images. It would be so easy to get lost here, I thought, so I hardly dared let go of his hand, but he wanted to explore all the little nooks and crannies. One shopkeeper, almost bald, but with an excuse for a moustache, bent down and said: "What's your name?"

"*Musa, ismee Musa.*" I had taught Musa how to say his name in Arabic, but I was quite surprised to hear him say it with such confidence. Then the man started to talk to him in Arabic, but of course we could not understand. Realising this he said: "I have a little boy at home and his name is Musa, too."

227

"Wow, can I meet him? Does he speak English? Does he go to school?"

"Wait a minute, I'll send for him." He beckoned to a young man from the back of the shop and within a few minutes, little Musa appeared. The man said something in Arabic to his son and the two boys looked at each other, but the other boy was too shy except to say 'Hello' in English. His father said something to him and he presented my Musa with a black and white chequered *kaffiya* headscarf and arranged it on his head. The shopkeeper laughed and I laughed, too. He handed him a small mirror and Musa stood proudly, arranging the scarf in different ways and changing his facial expressions to match, alternating between smiling and frowning. "Wow, wait till I show my friends."

"Now you are a real little Arab boy," I said, then whispering, "What can we give the boy?" Quick as a flash, Musa delved into his trouser pocket and fished out a badge which said 'I love London' (love in the shape of a heart) and a packet of chewing gum. It was not much to give but the little boy was delighted.

The two boys looked around the shop, speaking in sign language as far as I could see. Musa picked up a little camel carved in olive wood.

"Mummy, can I buy this for Jessie?"

"Of course," I said.

He then picked up a small drum and the other boy showed him how to strum with his fingers. It was a simple clay pot with some kind of animal skin stretched over the top. I bought him this, too. Then suddenly I had an idea. I spoke to the shopkeeper: "Do you think your Musa would be able to write letters in English with the help of his teacher? I know my Musa would love to have a pen-pal from Jerusalem."

"What a good idea," the shopkeeper said and immediately went to fetch a pad of paper and a pen. I wrote down our address and he gave me a business card with a Post Office box number in Jerusalem.

"My name is Yousef Kanafani and we are Christian Palestinians," he said. "Musa will look forward to hearing from you."

I had almost forgotten the way to the hostel. We took several wrong narrow turns until I finally spotted the hostel with its unimposing entrance. It would be easy to miss it. Sister Bridget was in the lobby talking to visitors when she spotted me. I had not warned her that I was coming. She came towards me with hands outstretched and enveloped me in a warm embrace, then looked at Musa.

"My, my, you're such a big boy now."

"Ismee Musa," he said, shaking her hand. I was amused that Musa wanted to try out the one and only Arabic word that he knew.

"I know who you are. I remember you this big," she held her hands to indicate his baby size.

"Rosa, why don't I take you and Musa to see some of the Christian sites?"

"Thank you, Sister, are you sure you have the time?"

"Of course. It would be a pleasure."

She took us along the Via Dolorosa, explaining the different Stations of the Cross until we reached the Church of the Holy Sepulchre. She also showed us the Wailing Wall where we saw many Jews putting little prayer notes into cracks of the stone wall and above that the Dome of the Rock, a sacred place for Muslims. Musa was not particularly impressed with the old stone structures, but was fascinated by the differences in people, the various religious uniforms of Christian priests, Muslim sheiks and ultra-orthodox Jews. I told

Sister that he was good with words and liked writing little stories.

"When you get back to London, you must write about this, Musa, and when you are grown up, you can perhaps show other people," she said.

"Yes," he said jumping up and down, excitedly. "When I grow up I want to write for the newspapers."

"You are a clever little boy, I can see," said Sister Bridget. We were passing by a shop that was selling school materials and text books. She stopped and bought him a beginner's book in Arabic, something like ABC. "Perhaps you can find a teacher in London to teach you Arabic," she said.

"Wow, look Mummy," he said, his eyes sparkling.

Sister turned over the first page. "See here, Musa, the letter A sounds like the English A, but it writes like number one. But it all reads backwards to English. You will soon learn."

"Then you can teach your Mummy," I said, laughing.

The next day we went to Bethlehem. Israeli soldiers in full gear with rifles at the ready were everywhere and we had to wait over half an hour at the checkpoint. Musa was clinging to me, nervously.

"Why are there so many guns?" he whispered. I explained quietly that this is Palestinian territory, occupied by Israel, though I'm not sure if he completely understood. We had to get out of the Israeli taxi and into another Arab taxi the other side of the checkpoint.

Musa was surprised to see the Church of the Nativity with the tiny entrance from outside, but with an enormous interior. The religious trappings and banners, lamps and statues were rather overwhelming. I think he had probably imagined a Christmas card scene, so was disappointed. Downstairs in the small dark grotto, he kissed the gold star, traditionally the place of the manger. I was quite touched to see how much he already understood and although I am not a Christian, I respect their beliefs and traditions.

We then went to the Hospital and I asked if Dr. Hussein was there. We waited for some time, sitting on a bench watching children with their mothers and old men on crutches. There was plenty of chattering in Arabic, but subdued. Musa just watched quietly. Eventually the doctor came and greeted me first. He looked older but walked with a more confident step.

"Musa," he said, bending down to Musa's height. "You are a very fortunate boy to have such a nice Mama who cared about you so much, that she came back for you. You know, I looked after you in this hospital for the first six months of your life."

Musa nodded. "I know, thank you," he said.

"What a well mannered boy! You are bringing him up so well, Mrs. Craig. I am so glad everything went well for his heart surgery. I was pleased that the hospital in London let me know the outcome. He keeps well does he?"

"Yes, very well, thank you Doctor."

But well mannered? I thought to myself; yes he is being polite here, but he can be bloody obstinate and stubborn too, even rude with tantrums at times.

"Do you go to school, Musa?"

"Yes, I'm in Class three, now."

"Are there any problems, Mrs. Craig?"

"No. Everything is fine. We just wanted to say thank you again, Doctor."

Musa interrupted: "Do you have any other Palestinian babies, like I was?"

"Not at the moment, Musa," the doctor said, looking amused. "Why?"

233

"I just hope they find a good Mummy, too!"

I squeezed him affectionately. After all my negative thoughts, I felt chastised. The doctor hugged Musa and shook my hand warmly.

"I will keep in touch," he said, as he waved us goodbye.

We walked to the taxi stop.

A few days later we said goodbye to Cassia, urging her to visit us in England.

"It's been lovely having you stay. I will be in touch and I do hope it will all come right for you and David," she said.

She had offered to drive us up north but we heard about a tour group leaving Jerusalem for the Galilee, so we decided to join them. Musa wanted to see the Lake of Galilee and all the Christian places that he had learnt about in Sunday School. We tramped around all the usual sites, with a guide explaining all the historical background and we stayed two nights in Nazareth. It was quite exhausting, even for an energetic little boy, but he loved it.

During the last couple of days, I felt queasy but put it down to the change of food, yet Musa was fine. In fact, I was surprised how easily he took to the different salads and rice dishes cooked with lentils or beans and served with plain yogurt, all so foreign to his palate. On the flight home I felt so nauseated and almost vomited. Also, my monthlies had not turned up. It can't be, I thought. This must be an early menopause, but I'm only 39 for goodness sake.

After a week at home, I decided to have a pregnancy test.

CHAPTER SIXTEEN

My pride told me not to inform David of my pregnancy immediately, but wait until he came to the house. He hadn't even enquired about our trip to Jerusalem. But I could not keep my secret to myself. I had to tell someone. I called Morag.

"Morag dear, how are you?"

"I'm much better thanks."

"How did the surgery go?"

"I've had surgery on one breast and now I'm having Chemo treatment."

"Is it all clear?"

"Yes, thank God. The doctor says he is pretty sure I'll be OK, so that's a blessing. I wish you could come up to see me."

"I'll try and come up to Scotland if I can. That's great news that you're much better. I can't imagine how traumatic it must have been to go through all that. I really feel for you. I do wish you lived nearer."

"I wish so too. Anyway, Rosa, what's more important is how are *you* holding up?"

"I'm OK Morag."

"Tell me, how did your trip go?"

236

"It was really good…" I paused. "But I have some news. What d'you think? You'll never believe this… I'm two months pregnant."

"No! Really! Wow, that's wonderful. Does David know? Is he happy?"

"David? I haven't told him yet. In fact, I haven't even seen him since we got back."

"What? The rotter! He's just the limit. Are you alright?"

"Kind of," I said, trying not to break down on the phone.

"Would you like me to tell David he must go and see you? I won't give the reason."

"Yes, I would appreciate that."

"I'll call you back." She hung up.

David arrived late that evening. I was glad that Musa was in bed. He gave me a peck on the cheek, took off his jacket, and went into the living room as if he had never left, settling himself on the settee with his arms outstretched over the back. He looked relaxed and yet I could not quite make out his bemused expression.

"Well, Rosa, you have to send a message to me through my sister in Scotland? Something important, she said?"

"Yes, I expected you to come and find out how we got on in Jerusalem, but we have been back now for two weeks. You have never enquired about me or whether I had a nice time with Cassia, or how Musa got on, nothing, nothing!"

"Oh, sorry about that," he said in a sarcastic tone. "Any drinks in this establishment?"

"Get your own," I said. "I'm not drinking."

He reluctantly went to the kitchen and found some red wine, opened the bottle and poured himself a glass. He came back with an air of indifference.

"Well, what do you want to tell me? About your trip to Jerusalem? Or...are you looking for a divorce?" He spoke softly with his head down to his chest as if he didn't really want me to hear nor for me to give an answer.

"David, just look at me and listen, will you." I stared at him. This was going to be his biggest bombshell yet and I didn't want to miss his facial reaction. "I'm pregnant."

He sat dumbstruck for a moment not knowing how to take this news. Then his screwed up eyebrows told me of utter disbelief followed by a quirky smile. "Wow, who's the lucky guy?"

"Don't be stupid, YOU are," I shouted.

"But I can't be. That's impossible."

"Why?"

"Look, I went to a doctor without telling you, remember, after you had the scans. The tests came back 'very low sperm count', which means I'm infertile."

"You never told me about that. Why didn't you tell me?"

"I guess it's not a manly thing to discuss." His lips were pursed together as if he didn't want to talk about it.

"Anyway, very low sperm count does not mean that you're completely infertile, as I am expecting a baby."

He sat there unable to say anything. I had nothing more to say. We just looked at each other. Eventually I said:

"Well?"

"What do you want me to do?"

"I want you to take responsibility. We're talking about *your* baby."

"I don't believe you."

"Do you honestly think I've had some other man in my bed after you left? *You've* got another woman but I'm not interested in taking another man. You think I'm making this up to get you back?" This statement made him open his mouth wide.

"Well, you and I haven't exactly been intimate for months. It does take two to make a baby you know!" He laughed cynically.

"Have you forgotten, already?"

"What?"

"The night before you moved out, we had quarrelled about Musa and how I told him he was adopted. Remember David? I made the first move, but you made love to me that night, even though you weren't exactly in the mood for it."

"Oh…" he paused as if he was trying to remember. "I admit I'd forgotten about that."

"I was trying to make it up to you. I had no idea that you were planning to leave me the next day."

"But have you had medical confirmation?"

"Yes." I said simply, watching him trying to dismiss the whole matter.

"It can't be true…"

He got up ready to leave and put his jacket on. He had only taken a small sip from his drink. I guess he was too shocked to even finish it. I did not accompany him to the door, but I gave him a parting shot: "You're a miserable heartless coward!"

"I'll be in touch," he shouted, as he let himself out, without looking back or responding to my anger.

After he'd gone, I just sat there for a long time thinking. I knew somehow, that I still loved David. Did he have any feelings for me anymore? Was he going to take responsibility for this child? Would he consider coming back to me now? Can I forgive him? I just went over and over his conversation with me, and his utter disbelief and denial. He had pretended to deny and wanted to give me the impression that he didn't care. Where was the loving man that I had married? Where was the David that had stood with me in the pressures and emotions of the adoption process? I realised he had not said a word or asked any questions about Musa or about how our trip went. But then I guess the news had driven away all other thoughts. I should be deliriously excited at the prospect of having my own baby. It was all I ever longed for. But I'm feeling absolutely wretched.

After sitting brooding for some time, I dragged myself upstairs, but could not sleep.

The next morning I got up late, but felt terrible. My head was spinning, my stomach was heaving and my eyes were red and swollen. I hugged my tatty old gown around me and with my hair uncombed I must have looked a sight. My image in the mirror was unrecognisable. Unconsciously, I made a mental note to treat myself to a new dressing gown, ready for the hospital.

Musa was already up, eating a bowl of cornflakes. He stared at me. "Mummy, you look crabby."

"I feel like crap, sorry!"

Just then we heard Dad's car draw up. Musa rushed to the back door to greet him.

"Grandpa, Mummy's sick."

Dad's paunch almost eclipsed his head as he bent down to me.

"Goddamnit girl, whatever's the matter?" He put his arms round me, looking worried. "I tried to call you this morning but there was no answer, so thought I'd better come round."

"Sorry Dad, my head was under the duvet."

"He's gone off again, hasn't he, the bastard?"

"He never came back. I'm just feeling sick and lousy."

"Come on, love. A cup 'o tea will buck you up. Musa, go and get your wellingtons, I'll take you for a ride into the country."

"Coo thanks, Grandpa. The neighbours are away, so I have no-one to play with."

"We'll let your Mummy rest. How about spending a couple of days with me?"

Musa let out a scream of delight and went upstairs to get ready. I followed Dad to put the kettle on and whispered, "I'm going to have a baby!"

He hugged me so tight. "That's the best news ever love, does David know?"

I wept on his shoulder.

~~~~~~

David had come back gradually. Like before, he crept into the house at different times, sometimes with barely a greeting, collecting the bills and whatever else he needed and then slipping out again. I felt like changing the locks so that he would have to ring the door bell, but I didn't want to send the message that I didn't want him. I needed him and I still loved the old David, the one I married, the kind caring husband...

243

Finally, he came one early evening when I was in my seventh month. It was just before Christmas. My bump was getting heavy and uncomfortable and I was feeling tired.

"How are you dear?" He had brought a bouquet of red roses and a LEGO set for Musa, which he set down on the coffee table.

Did I hear the word 'dear'? Did I smell roses? I was slumped down on the settee, feeling dizzy. Musa was sitting on the floor, watching a children's detective film. He turned round when David came in.

Musa gave him an intense look. "Can't you see how tired she is, Daddy?"

David sat down beside me, putting his arm around me. I let him, but did not look at him, straightening my back as if to give him a cool response.

"How are you coping?"

I shrugged. "OK. Once the baby comes I guess I'll survive without you."

He started to sob. "Rosa, I've been such a fool, can you ever forgive me?"

Musa got up from the floor and ran to David, putting his arms round his neck.

"Don't cry, Daddy, please." I was so astonished at Musa's wonderful spontaneous forgiveness, that I flung my arms round the two of them in a family embrace. I did not need to say anything.

"Does this mean we are going to be a family again?" Musa asked.

"Yes, if Mummy will have me back."

He looked at me, wide-eyed. "Will you, Mummy?"

"Yes, of course."

Musa was ecstatic. He started jumping up and down in excitement. "Soon we will be four with the new baby!"

Happiness so often comes after heartache, I thought. I wanted to believe that we could be a happy family again.

We decided not to go up to Scotland that Christmas as I couldn't face the journey, but instead we spent it with my Dad, which pleased him enormously. For Dad, it was the season of Hanukkah, or Festival of Lights, so we celebrated that first.

"Tell me the story, Grandpa," said Musa, when he saw the seven branched candlestick sitting in the window.

He gave Musa a taper to light the first candle, explaining: "A long, long time ago, there used to be a big Temple in Jerusalem. A wicked ruler was cruel to the Jews and set up heathen idols. Then after he died, the Jews cleaned out the Temple again, but only found one small jug of oil for the lamps. It was only enough oil to keep the lamps lit for one day, but God made a miracle so that the oil lasted a whole week. In those days there was no electricity you see. So that's why we celebrate."

"Wow, that's a lovely story, Grandpa. It reminds me of the story of Jesus who made buckets of wine out of a jug of water for a wedding."

"Buckets?" David laughed. "I don't think it was buckets!"

"Well, it was a lot, a lot of wine." He swept up his arms in a big circle.

"Bring on the buckets of wine, Ben!" We all laughed and I had to hold on tight to my tummy.

For Musa's sake, Dad bought a Christmas tree and let Musa decorate it with glass baubles and matchbox toys. It was a relief to enjoy a fun family Christmas.

My pregnancy was normal and our baby daughter was born on February 17th, '97 a winter baby, whom we named Margaret Joy. David gave her the name Margaret. He said Saint Margaret was the patron saint of expectant mothers and also it had associations with Scotland. Joy was my choice for obvious reasons.

The day after the hospital birth, I was surprised to receive a visit from Kevin. He had obviously seen my name on the admissions list. David and Musa were visiting at the same time.

"Rosa, congratulations. I'm so happy for you." He produced a box of chocolates and I could see Musa's expression willing me to open the box.

"Thank you so much. How good to see you again. David, open the box and hand the chocolates round."

He bent down to Musa. "My goodness, what a big boy you are now. I haven't seen you for some time." He ruffled Musa's curls affectionately. "I'm so glad to see you again, Rosa. I have a lot to tell you. You've changed my life!"

"What! You're the one who changed mine. You helped me bring Musa to London."

"No, you see, I think I told you I was taking trips to Israel and now I have been twice to the Holy Land in the last four years and am thinking of going again next year. You helped me see how important it was to visit Jerusalem and understand the politics of the current conflict. It has changed my whole way of thinking about Palestinians."

It was then that Musa piped up. "I went to Jerusalem with Mummy last year...*and* we went to Bethlehem." His face was shining with excitement.

That started a long conversation between Kevin, Musa and I. We shared so many experiences. David excused himself to go to the cafeteria for coffee. Before Kevin left, he asked me if I would mind if he said a simple prayer to thank God for the safe arrival of baby Margaret.

"Certainly," I said.

"O God our Creator, the birth of your child Jesus brought great joy to Mary and Joseph. We give thanks for the safe delivery of this child. May she ever grow in your faith, hope and love."

We all said *'Amen'*.

Musa was in one way delighted to have a baby sister, but on the other hand becoming more difficult in his behaviour. I think he felt that all my love had been transferred to the baby. His teachers were complaining that he wasn't concentrating, so his marks were poor. I knew he was intelligent, but sometimes he didn't even want to go to school.

Jane appeared at my door one day, holding Jessie's hand. "Rosa, Jessie tells me that Musa wasn't in class today. Is he sick?"

I instinctively covered my mouth. "Oh no! He left here with his school bag as usual this morning. I watched him walking along the road." I looked at Jessie. "Was he in the playground at lunchtime?"

"No," she said. "He was there first thing, but after the first class I think he went to the toilet and never came back. I thought he had gone to another class."

"Why didn't the teacher say something?"

She shook her head. I began to get alarmed, but just then I caught sight of Musa running round the back trying to avoid us.

Jessie spotted him. "There he is!" She lowered her voice. "I think he was a bit naughty."

I thanked Jane and went indoors to tackle him. What I didn't realise at first, was that he was being bullied by some of the other children.

Another day I was in the kitchen preparing tea with the door shut. Margaret was having a nap in the living room. I thought a bomb had dropped. Musa had come home from school and thrown his school bag full of books at the door with an almighty thud. I opened the door to find him standing in the hallway with his coat torn and a lump on his forehead.

"What on earth?"

His eyes were damp but I could see he was trying not to cry. "I hate you all, you bloody … Brits!" he came out with such swear words as I could not believe. He stamped his feet and picked up a vase of flowers ready to throw at me, but then thought better of it. It toppled over sending flowers and water over the carpet.

"What did you say?" I was trying not to lose it. I took hold of his arm and he tried to fight me, so I let go. "I'm going to wash your mouth out with soap!" I grabbed his coat collar. He tried to resist me, pushing me away, and even kicking his legs out, but missing my shins. "Bog off," he shouted.

I was tempted to smile, but managed to keep my face straight.

"Why are you so naughty these days?"

"I hate school. The boys hit me."

"And you hit them back, I suppose."

"I want to go home!"

250

I finally calmed him down and drew him to me. "Musa darling, you *are* home. You don't really hate us, do you?" I hugged him until his tears flowed. "But you're not my real Mummy are you? You are Mummy to Margaret. My real home is in Palestine, isn't it?"

"Here is your home right now. We don't know why your own mother left you, but perhaps when you grow up you can go to Palestine and try to find out." I dug into the pocket of my jeans. "Look what came for you in the post today. A picture postcard from Jerusalem."

He snatched the card from me and looked at the picture of the Damascus Gate. On it was a brief message: *'Hi Musa! How are u in London? Please send me a postcard. I fine. Luv Musa.'*

Musa was now quietly sitting down, reading his postcard over and over. Then the baby started to cry and I went to pick her up, but instead of putting her on my lap, I gave her to Musa.

"Here's Margaret. Look Musa she's stopped crying. She's smiling at you."

It somehow worked a miracle, at least temporarily. Musa looked at her and after a while started cooing to her like he had seen me do.

"Isn't it great, darling? You have a baby sister and Jessie has a baby brother. Now, please Musa, I don't ever want to hear any of those nasty words again. Are you going to say sorry?"

He handed over the baby and looked down at his shoes.

"Sorry Mummy," he mumbled.

"Now, let me have a look at your head."

We made an appointment to see the head teacher of Musa's school. David had taken the morning off and came with me which surprised me. It was a sunny, but cold morning in late spring, so I wrapped up Margaret warm and took her in the pram with us. The school was within a short walking distance. Mr. Whiting was a young, pleasant looking man whose obvious enthusiasm and vision for education was encouraging. He made us feel at ease immediately. He greeted us warmly and ordered coffee.

"You have come to discuss Musa's behaviour, I presume?"

David spoke up first: "Mr. Whiting, are you aware that Musa is adopted?"

"Yes of course, Mr. Craig. You know he is a very bright boy, in fact exceptionally bright, but he needs counselling to sort out his problems and perhaps a

252

school where he can somehow use his brain to a greater capacity."

"Are you saying that this school cannot meet his needs?"

"No, this is a good junior school. Musa is still young, of course, but in English he is far ahead of the class."

"I know he reads a lot," I said, "but I thought his problems were more to do with being confused about his identity. He doesn't know where he came from, you see." I proceeded to explain briefly how we found him as a baby, brought him to London for heart surgery and eventually adopted him.

"Thank you for telling me all of that. I didn't know the full story and that explains a lot of his behaviour. But also he hasn't found another boy who is a special friend. He hangs around a lot with Jessie and that's not healthy and he always has his head in a book. That's why the other kids tease him so. Then that starts a fight. He hits them and they hit him back."

"So what do you suggest?" David said.

"We will find an experienced counsellor and see if that helps. How about a Church school? Musa tells me he goes to church with Jessie?"

"Yes, he does, but we are not churchgoers. You see, I am Jewish. In any case I don't think we could afford a private school."

"I see," he said, showing surprise. "Anyway, we will do our best to help your son. I see you have a baby girl. How does Musa take to her?"

"He loves her," I said.

Musa was brought into the office at the same time as the coffee.

"Mr. Whiting has been telling us what a clever boy you are," I said, hugging him.

Later, at home, I asked him casually why he didn't have boys as friends.

"Those boys you invited to your birthday party, Johnny and Tom. Why don't you bring them home to play with you sometimes?"

"Mummy, I do have some boys who are friends, but Jessie is my best friend." What more could I say.

Meanwhile, it seemed that this episode brought David and I closer together. How ironic, I thought. It was Musa who had separated us in the first place, but now David realised that I needed his support and Musa needed a father. One evening I tackled him about his art studio.

"Have you given up painting canvases?"

"For the time being, yes. I realise that my talents are better used in the classroom and I couldn't sell my paintings. Nor did I have the money to pay for models." He laughed nervously.

"What about your lady friend?"

"Oh, Linda, (I made a note of the name). You see, she was my model and I guess I was turned on by her curvy body, breasts especially…"

I looked down at my almost flat chest and remembered seeing David's canvases with a prominence of breasts. No wonder Morag told me I needed to put on more flesh!

"Oh heck! Sorry I can't oblige with big boobs but I've got a bit more of those since Margaret was born." I said, laughing sarcastically and lifting up my bra.

"Darling, I've been so foolish. It's all over with her. You see, I was tired of hearing every day about Musa. I never felt that he belonged to me like he did to you."

"It's my fault too. I realise now that I became too possessive of him."

"I really don't deserve you, Rosa. Have you forgiven me?"

"Of course."

"You are always so calm and caring. I am truly sorry for last year but I want to make it up to you somehow." I put my arms round him. He stroked my hair fondly and then carried me up the stairs just as he did on our wedding night.

PART TWO
MUSA

CHAPTER SEVENTEEN

2002

It was a Saturday, a week before my thirteenth birthday. I thought of going to the library as I had run out of books to read. I had finished my homework, but the rain was coming down in torrents, so even the local football match had been cancelled. Not that I shall ever be an avid football fan, but it was important to support the local team.

"Mum, any good books in this house?" I could smell the luscious aromas coming from the oven, as I opened the kitchen door to find Mum with floury hands and Margaret with a floury face waving away the steam. I snatched a cinnamon roll from the table but it was just out of the oven and too hot to handle. I dropped it. "Ow, shit...!"

"M...U...S...A," they both screamed at me together, trying to look angry and amused at the same time.

"Wow," I said. "So much industry. What's going on? Starting a bakery, are we?"

"No, Mum's helping me make some cakes for the school fair. For charity."

"Charity, eh? What kind of charity?"

"For poor orphan children in Africa," said Margaret, dismissing me with the wave of her hands and trying to close the kitchen door.

I put my foot in the door. "Well, I'm a poor orphan kid. No cakes for me?" I laughed, but Mum looked at me as if I had committed a crime. Why does she always have to take me seriously?

"Get out, you scoundrel," she said.

"I just want a book to read."

"Well, go and browse through David's books."

David's bookshelves were stacked with books but mostly not the kind I would be interested in. 'Modern Art', 'Art in the Renaissance Period', 'Water colours of the Victorian Era', etc. also 'The Complete Works of Shakespeare', and other Classics. Then a few novels, 'Love in the Time of Cholera' and then 'The Joy of Sex'. I quickly tucked those under my shirt. I'll put those under my pillow! Finally I came across an old photo album, which I don't remember seeing before. I took it upstairs to flick through it. Pictures of David and Mum on their honeymoon in Italy, Mum looking stunning in her bikini by the beach; Mum in her graduation cap and gown with Grandpa and her Mother. Mum with her arm around another young man (not David!), then a few wedding photos. No photos of me in this album, I said to myself, until suddenly a newspaper cutting fell out. It was a bit faded, but there was a picture of Mum in a winter coat with a baby in her arms. The caption read: 'Christmas Baby arrives from Bethlehem'. It went on: 'Mrs. Craig would like to thank everyone who contributed so generously, so that this poor orphan baby from Bethlehem could come to London for his heart operation…..'

I was utterly gob smacked! My hands were trembling and I felt the entire colour drain from my face. Just then I heard David slam the front door and shake out his coat. He must have gone to the kitchen where Mum told him I was looking for a book, as I heard him sprinting up the stairs.

"You look like you've seen a ghost," he announced.

"Why have I never been shown this before, David?" I waved the cutting in his face. "You appealed for money for me?" ('Daddy' had been replaced by 'David' two years before.) I felt angry and betrayed.

"Mum told me she brought me to England because she loved me?

"I'm sorry Musa. I'd almost forgotten about it."

"You mean you got money for me?"

"No, no, no. That's not what you think. You see we had to find money for your operation. Mum had already spent a fortune in Jerusalem, staying in the Hostel, paying the lawyer, transport and many other expenses. We were almost bankrupt! We could have left you in Bethlehem. You might have died even. We had to find money somehow and it was Kevin's idea to tell the newspapers."

"Oh, I see."

"It was because we loved you we couldn't just leave you there, could we?"

I got up and hugged him, which took him by surprise.

"Steady on old chap!" We both laughed.

At last David has admitted that he loves me. He used the word 'we'. I reflected how David had often treated me with contempt or ignored me completely as if I didn't belong to him and was rather a nuisance and an embarrassment. I knew that Mum had gone through periods of hurt and feeling alienated and that I had been the cause of their splitting up. I too, had been hurt by his attitude, but now for the first time he was treating me like a son.

Mum suddenly appeared with a plateful of cakes and could see that David and I were showing signs of bridging a gap.

"What have you two been talking about?" she asked.

"Oh nothing," I said, trying to avoid looking her straight in the eye.

She looked like she didn't believe me, but dismissed it with a shake of her head. "Anyway, I've been thinking, what do you want to do for your birthday? Would you like to invite your friends here or go to the 'Shanghai Parlour'?"

"I'll think about it."

"OK, but please just tidy up a bit here, will you," said Mum, as she and David went downstairs. I hoped David would tell her about the article and my reaction to it.

I sat on the edge of my bed, still unmade, with the Pooh and Tigger duvet crumpled up in a messy heap on the carpet. I'm thirteen now, much too old for Pooh! Or am I? I still love the framed print on the wall of Pooh, Tigger and Piglet huddled together, laughing, with mouths wide open. 'Pooh and friends giggling,' it said. It always cheered me up. But my favourite poster amongst all the others, crowding my walls of Harry

262

Potter prints, map of the London underground, David's scribbles and some of mine, was of Bob Dylan, with the caption: '*All I can do is be me whoever that is.*' I may not look like Bob Dylan with his dark glasses and shaggy hair, but the sentiment fitted me exactly. Now that newspaper cutting had set me thinking. What sort of person was my real mother? Was she still alive? What would my life have been like had Mum not found me by the brook that day? Ending up as a nonentity in some orphanage, unloved and uncared for? We were not able to visit the village where Mum found me on our last trip because of the political barriers, but one day, maybe I could go. Then, perhaps it would be better if I don't find out. After all, why did my real parents throw me away? I know Mum loves me, but she can be so fussy. She still treats me like a baby sometimes.

I sat at my computer. The internet is a whole new world and I love it. I can go to websites which inform me of all the latest happenings in Palestine. Last year there were talks of peace and then the situation got steadily worse. Now there is this second intifada and as I keep telling myself I am a Palestinian! This is MY country they are talking about. Last year was 9/11 and now it looks like the troops are preparing for war in

Iraq. I try to keep abreast with all the news from the Middle East. Most of my classmates are not interested. All they talk about is football, girls, and Harry Potter.

An email from Musa. It's great that I can communicate with him instantly now without waiting for the postman to bring postcards. It is so easy with a computer in my bedroom. Musa has to go to an internet café. He told me that few people have computers at home, so they rely on coffee shops which have computers for the public to rent on an hourly basis. He said it's as cheap as a bottle of Cola!

Hi Musa Ben,

Do you like your new school? I have two best friends, Kareem and Samer. They live in the Old City to. But the soldiers make lots of trouble like the other day we had tear gas. Mama was so ill, she had to go to the hospital. The gas made her lose the baby. There r no tourists these days. Not enough bizness for my Dad. Thanks for inviting me to London but it is to difficult to get a visa and much, much money. I wish you come to Jerusalem again.

Happy Birthday!

Musa Yousef.

P.S. I print out all your emails, so that I can keep them at home. Please rite back.

This cheered me up in spite of the bad news. Poor Musa. My life is so much easier. He is becoming good in English. I decided to answer him later when I can tell him about my birthday celebration. I searched through my pile of CDs and put some music on. Gary Cooke's music was electric with bass drums and guitar and the lyrics were cool. I started to hum along, '*she doesn't know a thing about love...your beautiful face...it's not the end...*'

My new school is a modern mixed Comprehensive a long way away, but I like the fact that I have to take a bus and then the underground for a forty minute ride. My two best friends are very different. Ahmed is from Pakistani parents, who are devout Muslims, though Ahmed is full of fun and mischief. Robbie is a white, blond 'posh' guy, whom I had defended when he had been bullied by others for his proper English accent. It's funny how all three of us are so different, but kind of gang up together.

When Ahmed turned thirteen he invited me to a meal at his house and his mother had cooked the yummiest hot Indian curry. I was really impressed by

265

the wonderful smells of garlic and spices and I couldn't help noticing the cool choice of colours in the cushions. His mother was so welcoming and kind, dressed in a silk sari.

The meal was rather formal as we sat round the dining room table with fancy cutlery and posh plates. Like some old American film of the golden family except that instead of frilly dresses and starched collars, this family were wearing exotic Asian clothes. His father was at the head, his mother the other end, dishing out the food, Ahmed and I one side and two of his sisters the other side. The family wanted to know all about me. I guess they knew I didn't have English beginnings. Ahmed is the youngest of the family and the only boy.

"Musa, Ahmed tells me that you are adopted?" his father said.

"Yes I am."

"So where are your real family?"

"I don't know."

I could see, out of the corner of my eye, that Ahmed's mother was trying to give a message with her eyes to her husband. Maybe she didn't want him to ask too many questions, but I didn't really mind. Anyway,

Ahmed spoke up: "His mother just found him as a baby."

"Where, Musa?" said Ahmed's father.

"In Palestine. There was a little note in Arabic which said: 'my name is Musa'."

"Well, well! So you are Palestinian, a Muslim like us?" He leaned forward to snatch some more olives. He was doing all the talking.

"I think I am Christian, but I'm not sure. I was baptised as a baby by some Italian nuns. You see I was in a hospital in Bethlehem for the first six months of my life. Then Mum brought me to London for a heart operation."

"That's wonderful Musa! But just because those nuns baptised you doesn't mean anything. They were foreigners. No, no if you are Palestinian you must be Muslim."

He seemed quite sure about this, so who was I to contradict.

"How about going with Ahmed next Saturday to meet the Imam and take classes. You should definitely learn about the Koran and study some Arabic. You know we usually go to the Mosque on Fridays but since you have school, the children go on Saturdays. Do you know any Arabic?"

"I bought some CDs of the Arabic language, so I'm trying to learn Arabic phrases from the tapes but I've been told the Egyptian dialect is different. What kind of Arabic do you learn?"

"Oh, it's Koranic Arabic, which might be different from the spoken language."

"I'll have to ask my Mum about going to the mosque," I said.

Ahmed's father continued to talk about the importance of religion, so I was glad when his mother interrupted, "More curry Musa? Help yourself to pickles and salads. I hear you have a baby sister?"

"Margaret is five now. She has just started school," I said.

After the meal, Ahmed made the excuse that he wanted to show me his bedroom, so we went upstairs, played a card game, sat telling each other stories and giggling.

When I got home, I found Mum preparing Margaret for bed. She came down to greet me.

"Did you have a good time at Ahmed's?"

"Yes, we had a hot spicy curry and rice. You know how I love that. But Mum, I want to ask you. Do you think I might be a Muslim? Ahmed's father said all Palestinians are Muslims, so I should go to the Mosque and learn about the Koran. I am confused. What if I really am Muslim?"

In fact, going to Ahmed's home had made me question my identity more. Suppose I am a Muslim? I might have to change my lifestyle and get to read the Koran and learn more about Islam. I felt my brain being invaded by something alien. Not from outer space, but a new culture with a new set of values.

Mum patted me on the shoulder. "Musa, don't worry about it. You believe in God, don't you? You don't have to be religious. Besides, Christians, Muslims and Jews all believe in the same God. Not all Palestinians are Muslims. He's wrong about that, didn't your pen-friend Musa's father say they were Palestinian Christians?

"Mum, I'm so confused I've never really thought about it seriously."

"Then stop worrying. Here's David, talk to him about it."

"Talk to me about what?" David said, as he settled into his favourite chair, with the evening paper.

"Musa's friend Ahmed wants Musa to go to the Mosque because his father thinks he should be a Muslim," Mum said.

"No, it's Ahmed's father that told me," I said. "Ahmed only goes because his father makes him. He told me that as he was born into a Pakistani family, he has no choice but to be a Muslim. He cannot change even if he wanted to."

"But you have a choice. You don't need to belong to any religion. Look, I was born into a Christian family but I never go to church. I used to when I was little, though."

"Don't you believe in God, David?"

"I don't think anyone can be sure about that. Musa, just be yourself!"

I took some nuts from a dish and started munching on them without thinking what I was doing, but deep down I was upset and perturbed. "You know, I think I will go to the Mosque with Ahmed. Just out of curiosity, of course. Then next month, I've been invited to Jessie's Confirmation service at the church. She's having a little party afterwards too. The Vicar wanted me to take confirmation classes, but I told him I wasn't ready."

"Good for you. Don't commit yourself to anything at this stage of your life. You are still young. What's on TV tonight?" David said, looking for the entertainment page.

Why does David always manage to get out of talking about serious problems?

For my birthday, we went to the Chinese restaurant. Robbie, Ahmed and another friend from school, John, joined us as well as Grandpa Ben. Mum had sneaked in a birthday cake so they all sang 'Happy Birthday' after we had filled ourselves with food from the buffet. All the other people turned round to look at us and some even joined in the singing. I wanted to put my head under the table with embarrassment. Afterwards, Mum, David and Grandpa went home with Margaret and we boys went to the cinema. Robbie said it was his birthday treat for me. It was 'Harry Potter and the Sorcerer's Stone.' We sat completely spellbound, pure magic, witches, strange games and battles.

When we eventually emerged from the cinema, we rubbed our eyes and could hardly speak. It was difficult to come back to reality and run to the bus-stop.

271

"My Mum doesn't let me read Harry Potter books. For goodness sake, don't let her know I saw this movie," said John.

We all laughed and thumped him on the back. "Oo-ee, will she spank you, little boy?" teased Robbie. We could see poor John was on the verge of tears as he got on his bus, while each of us went our separate ways, Robbie on another bus and Ahmed and I to the underground. According to Grandpa Ben, thirteen was a very special birthday. It made me a man!

CHAPTER EIGHTEEN

Whoo..ah! The light was blinding me. My head hurts. My ears are buzzing. Where on earth! I covered my eyes under the sheet for a few seconds then gradually put my head up, rubbed my eyes and looked around. The first thing I noticed was a strange wriggly vine-like design on the walls. Wallpaper with crawling snakes? Where am I? I sat up in bed and found two strangers standing over me in an unfamiliar room. The purple clock by the bed said past two o'clock and I could see it was dark outside because the curtains had not been drawn across. My little alarm clock is yellow, not purple.

"Are you Robbie's friend, Musa?" the male voice said.

"Ye..es," I could hardly keep my eyes open and slumped back on the pillows. I must be dreaming.

"Don't worry, we've told your parents that you are safe here. Didn't you hear your mobile? They said they've been ringing you all night. Anyway, you can go back to sleep. Your parents will be collecting you in the morning. They were so worried when you didn't go home last night."

"What happened? What day is it?"

273

"Saturday. No school for another week, remember?"

"Where's Robbie?"

"Sleeping in the next room. We're his parents."

"Oh!"

They switched off the light but not before I noticed that the man had long wavy hair and the woman short bobbed hair, or had I got them mixed up? And why are they fully dressed in the middle of the night? She had a long black evening dress glittering with sequins and he had a formal suit with a black bow tie. Then I remembered what Robbie had told me. We were in the playground at school one day when I casually asked him what his parents did.

He had shrugged his shoulders and laughed. "O, they work at night in concert halls!"

He ran off and I felt he didn't want to pursue the subject.

But now here I was in Robbie's house, fully clothed in bed!

~~~~~~

It was the half term holiday. Mum, still treating me as a small child had told me again and again to tell her where I was at all times.

"Musa, take a scarf, it's a bit chilly today. And don't forget to tell me when you meet Ahmed."

"Yes, Mum."

"Take your hooded jacket, it's going to rain."

"Mum, don't fuss so. I'll be fine."

"Always let me know where you are."

"OK, Yes I know."

So I had called her from my mobile to tell her that Ahmed and his father had met me off the train at Regent's Park. I had promised Ahmed to spend the day with him. I think his father was determined to initiate me into the Islamic faith and since we had a little holiday, he said it was good to go on a Friday, the Muslim holy day.

We walked across the park and entered the big courtyard of the Mosque. I had seen the building many times before, but not actually entered. I had never seen so many men in one place in my life, hundreds of them. There were a few veiled women but the courtyard was packed with men and boys, even before we entered the mosque. Ahmed had explained to me some of the ritual worship beforehand so I just followed what he did and nobody glanced at me to enquire who I was. They didn't seem to notice that I was a stranger. This was

275

different from church where everyone greeted me by name. We slipped off our shoes and put them in a rack like a large letter rack. Then we went to a central fountain and washed or rather splashed our face, hands and feet.

"Now, don't talk till afterwards," Ahmed whispered, reminding me as we stepped inside.

The large hall-like space was filled with men kneeling in rows on the carpet with heads to the ground. There were no chairs or tables and no pictures, only written Arabic texts engraved on the walls. I watched Ahmed and his father carefully and copied what they did. There was no chatting or singing, just the bowing and chanting of Arabic prayers over and over. The Imam, dressed in a plain grey robe over his suit which matched the grey of his long beard, mounted some steps into a kind of pulpit and preached in English. You could have heard a pin drop, but I wasn't really listening. My mind was on other things. In fact, I was day-dreaming, comparing the Imam to a teacher at school who also sported a beard and was a joker. Here I sensed that everyone was deadly serious and in fearful awe of God.

After an hour, we went outside, grabbed our shoes and joined the throng of men walking towards the exit. Now there was plenty of noise as everyone was chatting and shouting to their friends. Some of the shoes seemed to have got mixed up and the men were quarrelling about taking the wrong ones.

"Why don't they put their names in the shoes?" I said. Ahmed just laughed.

"How did you like the Friday prayers, Musa? What did you think of the Imam's preaching? Powerful wasn't he?" his father said, looking at me intensely.

"I thought the prayers were awesome," I said bowing reverently...the Imam was good too."

"I must get Ahmed to take you to religious classes. I'll make an appointment for you to meet the Council."

"Let me see what my parents say before signing up for any classes."

"Alright. Let us know."

"Ahmed, treat your friend to some food and come home this afternoon. What do you boys want to do today?"

"I thought we could spend time in the library and then maybe visit Robbie."

"I'm not sure about Robbie. His parents are never at home are they?"

"They are only out at night," I said.

"OK, Ahmed, don't be late home and take care now." He handed Ahmed some pocket money and waved us goodbye as he walked to the bus-stop.

I was determined not to be persuaded into, what to me, was still a foreign religion.

What was it that attracted me to Christianity, I asked myself? Partly it was the wonderful music, missing in the Muslim prayers and partly it was the sense of reverence and awe, without the fear. I didn't want to say too much to Ahmed about my feelings as he would tell his father, but I asked him what religion meant to him.

"I don't take it too seriously," he said. "But I go along with it because it's what I've been brought up to do."

At MacDonald's we ate big Macs and chips. We were fooling around, snatching each other's chips and squeezing the little ketchup sachets into the air. Some of the red stuff landed on a neighbours table where an old man was sitting. He shouted at us, cursing and we had to run to the bathroom before the manager could tell us off. Then we spent a short time pretending to browse in the library, after which we took the bus to Robbie's. It was the first time we had been to his house, and was quite a long bus journey from where we were, but Ahmed and I were excited, trying to anticipate the home of 'Posh Rob', as they called him at school. Robbie was waiting for us and showed us round his grand mansion-like home.

"Wow! Wow!" Ahmed and I both chimed, in unison. The big entrance hall had a high ceiling with a large chandelier hanging from it. Robbie seemed to be alone. He showed us the sitting room with black leather sofas and white and red fluffy cushions. In one corner was a shiny black grand piano, with the lid hitched up to show the white piano notes. The dining room was through another door. The table had high backed chairs and French windows opened up to the garden. At the top of the wide staircase were six doors. Robbie showed us his room which not only had a computer and his own television, but also a gaming station, stacks of books, CDs and sheet music, most of it scattered around the floor. A guitar stood in the corner. Ahmed and I stared in wonder. All the time Robbie was bouncing from door to door as if he was trying to balance on a large rubber circus ball.

"Your folks must be pretty rich," Ahmed said.

Robbie shrugged his shoulders and laughed. "They pretend they are," he said, giving a dismissive wave of his arms and then raking his hand through his blond hair. "If they were really rich, they'd send me to a private school."

"Yes, I suppose so, but you like our school, don't you?" I said

"Not all of the time." He patted me on the back. "But I like you guys."

"Do your parents have a business?" Ahmed was curious.

"Oh no. They are musicians, you see. That's why they are never at home. They stay in bed until midday, then they have a meal, then all afternoon they are at rehearsals and in the evenings they play in the orchestra."

"Wow!" Ahmed said, looking at me. My mouth must have been hanging open. I had never come across musicians before except on the television.

"What do they play?"

"My mother plays the cello mostly, but sometimes the piano. My father is a percussionist."

"What's that?" piped in Ahmed.

"Drums, cymbals and anything that makes a loud noise, boom, boom, boom…" He drummed his fist against the door. "Come on, race you to the kitchen."

He slid down the banister and was at the bottom before we had started to run down the stairs. I couldn't help but notice that he referred to his parents as mother and father, not as Mum and Dad, but I didn't say anything. This was a whole new lifestyle.

"I bet you play the piano?" I asked when we had caught up with him, panting and out of breath.

"Yes. My parents make me practice all day on Sundays."

"Give us a tune, then," said Ahmed.

Robbie ran to the piano in the sitting room, swivelled the stool around and played a little tune without any music book. We followed.

"Wow!" I said. "That was great."

"Oh, that's nothing. I can play a proper concerto. I like Beethoven's Sonatas best. But not today." He bounced down from the stool and ran to the kitchen.

Robbie proceeded to make us popcorn in the microwave and filled up dishes with other snacks, nuts, crisps, biscuits and sweets. We sat on a comfortable sofa and turned on the television, all this in the kitchen.

"Are you always alone?" I asked Robbie.

"Nowadays, yes. We used to have a housekeeper who was also my baby-sitter when I was younger. Molly was lovely. I really miss her. Then we had a Swedish au-pair girl for a short time, until my parents found out she was sleeping with my brother!" He laughed, nervously, to see if we understood. We nodded, and giggled.

"She was really sexy," Robbie said, his eyes rolling. We laughed out loud, Ahmed poking me in the ribs which started us punching each other.

We had been munching snacks and watching silly children's programmes when we heard the front door open.

"That must be my brother, Gary, home for the weekend from University." He got up to greet him. They patted each other on the shoulders. Gary was eighteen, but looked older. He was tall with blond floppy hair like Robbie. It was the first time we had met the brother.

"Hiya, kids!" he said. "Anyone ready for a drink?" I did not like the way he said 'kids', but I was thirsty after all the salty snacks. I sucked my dry lips.

"Yes, please," we all chorused.

He went to a corner cupboard and I saw that it was filled with bottles of all kinds of alcohol. I knew my parents drank, but they did not keep anything in the house except a couple of bottles of wine, and sometimes a can or two of beer. Ahmed was horrified and started to make excuses about going home.

"Man, it's only four o'clock. You can't go yet," said Gary.

But Ahmed was determined. "I told my Dad, I'd be home early," he said. "Musa are you coming?"

"I'll stay a bit longer," I said. I was secretly interested in tasting drink. Besides, hadn't Grandpa Ben told me he drank wine at my age? I recalled the evening that we were left in the house together. He was the one person who treated me like a sensible boy almost grown-up. He told me all about the time when he was thirteen. Grandpa always had some interesting stories to tell of his younger days, how he had to be protected in the war because he was Jewish and how they had to sleep in the underground shelters.

"You know, Musa, when a Jewish boy is thirteen, he becomes a man. They have a special ceremony called the Bar Mitzvah when the lad has to recite a passage of Hebrew Scripture. It was quite scary as I had to carry

283

the Torah using my arms, not my hands and then I had to recite the Scripture passage in Hebrew, in front of all the people. Not read it, mind you. I had to learn it by heart. After my ceremony, at the family party, everyone was congratulating me, toasting me in champagne and my father handed me a small glass of wine. That was the first time I was allowed to drink."

I came back to the present when Gary clinked his glass against mine.

"Cheers!" he shouted.

Robbie laughed as I took my first sip and screwed up my face. "Great, eh…!" he said.

My biggest mistake was that I forgot to tell Mum and David where I was. They probably thought I was at Ahmed's. There was certainly no whiff of drink in his house.

The evening was hazy after that. I know we drank red wine and maybe a little Vodka and we watched a 'super-scary' video movie which was very frightening. Gary talked endlessly about all sorts of nonsense. I noticed he put a pill in his drink and was flinging his arms around, grabbing Robbie and dancing in a jig until Robbie pushed him away and he flopped down on to the sofa. Finally, he made us hot chocolate. Whether he put anything in the chocolate or who led or carried me up to bed, I have no memory at all. My only memories were seeing Gary, sitting on the edge of the couch with his long legs splayed out, his head held back, his eyes shut and a kind of groaning noise coming from his open mouth. I remember looking at Robbie, who instead of being his usual bouncy self was sitting at the table with his head in his hands. Goodness knows what I looked like!

The next morning, it must have been a dishevelled Robbie who heard the doorbell and opened the front door to David and Mum. I was still asleep, but he shook me and helped me put on my jacket and shoes. I did not even wash my face, so I must have looked terrible when they bundled me into the car. Not a word was spoken all the way home, but on arrival, David shouted at me using swear words I had never heard him speak before. In fact, he used all the bad words that I'm not allowed to use.

"Get up those stairs and stay in your room until we say so. Don't you dare come down, you wretched, ungrateful, good-for-nothing brat." He almost spat at me but Mum just sighed and frowned.

"If you wanted to stay the night with Robbie, all you had to do was let us know. What on earth were you doing?" she said. I just looked at her sorrowful face and said nothing as I climbed the stairs.

I lay on my bed and sobbed. David said I was grounded for the next three days with only books for company, except when Mum called me down for meals. They had even removed my computer. I could hear David and Mum quarrelling downstairs and picked up snippets of the conversation.

"I told you from the beginning that boy would bring us nothing but trouble," said David. "He's an Arab."

That hurt more than all the swearing. ARAB. Yes, I thought, Arabs were allegedly responsible for 9/11 and Arab Palestinians are carrying out suicide bombings. I'm an Arab but I'm not a terrorist! Only Margaret put her head round the door later that day.

"Dad said you've been a bad, bad boy. I can't even play with you."

She looked so sad, almost ready to cry. I had to get up and hug her.

"But I still love you!" she said.

CHAPTER NINETEEN

When I came down to a late breakfast on Sunday, David was there. Mum was busy at the stove and had her back to me. Margaret had already eaten and was sitting with her hairbrush waiting for Mum to help her brush her hair. I sat down and waited for someone to say something.

David looked up from his paper, removing his glasses. His mouth was stern, but his eyes crinkled as if he was smiling to himself. Ah, he's cooled down, I thought.

"Well, Musa, what have you got to say for yourself?"

"Sorr-ee."

"That's all you have to say?"

"It was Gary's fault."

"Blaming someone else, now, are you? Who's Gary, anyway?"

"He's Robbie's brother. He gave us some wine...only a bit."

David's face was as red as an over-ripe tomato. He stood up, raising his hands, then picked up his knife, dripping with marmalade and for a moment I thought he was going to hit me. I ducked my head. "You were drinking! What else?"

"Er…er…don't remember really. Cola with a kick! Gary was popping pills but I refused.

David's shouting became louder. They must have heard it next door.

Mum turned round and I could see her face when I glanced up. But I kept my face looking down at my lap.

"Mooou…sa!" was the only word she could shout.

Margaret started banging her hairbrush on the table, "Stop yelling, all of you."

"Where were Robbie's Mum and Dad?" Mum said, more calmly.

"They are musicians and they play in an orchestra late at night"

David pursed his lips in a cynical smile. I had noticed that look before. He was enjoying this interrogation.

"Musicians? What kind of musicians? A pop band?"

"No, classical music. His mother plays the cello."

"Och, toffs are they? Anyway the point is why didn't you call us or answer our messages?"

"I forgot. Then I was too dazed from the drink." I spoke quietly, but David started shouting again: "Are you sure you didn't take drugs as well?"

"No, I swear…unless Gary put something in the hot chocolate. I told you, I refused."

"So he might have done?"

"I don't think so. We were having fun watching videos, but now I feel awful and I swear it won't happen again."

"Don't you realise how worried we were. We almost rang the police. Then we found Ahmed's number. He told us he went home early. Why didn't you leave with Ahmed? He seems far more sensible and he was the one who told us where you were," said Mum.

"OK, I'm sorry. I guess I should have left with Ahmed. His parents don't drink but YOU do and I'm nearly grown-up. Besides, Grandpa Ben told me he drank wine at thirteen. I'm no longer a child and you're treating me like a criminal."

David turned to face Mum. "Your Dad making trouble again!"

"Oh, for goodness sake David, no need to bring my Dad into this."

I decided to face David squarely. I glared at him. Then I got up from my chair and started to go upstairs, "I hate you!" I shouted down, without turning round.

"Well, well, temper, temper! It better bloody well be the last time. If you were a bit younger, I'd like to give you a good spanking."

"Just you dare!" I shouted back.

"Don't you ever go to Robbie's again," David screamed after me. "What's more, I'm going to ring Robbie's parents and find out exactly how their boys have access to drinks. And drugs, too."

"Musa, come down and have something to eat," Mum called after me. I overheard her say something to David about not being too stern with me, but that they should investigate what Gary had given me. I really feared for Robbie getting into terrible trouble.

After a while, I came down and drank some tea but felt too sick to eat anything. The air was still thick with tension. Mum tried to coax me into eating something, but even the smell of her cooking made me want to heave and my head was throbbing like the chug-chug of a train.

"I know you said I can't go to Robbie's but do you think I could invite him here sometimes? He's a good boy but a poor rich kid."

"Poor rich!" laughed David. "We'll think about that, but how can someone be rich and poor at the same time, eh!"

"Well, he lives in a big house but he's lonely."

"Stupid boy! Sometimes you can be foolishly funny, if that makes sense." He walked away and reached for the telephone. He dialled several times but there was no answer, so finally gave up. "I'll call again later," he said.

Maybe they are still all in bed, it's Sunday today, I thought to myself. I was waiting for David to apologise for his language, but of course adults are not obliged to say sorry to children, are they? And right then I felt like a small child.

After David had gone out, Mum relaxed the rules and Margaret was allowed to play board games with me in my room. I still had some school homework to finish, so later I spent time studying. I found it difficult to concentrate as I was trying hard to recall memories of last evening. What had the movie been about? I vaguely remember it was about a boy being locked up in a shed, then tortured and killed by his stepfather. Then his ghost returned to enact revenge by torturing the murderer. Yet, although it was scary, I remember feeling foolish, happy, even a floating sensation. What if Robbie is influenced by his brother and goes the same way? I felt suddenly very afraid for Robbie. It's strange, in a way, how I feel so close to Robbie even

291

though we come from different backgrounds and have different lifestyles at home. I somehow know that we are going to be friends for life. I admire him for his gift of musical abilities and I think he admires me because I am clever in literature. As for Ahmed, we both love Ahmed for his mischievous nature and sense of humour. But, it's true that he is more sensible and mature than us.

I still feel hurt that David thinks of me as an ass and that Arabs are untrustworthy people. How can I change David's way of thinking about me and about Arabs in general? I do my best at school yet I never get a word of praise from David. Does he really care about me like he says he does? Mum is Jewish yet she doesn't share David's view. She had said that when David gets angry he says things he doesn't really mean. But I could not tell him that I had overheard what he had said to Mum. The next day, David told me he had had a nice talk with Mr. Langstaffe, Robbie's father. "When? What did he say?" I said, spluttering, in the middle of drinking my juice and almost choking.

"Late last night. You were asleep. He apologised for his son's behaviour and said he would punish Gary and that it would not happen again. But you know you were at fault for taking the drink and for not telling us you were going to Robbie's house."

"Yes, I suppose."

"Anyway, he said he still wanted you to be friends with Robbie, so next time you can invite him here. I'm sorry for what I said about Robbie's parents. They seem to be really nice people."

"Thanks David. Robbie and I are such good friends."

At the end of half-term holiday, I was in my room trying to write an essay about life in England more than a hundred years ago. I had done some research on the computer but found the subject difficult. David found me sitting at my desk with my head in my hands. He was smiling.

"Still got homework to do? How about a break? Where would you like to go today, Musa?" Mum and Margaret are going shopping for new clothes. Do you want to go with them or come out with me? Then tonight I'm treating you all out for dinner at your favourite place."

Wow, what a sudden turn of events I thought.

"Tell you what David, why don't we go round the Art Galleries? You can explain to me a bit about the history of art. Also, if there's time could I go and see the dinosaurs in the Science Museum?"

"Good idea. Get ready."

We had a great day. I asked David why the paintings of past centuries are so famous, so clever and have stood the test of time. Moreover, they are so much more valuable than present day art.

He put his arm on my shoulder as I was reading the titles of the paintings. This one had a colourful landscape with several half-nude girls in the foreground and a shepherd boy playing a flute. "This is so beautiful," I said.

"You see, in the old days, they didn't have photography, so we can learn at lot of history by these old paintings."

"But, David, if that was a photo, people would consider it rude. As a painting it's so cool!"

He laughed. "Yes, nowadays we use cameras to capture images, so artists try to express themselves in more abstract ways."

There were lots of paintings of London with cobble-stone streets, ragged children without shoes, horse-drawn carriages, ladies in crinoline dresses and lace bonnets, gas street lamps and poor women carrying sick babies. I studied the paintings carefully, noting the contrasts between rich and poor.

"David, these pictures are great. Life must have been so hard in the old days. This is going to help me with my homework."

"Glad you came out with me then?"

"Yes."

At the Science Museum we ate sandwiches in the cafeteria and surrounded by ugly dinosaurs, we discussed all the amazing animals and birds. I had been before with school, but there was so much more to see. David, of course, was in his element as a teacher, but I also found him trying hard to connect as a father.

"By the way, I see you have returned the photo album, but I'm missing two books?" David questioned.

I blushed.

"Books about sex?"

"Yes."

"I suppose I should give you a little talk about the birds and the bees, eh?"

"No need. We learn about that at school."

"They don't explain the emotional power, though. Sex can be a powerful tool or a force of love. Remember that Musa. It can destroy you or it can bring true happiness."

"I'll remember that," I said, squirming in my seat and feeling my face getting hot!

Back home, I found Margaret jumping up and down with excitement. She took hold of my hand and dragged me to her bedroom.

"Look Musa, Mum's bought me a new dress for Jessie's Confirmation party."

"That's lovely," I said. "Try it on."

She took off her trousers and jumper and put on the blue, embroidered dress.

"You look like a little princess," I said. "Are all the family going to the church first?"

"Yes, Mummy said we must all go as it is Jessie's special day!"

It took me by surprise. Except for Christmas Carol services in Scotland none of my family had ever gone to church with me before. It made me feel very happy.

Sunday arrived and I woke up with the sun shining. For once, David wore a gaudy tie which matched his mood. The church service was sombre, but the singing joyful, even Mum joined in, though it was all unfamiliar to her. The children to be confirmed knelt before the bishop one by one as they made their vows. The bishop put his hand on each of their heads and blessed them. It was awesome! Margaret was a bit fidgety but Mum managed to keep her from chattering. Afterwards the vicar greeted us, welcoming us as a family.

He whispered to me: "Good for you Musa, to bring all your family to church." I grinned from ear to ear.

"You seem to be well known here. Anyway, I enjoyed the singing," remarked Mum, patting me on the back and looking regal in her new dark red suit.

When we arrived home, David parked the car and smiled at me, cynically.

"What a lot of mumbo-jumbo! What do you see in it, Musa?"

"I like it," I said.

"Ha! What you really mean is that you like Jessie!"

I felt the colour rising from my neck up.

"Blushing are we?"

"Stop teasing, David," said Mum. "Jessie's lovely."

"OK, Jessie *is* lovely and she is someone special." I linked arms with Margaret and she gave me a squeeze of approval. "Well come on, it's party time," I said, skipping in step with Margaret.

Jessie was, of course, the centre of attraction with all her many relatives around her, but somehow I couldn't take my eyes off her. I had not seen her for some time as she was going to a different school and lately Sundays tended to be study days for exams. I had kind of taken her for granted as 'my friend next door', but on this day she looked so stunningly beautiful in her low cut white dress. Her long hair normally just tied back was styled in curls on top of her head and I couldn't help but notice her bright pink lipstick. And boy, she's got breasts!

Back at school there was plenty to talk about with Ahmed. Robbie was avoiding me at first but I managed to corner him in the lunch break.

"Robbie, did you get punished, too?"

"I got a good telling off, but Gary had a big row with my father about drinking and drugs of course. He should never have given you alcohol. I'm afraid he's very much a rebel.

"Did he put any drugs in our hot drink, d'you think? I felt ill afterwards."

"I'm not sure. I was sozzled, too."

"Sozzled? That's a good word!" I laughed.

"Anyway, we heard that Molly is coming back, so that will be great. Remember, I told you she was our housekeeper?"

"That's good news. Robbie, I've been thinking I would like to learn to play a musical instrument. You know, when I was seven, we bought a little drum in Jerusalem. I used to do strumming sounds on it with my hands. But, of course, that broke long ago. It was only a clay pot after all. You are so good on the piano but I'm not sure if I could learn that. What d'you think?"

"Don't be silly! You can learn anything. Why don't you speak to the music teacher?"

"Well, I couldn't do classical, but just some nice popular music."

"Isn't classical nice?"

"Yes, but too complicated. I like listening to the top ten pop tunes. They're so cool."

"Musa, pop music is just as complicated, but I can see you as a drummer, like my father!" Robbie laughed out loud. "You do like to make yourself heard, don't you?"

"Am I that noisy? I thought I was a quiet boy!"

"You noisy chump." Robbie chuckled and chased me round the yard. We ended up having a friendly tussle until Ahmed and John joined us.

John, who had come to my birthday, handed me a letter addressed to Mum.

"This is from my Mum. She told me, she is thanking your Mum for inviting me to your birthday."

I put it in my pocket and didn't remember until later, when I saw Mum reading a paper about supermarket offers. "Oh Mum, I almost forgot." I took out the crumpled envelope from my pocket. "Here is a letter from John's mother to thank you."

She opened it and I watched her expression change. First she seemed pleased, then surprised and then angry. "What kind of person writes a letter like this?" she said.

"What does she say?"

"It's a poison letter, Musa."

"What d'you mean?"

"The words are terrible." She handed me the letter. It read:

Dear Mrs. Craig,

Thank you very much for inviting John to your son's birthday. He said he enjoyed it. It is on my heart to tell you something that might upset you, but is necessary. I know you are Jewish and I am a strong Christian who believes that the Jews are God's chosen people and have a right to take over the land of Israel. I also believe that the Arabs have no place in that land. They

300

should go to other Arab countries. Do you not realise that you, as a Jew, raising an Arab child is contrary to the will of God? Some Arabs are calling for the destruction of Israel but the time will come when there will be a big battle and Christ will come back and claim His own people. Educating Musa will bring you nothing but devastating trouble. Please note I WARN YOU for your own good!

Liz Merriless

I could not believe it. I sat down with Mum on the settee and gave her a hug. Her face was crimson and her hands trembling.

"She must be a crackpot. Take no notice. I'll go and make you a cup of tea."

"Oh, thanks darling. You're a good boy!"

When I came back with the tea, Mum said: "This woman must be stopped spreading such racist propaganda. I've been thinking. You know what I'm going to do, Musa. I'm going to ring Kevin and see what he thinks of this. Maybe he can straighten her out."

"Yes, Kevin would know. I heard somewhere about a Christian sect who are Zionists who think that only the

Jews have a right to live in Israel but the vicar at our church said God loves everyone!"

"Well, I'm not a Christian but your vicar is right," Mum said.

Should I tell John? No, I decided not to say anything. It was obvious that he didn't know what his mother had written and I didn't want to spoil our friendship.

A few weeks later, I had an email from my pen-friend Musa. Although his English had many mistakes, I understood.

Dear Musa Ben,

Sorry for silence. So much trouble. You will not beleve. The Israeli soldiers broke the computers in most internet cafes. I don't have computer at house. Baba's shop closed and now he in prison. No reason. We are sad. Hope u happy.

Love, Musa Yousef.

I felt so helpless, and so sorry for Musa. How would I feel in that situation? I'm sure I would get so angry that I would want to take revenge. I started thumping on my desk, stamping my feet and cursing. I heard Mum shouting up the stairs: "What on earth is going on?"

I shouted down: "I just need a big drum."

It was supposed to be Spring but the weather was dull and damp. I trudged home from school feeling a bit down, but then I remembered it was my birthday the next day. Mum hadn't said anything about a party. David met me at the door smiling.

"Och Musa, what a long face! Your birthday tomorrow. Sweet sixteen, eh!" he teased. "But not, I suspect, never been kissed!"

"Well, David as a matter of fact, I've only kissed Jessie once and that was at the school dance. Anyway, she is dating another boy now.

"Ouch, heart-broken are you? Plenty more fish in the sea, you know!"

"David, I've got exams right now to study for. I doubt whether I shall have time swimming in the sea looking for fish! GCSEs are already on top of me. I have so much homework."

I was pretending outwardly that I didn't care about losing Jessie. I was, in fact, secretly nursing a broken heart.

I had told Jessie that I loved her at the summer school dance. I can still see her lips reaching out to mine and her arms round my neck. Her perfume had made my head spin. That was at the end of the last school year. I had come home from school one day and found Jessie hanging around the back door in her school uniform. Her chestnut hair was loosely tied back, and she seemed excited.

"Musa, can I ask you something?" For once she looked shy. We often exchanged opinions about our different schools or about problems with homework but I sensed that this was not about studies.

"Sure, what?"

"Would you like to come with me to the school dance?"

"You mean as your date?"

"Yes."

"Sorry Jessie."

"Why ever not?"

"I can't dance!"

"I'll teach you."

"Would you? Then, OK if I don't tread on your toes!"

She laughed and I just stood there like a dummy. Her hazel eyes were sparkling as she skipped away home. "See you then," she shouted. Since that day she had come round often in the evenings and showed me basic dance steps. Sometimes, we put some CDs on and Mum would join us, but often we were alone. We had grown up as children and played together almost from the time we were toddlers. We had read books, watched movies, ate picnics together. She was like one of the family. Yet now, alone, after being in each other's arms dancing with our cheeks touching, we suddenly felt embarrassed to be sitting on the couch together. My heart was telling me to squeeze her hand but my hormones were telling me to kiss her where I could just see the cups of her bra met, under her blouse. She smiled, got up quickly, touched my arm and gave me a peck on the cheek, as always.

"See you. I have to go. Mum wants me to help her, as we are having guests for dinner."

On the actual day we were having lots of fun with other young people. I enjoyed the music especially and my dance steps had improved considerably. We were sitting at a small table with another couple drinking Cola and tucking into strawberry ice-cream.

"Last one, will you take your partner for this final dance," announced the DJ as he turned up the music machine. The other guy, Roger, took hold of Jessie's hand and before she could say anything, he had dragged her on to the dance-floor. I found myself having to ask his girlfriend for the last dance. Neither of us was particularly pleased, as we held each other at arms length and twirled around. I could tell that Jessie was upset at not having danced the last one with me. As she rushed off to the cloakroom, I confronted Roger.

"Why did you…?"

He answered before I could finish, not even looking me in the eye. "All's fair in love and war," he said, laughing and running away.

I caught up with Jessie as we waited for her Dad to pick us up. "You know you're so beautiful, I got jealous seeing you with Roger." She slipped her arms around my neck, pulled me down tenderly and we kissed. It was like a warm electric current making my body tingle with happiness. I wanted to hug her like I used to hug my teddybear in bed when I first heard that Mum was not my real mother. A sort of comfort blanket.

"I want to teach you an Arabic word that means 'darling'. It will be our own little secret."

306

"What is it?"

"I call you *habibti* and you call me *habibi*."

"*Habibi, habibi*," she whispered, giggling, as we said goodnight.

I valued her friendship but did not want to get serious too soon. I know some of the kids in my class were already boasting of sexual adventures.

And now she's got another boyfriend!

Already, I had something else to get excited about. Music, music and more music! Mum loved me to sing to her one of her old favourites which went something like '...*Ooo, you'll be there... 'cause you're the best thing that ever happened to me.*' It was a pop song before my time but music had become the best thing that ever happened to me.

My friendship with Ahmed and Robbie had remained firm and we often went to one another's homes. Ahmed's father said he was disappointed that I hadn't pursued his invitation to attend religious classes, but I told him that I was always too busy. At Robbie's house I hardly saw Gary, but when I did, I felt he treated me like an ignorant little kid, as if he despised me and probably blamed me for him getting into

307

trouble. Robbie and I weren't grown up enough for the likes of him! On several occasions, I found Robbie's parents at home and had got to know them quite well. My first impression of them being posh, aloof and uncaring was totally wrong. They were actually kind and down to earth and were happy for Robbie to have me as a friend. Robbie presented me with a free ticket to go with him one evening to a concert in a large theatre. I got there early and waited for him in the foyer, watching all the people coming in, linking arms with their partners. Most were middle aged couples, the ladies wearing either long shiny dresses or minis with high heeled shoes. I felt out of place with my jeans and borrowed leather jacket. I could hear the orchestra tuning up. Robbie bounced in at the last minute, led me by my elbow and we raced up the stairs two at a time to be shown to seats at the front of the balcony.

Listening to classical CDs is nothing compared to the atmosphere of a concert hall. At the beginning there was absolute silence, then thunderous applause when the conductor walked in, bowing. The charged atmosphere of the crowd is one thing. But it was the sensing of a delirious tingling down my spine, like the first kiss, combined with almost a numbness of my arms and legs when the drums and cymbals strike up that make my heart race. One minute you are blasting off to the moon on the beat of the drums, the next you are being wrapped up in snug duvet clouds when the orchestra softens.

Robbie was already becoming well known as a young pianist, but for me it was the drums! Not that I will ever become expert, but I had been taking music lessons at school for almost three years. Now a local pop group band had become interested in my new skill and signed me on as a stand-in. They let me practice whenever I wanted and they had all the works; a proper five piece kit, tom toms, base drum with pedals, the lot.

When I first told Mum that I wanted to be a percussionist, she looked horror stricken. She placed her hands over her ears and squeezed her face. I just laughed.

"What, as a profession?"

"No, Mum, just as a fun thing to do."

"Well, not in the house, I hope. Besides you'll ruin your hearing. You'll be deaf before you're twenty and remember too, your heart is delicate."

I let out an exasperated sigh. "Mum, my heart is strong now and as for my hearing we always wear ear plugs, even though that doesn't prevent us from hearing the rhythm. Rhythm has become my passion."

"I'm glad to hear you have a talent for music but why don't you take up singing? You are always humming tunes around the house."

I laughed even more. "You must be joking," I said. "Who wants to listen to my cracked voice?"

"I'm remembering the day when you performed in a little play at school and you had to sing a solo. You were about five or six, I think."

"And I had to wear a silly Peter Pan outfit! I remember. Do you wish I was still a little boy, Mum?"

"No, of course not. You have to grow up and your voice has changed, but you will always be my little boy!"

"And you will always be my Mum." I gave her a hug and she had to reach up to kiss me. I was already taller than her!

On a recent visit to Scotland for a family wedding, David's family learnt about my sudden passion for music. Grandpa Craig told me he used to be a jazz fan, so I persuaded him to take me to a jazz concert in Edinburgh and it was one of the most wonderful performances I had ever been to. I was enraptured and told Robbie about it when I got home.

"So are you going to take up jazz, now?" Robbie said. "I thought maybe we could join forces to start a kind of classy-modern-pop band. I would be the pianist and you the percussionist. We just need a vocalist!"

"Wow, that sounds great," I said. "But first come our exams, right?"

"OK, OK." He shrugged his shoulders.

One day, towards the end of the spring term, Robbie galloped up to me at school.

"Musa, what do you think?" His face was glowing and I thought he was going to tell me about a new girlfriend. The girls thought his good looks were something to die for!

"What?"

"My parents have been invited to join an Israeli orchestra which has Jews and Arabs, Israelis and Palestinians, for a whole month, maybe longer."

"Wow, that's exciting," I said.

He grabbed me by the arm. "You and I are going with them!" He was literally lifting me up and jumping me up and down like a salt shaker.

"What, how, when?" I almost shouted.

311

"Probably end of June. We'll be finished with our exams by then."

"Where?"

"Tel Aviv, Jerusalem and Ramallah."

"Ramallah, did you say Ramallah?"

It was my turn to hug him and jump. I could not believe it. My mind was running with so many questions and my pulse racing like an express train. I knew Mum would be pleased but would David agree? How was I going to pay for it all?

"Robbie, that would be totally cool, but I doubt if my folks could afford it."

"Musa, don't worry. All expenses will be paid for. You only have to find the plane fare."

"Who's paying?"

"The orchestra are paying for my parents, and my father said he will cover all costs for you and me. He wants you to go as my companion to keep me out of trouble!"

We both laughed. The other boys were wondering what was making us both so excited but we let their questions go unanswered. This was our secret, at least for the time being.

I could hardly wait to tell Mum and David. They were thrilled about the idea. "Let's invite Robbie and his parents for dinner one day, so as to get to know them better. When would be a good time, Musa?" said Mum, spontaneously.

"I will ask Robbie, but probably a late Sunday lunch."

"Do we have to?" David moaned.

"Don't be so mean. They are offering Musa a wonderful opportunity."

"Well, our house doesn't exactly come up to their standards, does it?"

"David, they may have a posh house but they are very ordinary people," I said.

"And you mean Robbie's parents are going to be responsible for you? Do they know what kind of troublemaker they are taking on?" David smiled wickedly.

"Am I that bad?"

"Well, you could be. You are still only sixteen, remember."

"Robbie says his father wants me to go with them to keep Robbie in check. And besides, they said as I have been to Jerusalem before, I can show him round."

"That was a long time ago. Can you remember?"

313

"Of course I remember. I shall never forget Jerusalem. Besides, I'll be able to meet up with my pen-friend again."

"Well, I reckon Robbie will help to keep *you* from getting into mischief. And going to Ramallah, I can imagine you stopping people in the street to ask if they know anything about your babyhood. Are you going to take the little note with you that Mum has preserved so carefully?"

"Yes, but I won't be asking people in the street, silly!"

David was laughing, but I didn't even smile at him. How could he? I walked away and hoped that he would realise how much he had upset me. It was not a subject for joking about. I found his attitude not just annoying and too light-hearted but hurtful in a way. Surely to look for one's parentage is a very serious matter, especially when there is no clue except a scrap of paper with your name on it. It wasn't the first time that David had hurt my feelings, but I am determined to prove to him one day, that my ancestry was every bit as good as his!

I had thought of nothing else, of course, ever since Robbie had mentioned the town Ramallah. I lay awake at night trying to work out how I could go about getting information and who I could ask.

Two weeks later on a Sunday, Robbie brought his parents. They presented Mum with a big bouquet of lilies. Harry and Louise were dressed in very casual clothes whereas David on the other hand, was wearing a suit and tie. Immediately, they were conversing together happily without any of the 'airs and graces' that David had imagined. Mum had cooked a roast chicken, which they tucked into, like it was a special treat, after which Robbie and I larked around in the kitchen while doing the washing up, leaving the adults to drink their aperitifs. Margaret had gone to spend the day with one of her little friends from school.

Back to school and hard slog, studying, revising, swatting for exams. I made myself concentrate, because I knew that my coming trip depended on it.

Before each exam, the teacher tried to calm our nerves and help us relax, as we sat at the desks with pen and papers in front of us. She went over the rules for answering questions and told us to take a deep breath before we started to write. I found we had three or even four choices for each question about classical novels

315

and poetry. I had always been an avid reader so I did not find it too difficult.

The section about writing to 'argue, persuade or advise' was a little harder because we had to give our own opinions for or against other people's. We had to distinguish between fact and opinion and evaluate information concerning various modern lifestyles, such as: Is television good or bad for children? How can we improve the environment?

I kept looking out of the classroom window and imagining all sorts of scenarios, which had nothing to do with the exam paper. I tried hard to concentrate but sometimes my stomach felt tight with worry, although not so much about the exams. I was fairly confident that I would pass the grade, but anxious about the coming trip, especially about going to Ramallah. Two hours had passed and I had finished the paper.

One exam over, eight more to go.

CHAPTER TWENTY ONE

My luggage was in the boot of the car, Mum was sitting in the front, David at the front door of the house, jangling his keys, waiting to lock up, and only Margaret was delaying us. I went to join David and hollered up the stairs: "Come on, Sis, I'll be late!"

"What kept you," I asked when she finally appeared, and we all settled down in the car. She presented me with a photo of herself in her favourite dress with me at her side, both of us grinning at some joke David had made. I think the occasion was Jessie's party. It reminded me that Jessie and her family had come round yesterday to say their goodbyes, as if I was going on a world tour! Jessie had discretely tucked a tiny card in my trouser pocket with only one word on it: *Habibi!* That one little word made my heart glow with happiness. Now Margaret was chatting beside me:

"I was hunting for this picture and I wanted you to take it with you."

"I'm not going away for good, you know, but thanks anyway."

"I wish I was going with you."

317

"Margaret darling, Musa will be back before we know it. And maybe next year, I can take you to Jerusalem."

"Oo, really Mummy?" She was bouncing up and down in the seat next to me with her big-eyed rag doll.

"For, goodness sake, sit still. The traffic is bad today and we are late," I could see that David was driving erratically. "We should have gotten a taxi," he said.

"Steady on, dear, it's more important to get there in one piece," Mum shouted. She was gripping her seat, nervously, turning round to check up on us from time to time.

Robbie and his parents were waiting for us at Heathrow and we went straight to check in the luggage. Again Margaret was the one who delayed us. She was doing a little jig and wouldn't keep still.

"Mummy, I need the loo!"

So Mum had to run away with her, annoyed at having to leave us. They returned just as I was ready to go through the gate to the departure section. Mum was puffing, almost out of breath. Her face was flushed and her hands trembled as she was gripping hold of Margaret then letting go to hug me. She did not say much, but I imagined that she was conjuring up all the indelible memories of finding me and then going back

318

to bring me home as a baby. The thought crossed my mind that maybe she thought I would locate my parents and stay there for good. She hugged me so hard I found it hard to break free and her tears were wetting my jacket.

"Do take care, darling," she said, her voice cracking. "Remember to keep your passport with you at all times and if there is any trouble you have Cassia's telephone."

"I'll be fine Mum."

"We'll look after him, Rosa. Don't worry," said Louise. David had been chatting with Harry as if they had become old buddies.

"Thank you so much Louise and Harry for everything," called David, as he waved us through the barriers. I saw Mum crying on David's shoulder, as I waved back. Robbie had his arm around my shoulder, while my stomach was doing somersaults.

At the London security check-in counter, I was asked if I had been to Israel before, if I had packed my luggage by myself (Mum had helped me but I did not tell them that) and if my bag had been with me all the time.

"Are you sure that no-one could have had access to your bag or added anything to it?"

"No," I said, emphatically.

"Are you taking anything for anyone living there?"

"No, only a sweat shirt for a young boy as a present."

"Who is he?"

"Just a school boy I met in Jerusalem."

"What's his name?"

"Musa, same as mine."

The last email I had had about two weeks ago from my pen-friend was that his father was out of prison after six months 'administrative detention,' without any charge or trial. He had sent me his telephone number, so I looked forward to contacting him.

Eventually the official waved me through and I joined the others who had not had any such questioning.

"What on earth was all that about?" asked Robbie.

"Oh, you know the usual questioning. It must be my Arab looks or curly hair. I'm always suspect!" I laughed, trying to make a joke out of it, but it was rather irritating.

Why couldn't I have had blond hair and blue eyes like Robbie?

"Wait until we get to Tel Aviv," I said. "If it's anything like last time we will be questioned for over an hour. I guess I'm the one who's going to cause *you* trouble, not the other way around."

"Surely not," said Robbie. "You have a British passport."

"Yes, but I was probably born in Ramallah. My new passport says Ramallah for place of birth."

"Let me see," said Harry. I handed over my passport and turned to the page for my details. *Citizenship: British Citizen.* "You shouldn't have any problem," he said, shrugging his shoulders.

The flight was uneventful. Robbie and I passed the time playing card games and watching videos. His parents napped a lot of the way. I knew that they had a very busy schedule ahead of them. We arrived late afternoon to blazing hot weather. It was the middle of summer and I remembered my last trip when Cassia met us in Tel Aviv and as a child I had never before experienced such heat. Harry had told us that there would be a hotel car waiting for us to take us straight to the hotel.

As I expected, no sooner had we reached the passport immigration desk, the questioning started.

Where was I born, who were my real parents, why was I on this journey, why did my adoptive parents not come with me, why was I with a concert group, what was my relationship with them...and on and on. The questions were endless and repetitive. They asked the same questions several times as if they were trying to trip me up. Harry tried to intervene and speak up for me.

"Madam, Musa is in my care. I am responsible for him. He is my son's friend."

"Sir, you must understand that this is for your security as well as ours."

"He's just a school boy. We have known him for years."

"Maybe Sir, but we have rules and I'm afraid we have to take Mr. Craig with us to another room for further questioning."

Harry began to raise his voice a notch. I could see his face going crimson and heard him cracking his knuckles noisily. He clenched his fists as if ready to strike, but he managed to speak politely. "My wife and I have a very important appointment this evening. We are here on a concert tour and it is imperative that we keep this appointment. You must let Musa come with us."

She went off to confer with some senior officials and I could see the three of them discussing me in Hebrew and looking at my face time and again. I felt so helpless and humiliated. Surely they won't send me back to London, will they? I had taken off my jacket with the heat, but now the armpits of my shirt were wet through. I began to tremble with fear.

She came back with a senior officer and addressed Harry: "Mr Langstaffe, I'm sorry this will cause you delay, but we have to go through Musa's luggage. I promise you it will only take a few more minutes."

"But the luggage has already gone through the X-ray machines. I can see it waiting for us to pick up," Harry said, exasperated.

She took no notice and now it was the man's turn to speak in a very authoritative voice: "Pick up your case and come with me." Then to Harry and his family he said:

"Mr. Langstaffe, you can leave with your luggage and Musa will follow."

"We're not leaving until Musa is with us," Harry said. Robbie and Louise already had their luggage on a trolley. Louise's cello was a large item on its own.

They took me aside and led me to the little room. I had vague memories of that small, bare room when Mum was with me. It smelt of disinfectant, like Mum uses for the toilet. They asked me to open my case, so I unzipped it. With nylon gloves, one of the two girls first felt down the sides, then removed every item, putting them carefully on a bench. She even folded my pyjamas which I had put in at the last minute, untidily. Her face was blank, showing no emotion at all. Then they took away my bag of toiletries, toothbrush, hairbrush, toothpaste, soap etc. They asked me to take off my shoes and they took those away also. Everyone had had to take off their shoes in London to go through the X-ray machine but this time the shoes were taken away out of my sight. After a while they brought everything back and told me to pack it all again. I stuffed everything back hurriedly and finally they let me go. I breathed a sigh of relief and the family literally marched through the exit with the trolley, without saying another word. Thankfully the taxi had been waiting and we were driven straight to the hotel in Jerusalem.

I was so happy to see the location of the hotel. It straddled the Old City nearby and the New Jerusalem. Within walking distance of the Old City it would be easy to find my way around. Even though I was only seven on my last visit, I still had so many vivid memories. Robbie and I shared a room on the top floor, his parents next door. I was so excited that even before we unpacked we ran up the stairs to the flat roof to view the panoramic view of all Jerusalem. We could see the spires of churches, The Dome of the Rock central mosque, the palm trees lining the street and old stone buildings built so close together that you couldn't see any spaces in between. The sun was beginning to set and I remembered that there are no long evenings here, even in summer. The sky was a bright yellow to start with, then turned to shades of crimson, orange, dark gold and finally pink. Robbie kept exclaiming: "Wow! My God, wow!"

We returned to our room which had a high ceiling and tall sash windows with outside shutters, a ceramic tiled patterned floor in blue and white covered by colourful oriental rugs. There was a plain en-suite bathroom. The leaflet welcomed us with words like: *'pilgrimage,'* *'deep spiritual experience,'* *'Holy Land Tours,'* *'life changing,'* *'Jerusalem's past history and present conflict,'* *etc.* We are not really here on a pilgrimage, I thought to myself, but maybe this is going to be a life changing experience. Who knows? I was so overwhelmed with excitement that I hardly slept that first night.

The next morning a buffet feast awaited us. Every kind of fruit and some I had never tried before, pineapples, mangos, kiwis, star-fruit, figs, and cactus fruit dripping in luscious red juice as well as the familiar apples, peaches and bananas; every kind of cereal, cheeses galore, cold meats and bacon and a large variety of breads were on display. We were spoilt for choice. Robbie wanted to try everything until his mother told him off for stuffing himself! The waiters were all Palestinians and I was eager to try out my Arabic phrases with them. They beamed as they answered me in Arabic and somehow I felt right at home.

"This is going to be fun," I told Robbie.

"Yeah! This is going to be the coolest of the cool!"

After breakfast, I telephoned my friend Musa and arranged to meet him outside the Damascus Gate just before noon. We had to cross the busy main road and it was just a stone's throw away. Robbie went with me. I knew that I would have difficulty in recognising my friend as in nine years we had both grown up. We spotted a boy standing alone, his eyes darting everywhere, so I went up to him.

"*Marhaba*, (Hello) Musa?" He smiled and came forward to greet us. He was dressed in faded jeans and a tee-shirt advertising Coca Cola and he was slightly shorter than me. I blushed with embarrassment that he gave me such a close hug, realising, of course, that this was usual in the Arab culture. He shook Robbie's hand and the three of us walked down the stone steps and under the gate archway, with soldiers looking down from the battlements, then pushed our way through the crowds into the Old City. After many twists and turns through the maze of alleyways, and up two flights of stairs, we followed him into his family home. It was just a cramped small apartment, but really clean in the midst of all the dirty streets. His father looked tired and thin in contrast to his mother who was plump and rosy faced. They welcomed us so effusively and kept on serving us with nuts, fruit and mint tea that I felt ashamed to have brought such a small gift of a sweat shirt. They were obviously poor and I knew from the letters that they had suffered. After a while we got up to take our leave, but were hastily sat down again to be served lunch which was spicy meat balls with various kinds of salads. We were not really hungry, but knew that it would offend them to refuse. The reputation of Arab hospitality was overwhelming. I asked Musa's father about the prison but he didn't want to talk about it, except to continually thank Allah for his release. They had Christian religious pictures and a big, roughly carved wooden cross adorning the otherwise bare whitewashed walls and they were continually exclaiming *'Nushkur Allah.'*

"What do they mean?" asked Robbie.

"They are thanking God."

"But I thought they were Christians."

"They are," I said. "Allah is used by the Christians too, not just the Muslims."

After more chatting and sweet tea with sprigs of mint, Musa took us to the shop, now open again, with his elder brother in charge. I tried to remember the shop but it looked different, somehow smaller and stacked with dusty tee-shirts piled high. Robbie and I bought a few olive wood souvenirs and I showed him some similar clay-pot drums of the kind that I had once owned. He decided to buy one for his father.

"Ma'salameh, Allah ma'cum." Musa and his brother hugged both of us goodbye and we arranged to meet the next day in the afternoon.

"What did they say?"

"Something like, 'May the Peace of God go with us,'" I explained to Robbie.

"Wow, religion is so heavy here!" he said.

The next day, as promised, Robbie and I went to Musa's shop. We found his brother, Sulieman, trying to sell some silver crosses to a couple of American lady tourists. They were bargaining the price with him but eventually settled on a purchase and went away looking pleased.

"Business is slow, these days," he said. "Not many tourists because of all the troubles." Then he turned to his younger brother, Musa, speaking in Arabic but I understood the word *'Kaneeseh'* meaning church. So we followed Musa through the old covered market place until we came to an open court yard and the ancient Church of the Holy Sepulchre. There was a crowd of women and girls outside waving banners of pictures of saints.

"Today is a special day for Saint Peter," he explained. It all seemed very foreign to Robbie and I, but we just silently followed Musa into the church and were awestruck by the thick smell of incense and the small lamps illuminating the dark interior.

"Let's get out of here," whispered Robbie. He was continually sneezing and I realised he must have an allergy to the incense. I wanted to laugh. "It's no laughing matter," he said, his eyes and nose streaming.

Musa led us to another part and down a side alleyway; we came across a crowd of young men and boys, highly excited, shouting in Hebrew at the tops of their voices. Musa held us back with his hand until we were hugging the wall as they passed. I could see they were Jews with their little skull caps and cotton strings hanging from the waists of their trousers. The majority of them were only high school kids who were armed with sticks which were branches of trees whittled down to look like spears. They poked some passers-by with their 'spears' and threatened us, laughing. The older men carried rifles which they held as if ready to shoot, their hands on the triggers. One kid picked up a stone and threw it at a shop window, shattering the glass, which they found really funny, laughing louder. We glared at them but Robbie was quivering with fright.

"Settlers, we despise settlers," breathed Musa. "They think they have a right to claim all these old Arab properties as their own!"

Some shopkeepers came out and spat on the ground where the settlers had passed.

"So much hatred…" observed Robbie.

"And so much injustice!" I added, as we said goodbye to Musa and made our way back to the hotel.

On the evening of the fourth day, we were relaxing in Robbie's parents' room and about to say goodnight. We had returned from a most exhilarating concert and a fab meal in a posh restaurant with all the members of the orchestra. Harry had taken off his suit and Louise was in the bathroom. There was a sharp knock on the door. It was the Hotel Manager, looking very troubled.

"Excuse me Sir, Musa Craig is needed downstairs."

"Who needs him?" asked Harry.

"I cannot tell you. Just come down with the boy immediately, if you please."

Harry hurriedly went down with me in the elevator.

"Who could it be? My pen-friend wouldn't come to the hotel this late, unless there was some serious trouble."

Harry shrugged his shoulders. "We'll soon see."

"Are you Musa Craig?" The stranger spoke English but with a Hebrew accent.

"Yes."

"You must come with us," he said, who was a giant of a man with a shiny bald head. Another shorter man took hold of my arm roughly and marched me towards the exit door. Fortunately, I had not undressed as yet. I still had my trousers and shirt on, but had removed my tie. Harry had insisted that we dress formally as we were given VIP seats in the concert auditorium.

Harry ran ahead and tried to block the exit. "Hang on," he shouted. "I'm responsible for that boy. Where are you taking him?"

"Who are you?"

"Harry Langstaffe."

"Sir, this is police business." He produced a police identity tag in Hebrew and English. "We will bring him back soon."

"Look here, this young man is a British Citizen, he is underage and he is a tourist under my care."

I shall always remember my last sight of Harry. He was wearing blue boxer shorts and a white tee shirt, his long silvery hair all dishevelled and his bare feet pushed into trainers.

He was literally screaming: "Damn your bloody security!"

"You can contact the British Consulate," was their calm retort.

I then remembered that my British passport was in my room. I had come downstairs without anything.

CHAPTER TWENTY TWO

They bundled me into the car and sat me in the back seat between two men who I presumed were policemen. The windows of the car were blacked out.

"Where are you taking me?" I squeaked, terrified.

"Not far, we're almost there," Mr. big man said who was sitting in the front, next to the driver.

"Wh...y? What...? My voice cracked. I tried to ask more questions but somehow my tongue was stuck to the roof of my mouth and my teeth clattered like a typewriter. At least they hadn't tied up my hands so I tried to put one hand over my mouth, but the man beside me pulled my hand down sharply, pressing against it with his body. The man on the other side of me pushed closer to me to stop me moving my other arm.

They did not answer. The two men beside me spoke Hebrew to each other but ignored me. Should I try some Arabic? No, I couldn't even speak. It was not cold but my shivering had reached such a pitch that my two companions were pressing their bodies firm against mine in an attempt to calm me. That only raised my fears and I felt like screaming. Indeed I *was* screaming inside. There was something hard and lumpish against my thigh and I realised with horror that it was a pistol. Am I going to come out of this alive? I've read so many stories…

"A…ggh…kh…!" Some animal noise escaped from my throat. Oh God, please don't let me wet my pants! My head was spinning and I felt faint. I'm going to die! They are kidnapping me for ransom! Then one of the men must have farted as the body odour was almost unbearable. And that mixed with the stench of sweat. My own shirt was soaking wet. I tried to hold my breath. I wanted to stop breathing.

I was imagining Harry and his family going berserk with worry. Would he phone David or leave it until the morning? Mum will go crazy. I couldn't understand what was going on. Will they demand a ransom for my release? Why? Why? Why? Give me a clue, I silently shrieked.

The car stopped and the big man got out first. I felt so weak the other two men almost dragged me out. All I could make out was a light over a big wooden door and a large sign in Hebrew, which of course, I couldn't read. They took hold of my arms each side and I struggled to walk with them down a long corridor to a small room like a prison cell. It was not big enough for two people. They escorted me to a cot-like bed and I was relieved to sit down in the glare of a very bright electric light.

"Do you need a drink?" Mr. big man asked, before the three of them all left.

"Just water," I managed to say.

Someone brought me a plastic cup of water then shut the door and turned the lock. I looked around at the whitewashed walls covered in Arabic and Hebrew graffiti, none of which I could read. Some of it had been rubbed over leaving dirty smudges. There was a primitive Arabic (floor level) toilet and small washbasin in one corner and a tiny bedside cupboard, but that was all. I tried to switch off the light but couldn't find the switch. Eventually, I undressed and lay down in my underwear. I tried to cry to relieve the tension, but the tears would not come and I must have slept, as the next thing I remember was the dawn light coming through the little window high up. The electric light was no longer glaring in my face, so I figured the switch must be on the outside.

My pillow was damp when I roused myself properly. Had I cried in my sleep or was it just the heat that made me sweat profusely?

I decided to get up and splash my face. I was dressed when someone brought me a tray of breakfast. On it was a cup of sweet tea, without milk, two halves of a dry pita bread, some olives and a small piece of goat's cheese. It was such a contrast to the elaborate breakfast at the Hotel, I found it almost laughable. I suppose in a way it made me think of the 'haves' and the 'have-nots' of this world. I was learning.

I ate everything quickly, still feeling hungry and waited...and waited ... and waited. Meanwhile I was trying to answer my own question as to why. What had I done wrong? Had Robbie's brother put anything in my suitcase via Robbie, like a drug or something? But I knew Gary had not had access to my bag and Robbie would certainly not do that. Besides, had there been a drug problem they would have confronted me with it at the airport. No it was not that. I had brought two school books with me to do further study. Had I included any Palestinian political material in these books? No, I was sure I had not. Had the secret police followed me to my pen-friend's house? Surely not. I had nothing to hide anyway.

I thought about Mum and started to worry more about her than about myself.

Eventually Mr. big man arrived. I assumed he must be the commander.

"Did you have a good night's sleep?" He seemed to be trying to lighten my mood.

"I would have slept better if you'd told me why I am here."

"Come now, dear boy. We only need your cooperation and all will be revealed. You will not be harmed, I promise you." He coughed as if to suppress a laugh.

I decided to keep quiet. He motioned for me to follow him. He certainly was a big man. He seemed to have an enormous head without hair and huge hands and feet.

After walking along several corridors we arrived at a large room, almost like a court but without seating for a gallery of people. There were several men waiting to question me including two uniformed soldiers with rifles at the ready. I was given a chair and noticed that one man in civvies was ready to record everything on a laptop. The chair was hard and uncomfortable. I tried to sit on my hands from time to time.

"Your full name?"

"Musa Benjamin Craig."

"Address? Names of adoptive parents? Date of adoption? Passport details?"

"My passport is in my room at the Hotel. I'm sure Mr. Langstaffe would be happy to bring it." How I would love to see Harry right now, I thought.

They ignored this and started to question me about my friend Musa. How did they know I had a pen-friend?

"We hear you have a friend in Jerusalem? How do you know him?"

"I met him nine years ago when I came to Jerusalem and he became a pen friend."

"What is his full name?"

"Umm.. Musa Yousef Kanafi, I think. I can't remember how to pronounce his surname as we email each other." They all laughed. "Ha, ha, kanafi is a sweet cake, not a name!" Then I remembered that Robbie and I had bought some kanafi just yesterday. I could still feel the sticky syrupy taste and cheesy base in my mouth. They told us it was necessary to eat it hot. It was good!

One of the soldiers spoke up. "We know this family. They are instigators of violence. Did you know Musa that Mr. Kanafani was in prison for hiding young Palestinian trouble makers in his shop?"

"No."

"Come now, Musa Craig, you must have known that we are watching you. Why would you befriend a family that sympathise with militants? Do you support the Palestinian insurrection?"

I decided to be honest. "I am Palestinian by birth, but I don't believe in armed struggle."

"But you believe in an independent Palestinian State?"

I hesitated. "Yes, of course."

They paused, writing down goodness knows what in Hebrew and then they handed me a paper to sign.

"I do not read Hebrew. I cannot sign this."

"It is only a statement of what you have told us."

I shook my head. How could I trust them? One of the soldiers came close to striking me with the butt of his gun but the commander stopped him. After conferring with each other, they decided not to force me to sign.

Mr. big man leaned forward: "Now then, Musa, did your adoptive mother tell you why and how she took you from here?"

"Yes, Sir."

"Why did she give you an Arabic name?"

"There was a note pinned to my baby shawl which said in Arabic '*Ismee Musa*'. I still have that note but it is in my wallet at the hotel."

"Well, did she tell you where she found you?"

"Yes, Sir."

"Well, Musa I want you to tell us the full story. Take your time. Let's start with the place where they found you. Where was that?"

Thinking of Mum, I burst into tears.

Mr. big man spoke Hebrew to his assistants and one of them brought me a cup of water. Then there was silence while they waited for me to control my sobbing. Here was I, a confident young man who had been showing off some of the holy sites to Robbie and boasting about my knowledge of Jerusalem, reduced to a snivelling, frightened little boy. Meanwhile, Mr. big man sat back in his padded swivel chair with his arms folded. I did not look at his face.

After a while I managed to control myself.

"I do not know anything about my birth, but my mother told me that they found me by a brook in a village just outside Ramallah. My mother is Jewish, you see (would that help, I wondered, but they probably knew

341

already) and she was staying on a settlement with an Israeli couple who were friends."

"What was the name of these friends?" Mr. big man interrupted.

"Mr and Mrs Amos Steiner."

"Go on, Musa."

"They looked around for someone who might be related to me and they asked everyone in the village, but no-one knew anything. So they took me to Jerusalem and asked some Italian nuns. They then took me to Bethlehem and left me in a hospital there, but the Doctor told them I needed a heart operation. So when I was six months old my mother came back to Bethlehem and took me to London, where eventually I was adopted." Why do they need to know all of this? I asked myself.

"Did you have the heart operation?"

"Yes, in London, but of course I don't remember anything."

"Good, Musa. Can you remember the name of the doctor in Bethlehem? He would have your records, I suppose?"

"I don't know his name. My mother might remember."

"How is your heart now? Are you strong physically?"

"Oh yes, I'm fine now."

"Good."

The commander spoke at length to his aides in Hebrew and then he said: "You can go back to your room now."

"Can my friends visit me?" I spoke hesitatingly.

"No, not yet, but you are allowed a two minute phone call. Who do you want to call?"

"Harry, er… Mr. Langstaffe."

"What's his mobile number?"

"Oh, I can't remember. It's in my notebook at the Hotel."

"Oh too bad!" he sneered.

I was taken back to my room under guard and given a prison uniform instead of my trousers and shirt. I was embarrassed to undress in front of the guard and my underwear was already wet with perspiration. It seems I will have to wear those day and night. The uniform was like a plumber's all in one suit in a kind of dull brown. I sat on the bed and waited for lunch which was some kind of vegetable stew with rice and a small piece of meat. Was it chicken? I was not allowed to mix with the other prisoners, but occasionally I saw glimpses of them when I was walked along the corridors. They

343

were all wearing the same uniform. Why? Why? Am I a prisoner like them? What crime have I committed?

The next day someone brought me a pad of writing paper and pen, also reading material. I had to chuckle when I saw what they had brought, but it was probably the only stuff they had in English in their 'library'. One was an English phrase book for Israeli tourists visiting London. The other was a slim paper back of romantic fiction that was so erotic it was borderline pornographic! It made me squirm with sexual fantasies. Anyway it relieved the boredom until I got bored with it. At least I had some paper and a pen to write my thoughts down. I started to write a kind of diary but the days were all the same and nothing of note was happening. So I wrote some personal thoughts down, a kind of memoirs of musings… the family, Mum especially…sorry Mum for calling you a dim-wit, a stick-insect, a fuss-pot. You are the best cook in the world, especially when it comes to making cakes and pies. My mouth started watering thinking of those raspberry sponges and chocolate chip cookies. Usually cakes for her ladies' circles or charity coffees. I thought of Grandpa Ben, such a diminutive big bellied old man yet the dearest Grandpa in the world…he loves the internet and taught himself with a book called 'Computers for Dummies'…I love him…and he's a Jew! But Mum certainly didn't get her beauty from you! Robbie, my best friend yet so different, music my passion and Jessie my heart-throb…I would write something and then cross it all out again. I didn't want anyone else to read it. Perhaps I should write letters but would they ever reach their destination? The minutes ticked by (I still had my watch on, fortunately), then the hours and the days.

I began looking at some Arabic scribbles on the wall and watching ants and cockroaches scuttling about. I played a kind of game with myself by comparing the tiles of the floor. They were of a motley grey colour like ink smudges but if I stared at them, I could see faces in the design, some with very long noses, some with big ears, some with skinny cheeks and so on. Sometimes, I tried to draw them on paper. It amused me and passed the time.

When can I go home and why am I here? I grew tired of asking the same questions to the guards. There was never any answer and the commander did not come every day.

The only clue he had given me was: "Musa, be patient, we are trying to locate someone." Who the someone was they wouldn't tell me.

I was sure that Harry was trying to investigate but I desperately wanted to know if he knew where I was or what the Consulate had told him. He must have felt bad since he was responsible for me and Louise had promised Mum that she would take care of me. But I had no idea what was going on outside of my four walls. Only the sun rose every morning and set every evening. I had been told that the Israelis were a law unto themselves. If they don't implement or even respect the hundreds of United Nations Resolutions I figured, why would they listen to local Consular representatives? I had read about the many UN resolutions concerning returning occupied land to the Palestinians and about the return of the refugees; about using illegal weapons; about imprisoning children (I am one!) and so many other justice issues.

Everything in this world has to come to an end, I said to myself. All life has a beginning and an ending. This situation *will* come to an end, but how long? I recalled all the questions and my answers. Yes, I certainly did believe the Palestinians needed freedom and justice to rule themselves. Now I could understand what freedom really means. In England, people have no idea. It is a free country.

I also thought a lot about God and decided to pray. I discovered that prayer helped to keep me calm and brought a sense of peace.

On the sixth morning, I felt tired. Tired of having nothing to do, tired of not knowing anything, tired of banging my fists on the bed, tired of being so utterly helpless. Should I try kicking the door or yelling swear words? What good would that do? I ate my lunch and was dozing when I heard the guard announce *'Mifaked'*. I discovered this is Hebrew for commanding officer. It was the big man again, who suddenly barged into my room. I hadn't even heard the turn of the lock.

"Musa, what would you say if I told you that your real father is a terrorist? Would you still want to meet him? If so, prepare yourself now!"

CHAPTER TWENTY THREE

The commander, Mr. big man, stood in the doorway of my room filling the frame.

"Musa, put on your own clothes and come with me now."

I saw utter contempt in his facial expression, the corners of his mouth turned down but his chin up as if he despised me. He watched me button up my shirt, my hands shaking.

"You're kidding me, aren't you? Why are you torturing me?"

"No Musa. You are going to meet your father."

My whole body was trembling, my mind numb. Was this how I was going to meet my father? In a prison? Maybe this was all some kind of trick? I still did not believe and felt like I was being marched to my execution. My imagination was working overtime as I looked for clues of instruments of torture. We entered a room just big enough for two chairs and a small table but without any windows. There was a bright electric light and cameras hung from the ceiling. I imagined this to be a solitary interrogation room.

"Sit down," he ordered, gruffly.

I sat down anxiously, feeling my pulse quicken, my chest tighten and waited. The commander left me, shutting the door. If this is real, how will we communicate? I don't suppose he speaks English and my Arabic is only rudimentary.

About ten minutes later, spent playing with my hands, clasping and unclasping them, a man limped in. He had dark curly hair, peppered with grey, and a small moustache. As I stood up, I noticed he was slightly shorter than me. We were left alone and I heard the door lock click. We both sat down with the table in between as we studied each other, our mouths slightly open but without a word. I noticed he wore glasses and he rubbed his thigh as he sat down. He wore plain grey trousers and a white shirt unbuttoned at the neck. His hair was neatly combed back with a parting each side. I was conscious that my hair was uncombed, but his parting was the same as mine!

"*Marhaba*," I ventured. I knew the Arabic word for 'Hello.'

"*Marhaba* Musa," He reached for a handkerchief as he took off his glasses to wipe a tear away.

"My name is Abdullah, but would you like to call me Baba?" He reached out for my hand across the table.

"Yes, Baba, I would." I knew that Baba was Arabic for Dad. Was this really my Dad? I didn't know he existed before this minute, and now he is acknowledging me as his son. How? He certainly didn't look like a terrorist. I could see his lips quivering and his chest heaving, almost holding his breath, his eyes damp but trying not to cry. He still held on to my hand and squeezed it.

There was a pause as I watched him square up his shoulders and take a deep breath. "Musa, I guess you are just as surprised as I am. I didn't know you existed until this morning."

"Neither did I…Can this be true?"

"I will try to explain but it's still a mystery."

"Wow! Baba, you speak good English!"

"Yani, I've studied you know.' He paused. "Musa, the army came to my house this morning and I knew they were Israeli soldiers, but no uniforms. I thought, no, not again. Are they going to arrest me again? Instead the officer said he had some good news for me. Well, why would the Israeli army bring good news, I asked myself. They are nothing but bad news! They showed me a photograph of a young man. They said: 'Do you know this boy'? I looked at the photo and shook my head. 'No', I said."

"Well?" I was watching him shake his head and then his face creased into a smile, his eyes crinkling.

"You see, *yani*, I thought they wanted me to give them a name, so they could arrest the boy. But even if I had known the face, I would never have said so. They told me to look closer. 'This is your son, Musa,' they said. 'I don't have a son', I said. I couldn't believe it, until they explained. Then they took me in their car and brought me to Jerusalem. People in the Camp were looking at me thinking I was being arrested again."

"My God, *again*, you say. You have been arrested before?" Was it true what the big man had told me, my father a terrorist? '*Camp,*' what does he mean?

"Yes, I have been arrested before. *Nushkur Allah*, Thank God I am alive!"

So many things I didn't understand. My brows creased with questions.

"Go on," I said.

"You see, Musa, I live in a refugee camp in Ramallah. I was afraid that it all might be a trick and kept wondering where they were taking me. But it wasn't a trick because here I am meeting you!"

He paused, as I tried to absorb it all. "How did they know?" was all I managed to stutter.

"You want to know how? Well, you see when you arrived at the airport one of the security girls told her senior officer that you looked like one of the photos in their computer album of Palestinian trouble makers. Then your passport stated that you were born in Ramallah but you had no record of your real parents. My picture is one of those on their computer list. You see, *Allah,* I have been in prison for almost fifteen years and only came out six months ago."

"No! that's almost as long as my lifetime. How did you survive? And how could they prove that we are related?" I exclaimed, shaking my head with disbelief.

He leaned across the table until our faces almost touched and looked into my eyes. "You see, *yani*, they took away your hairbrush and removed some hairs. Then, they sent them away for DNA testing. It seems that it matched almost one hundred per cent with my DNA, which of course, they had on a file. So there you are Musa. You are my son!"

I could not believe it. Was I dreaming? "Wow! Where did they get my picture they showed you from?"

"From your passport, or maybe they took a photo of you when you were at the airport without you noticing."

"That means that they didn't need any of my passport information, when they were questioning me here?"

"No, of course not. They don't need to ask any questions about your identity. They know everything."

"But, how come you didn't know about my existence?" He paused to catch his breath and wiped his glasses. "You see, I was told you died at birth." He moved his chair to my side of the table until our shoulders were touching and he held on to both my hands. "Amira…that's your mother's name. She and I were both studying at the University just outside Ramallah. She was only eighteen and in her first year. I was twenty and in my third year. Oh Musa, she was so lovely, so full of life. It was a case of love at first sight." He let go of my hands to touch his heart, his voice breaking. I kept silent waiting for him to continue.

"We used to meet in the library or the cafeteria. I couldn't get her out of my mind. We met secretly in a friend's empty house and we made love. But, *yani*, only a few times. After the last time, I never saw her again. The Israelis closed the university for almost a year because of the intifada and blocked all the roads. I was afraid to telephone her because she had not told her family about me. So I didn't even know she was pregnant."

"Amira, Amira, my mother's name *is* Amira!"

"*Was.* When the university opened again, I asked a friend of Amira's where she was. This friend started to cry when I mentioned her name. 'Didn't you know?' she had said. *Allah!* She told me that Amira had had a baby boy at home, helped I think by a local woman for the birth, but that on the fourth day she had a bad complication. Much bleeding, she said. Amira's brother tried to take her to the hospital, but the Israeli soldiers blocked the road. In fact, there was a curfew all over the town, so nobody could leave their home not even for medical emergencies and soldiers would shoot at the ambulances."

"No!" I gasped, my hand over my mouth. "How terrible!"

Here he paused again and I could see he was biting his lip as if trying to hold back tears.

"So what happened?"

"She died," he whispered, gulping.

"No, God! She's dead? My mother's dead?" I covered my face with one hand and held on to Baba with the other. We were both crying, quietly, the tears

354

streaming down our faces. Baba buried his head in my shoulder.

"Yes, my beautiful Amira. She had such a pretty little mouth but large dark eyes, like you, Musa. She was too young to die. I couldn't speak to anyone for days. What's more she told me that the baby had died too. *Allah!* what a shock to hear you are alive and I have a son!"

"I would be dead if Mum hadn't found me," I said, suddenly realising that's what David had said about how I could have died if they had left me."

"Tell me Musa about the woman you call Mum. I want to know all about where and how you were found?"

"My adoptive mother, Mum, found me by a brook just outside a village near Ramallah. I was wrapped in a knitted shawl and there was a note pinned to it which said '*Ismee Musa*'. Of course she couldn't read the Arabic words but she was told what it meant. Those are the first two words of Arabic that I learned. She told me that my father, whom I call David, knocked on every door in the village to ask if they knew anything about me, but nobody knew. They took me to a hospital in Bethlehem where the doctor told them I needed a heart operation. Then later that year, Mum came back to

355

Bethlehem and took me to London for surgery. They adopted me because my Mum said she really loved me from when she first saw me."

"*Al hamdolillah*, God be praised, your Mum must be very special. I don't suppose, *yani*, that she kept that knitted shawl?"

"Yes, she did. She has often wondered who knitted it."

"Amira must have made it. She was clever in all sorts of ways. How I would love to touch it! It's the only thing left of Amira." His face creased into a big smile.

"Baba, you will one day, I promise. Yes, my Mum is someone special." I paused, worried how I could tell him.

"My Mum is Jewish you know. Do you hate the Jews?" I lowered my voice to a whisper avoiding his eyes.

Baba lifted up my chin. "Look at me, Musa, I don't hate Jews. I only hate what the Israelis are doing to the Palestinian people."

"My Mum knows all about that too and she would agree with you," I sighed, relieved, then continued: "She is not religious and she understands all about the suffering of the Palestinian people. She was staying on a Jewish settlement when she found me, but now that she understands the situation, she is against the settlements."

"That is remarkable. Fortunately, there are a few Jews who are like your Mum but I wish more would speak out."

"What religion are you, Baba?"

"I am Muslim as all my family, of course. But your mother was a Christian and that's why we knew that our families would never agree to our marriage."

"I would like to be a Christian. In fact the nuns in Bethlehem baptised me as a baby, because I was not well, and no-one knew who my parents were."

Musa, religion can cause problems which is a pity. Amira knew that our deep love for each other was really without a future. Her family would never agree to their daughter joining my family. *Yani*, it is generally not accepted"

I just had to interrupt. I needed to know. "What does *yani* mean?"

Baba chuckled. "It means, 'you see' or 'it means' or many other things. It's a very useful little Arabic word.

"Like we say 'Well' at the beginning of speech?"

"Well, something like that, I suppose." We both smiled.

All this time, I was sitting studying his face, watching his every expression, his dimpled smile, the movement of his eyebrows and eyes, his quivering moustache and trembling lips. He had the same shaped nose as me, with a slight hump in the middle. Some people say it is a Jewish nose and after all Jews and Arabs go back to the same roots, I'm told. His hair the same parting, his fingers long and thin like mine…All these thoughts were racing through my mind, as I tried to take it all in.

"Baba, does it bother you me being a Christian? I suppose I should be a Muslim like you?"

"No, *ibnee,* my son. It makes no difference at all. I have friends who are Christians and admire their faith."

After a pause I asked him: "Why did it take them six days to find you?"

"Who knows? They know where I live. They didn't have to go looking for me. Maybe they had to verify the DNA tests or maybe they just wanted to monitor your behaviour."

"You don't look like a terrorist!"

"Is that what they said about me?" He laughed out loud at this and I had to laugh with him. It felt like the bursting of a balloon.

Do you want to tell me why you were in prison?"

"Not now, I will talk another time about that. This is not the time or the place."

I simply nodded.

"Now my dear boy, we have sixteen years to catch up on. I expect the army will take me back to my home as I am not really allowed into Jerusalem. I live with my mother, brothers and sister in a refugee camp on the outskirts of Ramallah. My father was killed, you see."

"How?"

"It was during a curfew. He was walking in the street trying to find a shop to buy a gas cylinder. We had run out of gas for cooking. They just shot him in cold blood."

"How terrible! Your family have suffered so much. I have lived such a comfortable life. It's just not fair!"

"Musa, I'm glad you have been spared."

"Tell me, Baba, about my mother's family?"

"Amira's father was in prison, just because he belonged to a certain political party and her mother had died young, so she was only living with a brother when you were born."

"Then her brother is my Uncle. What's his name?"

"I think it was Tariq. I'm not sure. I have never spoken to him because he would blame me for Amira's pregnancy and death."

"But he would be the one who left me in the village by the brook, d'you think?"

"Yes, probably. He abandoned you, but at least he protected his sister when she was carrying you. That is a small miracle. Some girls are killed if they are not married."

"Wow, so much to think about."

"Here you are Musa, the biggest miracle of all. My life will never be the same. I have a son!"

"And I have a father!"

There was so much more that I wanted to know but I felt physically and emotionally exhausted. My legs felt quite weak and my head dizzy. It was too much all at once. I still couldn't quite believe that I had met my real father and now I understood why he did not know anything about me either. David has been a father-figure to me but Abdullah is my real Abuee. Wow, it's all mind blowing!

"Baba, you must be wondering what kind of a boy I am." I rubbed my chin and felt the stubble. "Right now, I feel very scruffy and dirty because they have kept me here for six days and I haven't had a shower. I must stink!"

"Mah-lish, never mind. It's not important."

"And my family don't even know where I am. Tell me this is all just a dream and I shall soon wake up!"

"No, Musa, you're not dreaming." He grabbed hold of both my arms and shook them. Then he gave me a broad smile and chuckled.

"Oh Baba… I have so much more to ask you and to tell you about my life. And I want to hear all about your family and your life."

"Musa, I'm lost for words too. This has been the biggest shock of my life. Forgive my tears. There are so many memories flooding back of my time with your dear mother that I had pushed out of my mind. She was so kind and so sensitive. I could never have imagined that she gave me a son. But we will see each other again. How long are you in Jerusalem?"

"Another two weeks, I think."

We both stood up and clung to each other. We were not strangers any more and I felt as if my life had suddenly come together. We clung to each other. Neither of us wanted to let go. There was so much to catch up on.

The door suddenly burst open. Mr. big man stood there, his hands on his hips.

"Well, have you two got acquainted? Like father, like son, eh! Will you be following in your father's footsteps, Musa?" He laughed cynically.

"Abdullah, get in the jeep, we will take you as far as the checkpoint. And Musa, your taxi is waiting for you to go back to the hotel."

Baba handed me a slip of paper with his telephone number and email address, as we said goodbye. "Call me soon," were his last words.

I arrived at the hotel just before evening dinner and everyone was making their way into the dining room. I felt very dirty and was conscious that my clothes stank. Robbie spotted me and called out to me, but it was my Mum's pained face I saw first.

CHAPTER TWENTY FOUR

Robbie screamed and everyone came running. He gave me a bear hug first, then my Mum pushed through and enveloped me. I brushed my hands over her damp face, "Mum you're here!"

"Darling, are you OK?" She was all choked up as she put her hand to my stubbly chin.

"I feel like a tramp," I said, somehow managing to pull myself away from her embrace. "Let me first go and have a shower. I'm not fit to meet anyone now."

Robbie threw me the key to our room. "We'll wait for you in the dining room."

"I'll join you when I'm more presentable. Then I'll tell you all about it."

I had only been away for six days but it felt like six years. I was completely disorientated. I revelled in the shower, scrubbing myself with scented soap and singing with joy. Fancy Mum coming all the way to Jerusalem! I did not expect to see her here and was wondering what she is going to say about my meeting my father. I have to reassure her that she is still my mother.

Returning downstairs, I asked her when she got here. "I got on the next plane to Tel Aviv, after I got the phone call from Harry to say you had been taken away by the police. He didn't want to use the word arrest. I couldn't for the life of me think what trouble you had got yourself into after only four days. Whatever happened?"

"Why don't we all leave the poor boy to eat!?" said Harry.

The others left to sit in the lobby but Mum still hovered over me, telling the waiter to look after me and ordering steak and chips. She knows what I like. I had to smile! The waiter started filling up the table with small dishes of lemony Arabic salads such as humus, fried aubergine, mushrooms in tahini sauce, parsley and mint tabouli with olive oil and a basket of fresh warm pitta bread, tasting of heaven! I was already full when they brought me steak and chips but I managed to eat chocolate ice-cream as well. What a feast! I must have appeared rude and greedy the way I was stuffing myself!

I could hear quiet piano music in the background, becoming louder as if someone was darting up and down the keys in an excitable arpeggio rhythm. That sounds like Robbie! I thought. He finished with a flourish and ran towards me bowing like a pro. We all laughed and clapped.

Afterwards we all sat together in the lobby, waiting for my story.

"Shall I start at the beginning or tell you the end?"

"Both!" shouted Robbie.

"Well, in a nutshell, I've finally found out who I am! But first of all, I was kidnapped by a giant who put me in a tiny cell… crawling cockroaches for company and only rice and broth to eat. I had guns to my head and was shivering with fright."

I looked at their faces. I could see Mum with her mouth open, but it was Robbie who was the first to respond.

"That's a fairy story. You're kidding, of course," he said, giggling.

"No, I'm not joking. It's true. I had no idea why they were keeping me in a prison cell until this morning. I asked questions for six days but the giant man refused to tell me, that is, until today. They took me to a small room where they interrogate prisoners and there I met my real father, Baba Abdullah."

"How could they know it was your real father?" asked Mum, her brow furrowed with worry.

"At the airport they suspected I was related to a Palestinian man known to them so they took some hairs from my brush and tested them for DNA. It matched my father's."

"Was he a prisoner?"

"He was, but not now. You see, he was in university and fell in love with a girl, also a student. When the university closed during the intifada, he didn't see her again."

"Go on," urged Mum.

"A year later he was told she had had a baby and that both she and the baby had died... I am that baby but I am alive! Baba...that means Dad, said that she had probably knitted the shawl you found me in."

Mum squeezed my hand. "I really don't know what to say, except that my mind is going back to that day when I found you, wrapped in that shawl. You say your mother knitted it and now she is dead? How terribly sad."

"I'm sad too, that I never met my real mother but I wouldn't be here today if you hadn't picked me up, Mum.

Louise was dabbing her eyes with a handkerchief. "That's more amazing than any soppy story on the TV. I've never heard anything like it."

"Wow, wow, wow," was all Robbie could utter.

"Gosh! Unbelievable. We have to celebrate," shouted Harry. He ordered a bottle of champagne. They made me feel like a celebrity who had won the lottery. I didn't deserve any such glory. Actually, as we were clinking glasses, I didn't really feel we had anything to toast in drink. To know that I have a real family might complicate my future.

"The British Consul did his best to make contact with you but it seems the Israelis weren't going to co-operate." said Harry.

"Yes, we tried everything," added Mum. "I contacted Cassia and she called her friends. I even rang Amos. Remember I told you about him where we stayed in that settlement? Nobody could help. They all just said we have to wait. You don't know how sick I've been worrying about you."

"I know how you must have felt, Mum."

I was sitting down, relaxed, and she was standing over me, like a mother hen trying to protect me with her wings! "You'll be the death of me, but I still love you!"

she said, not knowing whether to laugh or cry as she sat down and hugged me again. I attempted to distance myself from her emotional clinginess in front of everyone. I could not imagine Louise clinging to Robbie. At the same time, I realised that Mum was probably feeling a little insecure at this revelation. Was she going to lose me now to another family were probably thoughts going through her mind. I had to reassure her that she was still my Mum.

"Calm down, for goodness sake Mum. Nothing has changed. I am still your son!"

"Bless you, darling," was all she could say, blowing her nose.

"Remember that letter you had years ago from John's mother? Her prophecy came true. Didn't she say I would bring you 'devastating trouble'?"

"Oh, I'd forgotten about that. Fancy you remembering," Mum said. It made her laugh through her tears.

There were other guests at the hotel who were witnessing this big family drama unfold. They probably thought the prodigal son had returned from a far country and that's just how I felt. Many smiling faces were turned towards us.

"How are David and Margaret?"

"They've been so worried," Mum replied. And you know what? Jessie came round and asked me to remind you of the secret little Arabic word. She said you would know what she meant."

I laughed. "Thanks. Go and give them a call."

She went over to the reception desk and I watched as she made the call, then we all went back to our rooms.

Robbie started to bombard me with questions as we sat on our beds.

"What's your real father like?"

"Like me I guess! Only he walks with a limp, don't know why. He hasn't told me everything."

"And what was your mother's name?"

"Amira. She was only eighteen."

"Wow, that's too young to die." Robbie paused; his head bowed thinking, and then lightened up.

"Did you really have a room full of cockroaches?"

"The floor and walls were black with them …even in my soup…" I joked.

"Go on…" He pushed me down, punching me playfully. "Tell me more…did you have anything to read?"

"Oooo! Girls…Sex…Porn!"

369

"You devil!"

There was a knock on the door. It was Harry. We had to quickly straighten up. He came in and sat on my bed with his arm round my shoulders.

"We are so thankful to have you back, Musa. What a story! Anyway, I wanted to tell you about a friend of mine in the orchestra. He can give you a teaching session on the drums, if you would like that? His name is Avram."

"That sounds great. Boy! I would love that. I've missed some of the concerts. How have they been going?"

"Wonderful…" He was interrupted by a call on his mobile, which he answered, then turned to me again. "It's confirmed. Tomorrow afternoon we will be in Ramallah in the hall of the Friends High School. How about telling your father to be there?" He jotted down the time and location while I fished out the scrap of paper with Baba's number.

Borrowing Robbie's mobile, I dialled the number in Ramallah. An elderly female voice answered.

"Is Abdullah there?" I asked.

"No," then some words in Arabic which I didn't understand. She put the phone down.

I thought I would try again later, but after a few minutes, I heard some piano music. It was Robbie's mobile. "For you," he said, handing me the phone.

"Musa?"

"Yes, Baba it's me."

"I got your number after my mother put down the phone," he said.

We talked for some time. I told him about the concert in Ramallah and had to explain about my friends. This was something I had not told him about in the prison room.

"Musa, *Inshallah*, God willing, I hope to be at the concert but my family want to invite you to our home for a celebration meal. When can you come?"

"Baba, my Mum came to look for me in Jerusalem so she is here too."

"That's great," he said. "And bring Robbie with you too. I will tell you how to get to the checkpoint and I will meet you on the other side. Hopefully, I will explain everything when I see you at the concert."

The next day in the afternoon a coach arrived at the hotel with all the members of the orchestra and their instruments. In fact, there were so many instruments of one sort and another that they had to hire a van as well.

371

As Harry explained in some of the other venues, there was already a full set of drums and sounding board, but for Ramallah they had to take everything.

"Musa, come here," beckoned Harry. "I want you to meet Avram."

A middle-aged man with dark complexion and deep-set eyes, almost hidden under thick bushy eyebrows, extended his hand. "Delighted to meet you, Musa."

"I'm happy to meet you too." He gave me a firm handshake and took my arm as we stepped up into the coach, then sat down beside me. I noticed Robbie had already struck up a friendship with a blond flutist and Mum was sitting with Louise, chatting away.

"I've heard so much about you, but I want to know more," said Avram. "I am Jewish but very involved with groups who seek justice for the Palestinians. I am persecuted for my anti-Zionist stand."

We talked non-stop all the way to Ramallah. I was so eager to hear more of his activities and also to have his promised session on the drums. In turn he wanted to know all about my background.

"Musa, if you are in any trouble, just get in touch." He gave me his business card, which had his name and address in English on one side and Hebrew on the other. 'Jews for Justice,' was the name of the group.

Half-way to Ramallah, we were stopped at a checkpoint, but as we were tourists we did not have to get down. Instead an armed Israeli officer came on the bus and checked each individual passport.

The Concert was in a school hall, not as grand as the venues in West Jerusalem. I noticed the stage was smaller and the red velvet curtains much faded, the metal chairs linked together in rows but not upholstered.

"Not half as posh as Jerusalem," observed Robbie.

"Of course not, this is occupied territory, but here I am in Ramallah. Robbie I was born here!"

"Wow…" he said, as we caught up with Mum and decided to go for a walk around.

We had plenty of time while the orchestra were setting up their instruments and rehearsing. Even in central London I hadn't seen so many people crammed on to the pavements. Many were walking in the roads as there was hardly room, with cars lined up somehow trying to avoid the people and the potholes. Smart city business men in Western-styled suits mingled with village men in their long dish-dashes and black and white chequered kaffiyas; some women who were completely covered up and carrying babies brushed alongside girls in short skirts and blouses. And parking was utterly chaotic! Everyone seemed to be in a hurry, as we wandered round the streets looking at all the fancy dresses, multicoloured scarves, electrical goods, and coffee shops. Then there were several small booths where they were selling roasting meat on a kind of drum.

Robbie was intrigued by the revolving spit. He pointed to the meat. "Camel?"

The man laughed. "No, not camel, goat! *Shawrameh,* he said, handing him a sandwich full of onions and meat. Others were frying falafel out on the street and putting it into pitta sandwiches with pickles and a spicy sesame sauce. They smelt so temptingly delicious Mum and I bought some sandwiches for ourselves, while Robbie had the meat. The tastes were all foreign to Robbie but to Mum they were familiar from her times in Jerusalem. I tried out some of my Arabic on the shopkeepers, *"Keif Halkum?"* (How are you all?)

"Al hamdulillah, Fine, thank God. Speak Arabic?"

"Shwei (a little), I said. Everyone was so friendly and helpful.

We also noticed lots of war damage to buildings, some of the metal shop signs were rusty and hanging by a piece of wire, while other stores had bullet holes in the brickwork, windows were boarded up, and trashed cars were piled up on top of each other at the roadside, like an elaborate symbolic sculpture. I sensed Mum's fear as she tried to hold on to my arm several times, but I shook her off. "I don't want you kidnapped again," she said.

"Don't be ridiculous," I shivered at the memory.

Mum was admiring some silk scarves and made a comment about her experience in Bethlehem. The shopkeeper, who spoke good English, picked up on our conversation and told us that the Israeli army come into the town anytime they feel like it, fully armed, of course.

"They barge into the town like conquering warriors, flying the blue and white Israeli flag," he said, waving his arms around. "They never give any warning and people have to scatter into shops or doorways. Sometimes they use their armoured vehicles to crush any private cars parked on the side of the road."

"Yes, like they did in Bethlehem, but that was sixteen years ago. I thought the intifada was over now?" Mum commented.

"It is, but we are still under occupation."

Mum still had her eye on the scarf and decided to buy it. It was white with streaks of red and pink in a kind of zigzag design. When we left the shop, Mum recounted to Robbie the story of the boy shot in Bethlehem.

"You see this scarf, it reminds me. The poor mother was wiping his blood with her hair," she said. I had heard this story before, but I could tell that Robbie was visibly shocked by the way he went silent.

The concert was magical but I wasn't giving the music my full attention as I was anxiously scanning the audience time and again to look for my father. Eventually I found him during the interval. He was reticent to greet me enthusiastically in a public place, and I could tell he was a little embarrassed. Maybe the concert audience were not the usual crowd he associated with. After the first part of the show we were able to meet in a quiet corner of the school courtyard.

"Meet Baba Abdullah," I announced to Mum and Robbie.

Mum shook his hand. "Glad to meet you at last."

376

"I have to thank you for raising my son; er…can I call you Um Musa?"

"My name is Rosa, but if you like I can be Um Musa."

They gave each other a huge smile.

"My mother will be so happy to meet you, Musa. As you can imagine it is a big shock for all the family to know I have a son. They will need time to get used to the idea. In fact my brothers still do not believe me."

"Baba, I don't want to be an embarrassment."

Baba patted me on the shoulder. "No you won't be. Now let me explain how we can meet up tomorrow at the checkpoint. You will take a service taxi from Damascus Gate to Kalandia, follow the crowd to cross over and I will meet you. Can you be there by midday, tomorrow? Is that OK Um Musa?

"Are you inviting me, too?"

"Of course, and Robbie too."

"We'd love to. Thanks. By the way, what do I call you?" asked Mum.

"You can call me Abu Musa if you like, but that might sound strange, so just call me Abdullah. My mother is known as Um Abdullah."

After talking for a while, Baba waved us goodbye as we returned to the Hall for the second half of the concert.

At the end of the concert, there was thunderous applause and some speeches. The members of the orchestra and ourselves were then taken to a very grand restaurant in a residential part of the city. The waiters were all in smart black and white uniforms and the tables laid with gleaming cutlery and blue check serviettes. From the windows we could see a different view of Ramallah, huge apartment blocks built out of white stone and beautiful villas with gardens.

"You see that cluster of houses with red roofs on the hill not far away? See how different they are from these houses in Ramallah?" said Avram, who was sitting with us and explaining everything. "That's a Jewish settlement, on land stolen from Palestinians."

"Yes, we can see that," commented Robbie.

"How can they live surrounded by guards and barbed wire?" Mum said. She felt free to talk. "I know how intimidated I felt all those years ago. But, then again, if I hadn't gone to stay on a settlement Musa wouldn't be sitting here now. I suppose you've heard his story?"

"Yes, indeed Rosa, I am full of admiration for you and your husband."

It had been an exhausting two days and I quickly fell asleep on the bus returning to Jerusalem.

The following day, the three of us boarded a service taxi at the Damascus Gate to make our own way to Ramallah. We had to get out and cross over by foot at the checkpoint. A bunch of young Israeli soldiers manned the checkpoint and looked at our passports. They had their rifles pointing at the people as if ready to shoot at any disturbance. We could see by the long lines of commuters going the other way, that going back to Jerusalem would not be so easy.

"But look at the soldiers in the watchtowers with their guns pointing at us," said Robbie, ducking his head and eager to move on.

"You think ducking your head will make you less obvious!" I giggled, slapping him on the back. "See that wall. That's what the Israelis call the Security Barrier, but what the Arabs call the Apartheid Wall."

"It certainly is scary," Mum said. "Years ago, when we came before, there was no wall." The Wall, as everybody called it, was covered in drawings and graffiti, 'Make peace not war' and 'The wall must fall'.

It was then, that I spotted my father, trying to attract our attention in the middle of a crowd.

My father greeted us and took us in a taxi to the refugee camp, which was only a short distance away. Here again was another contrasting scene. Small box-like concrete houses, crammed together in a tiny space with only dirt roads, open gutters for sanitation, rubbish everywhere and scores of ragged children playing, a real shanty town. A crowd of little boys followed us shouting *'Yahood, yahood* (Jew) and I realised that Robbie with his blond complexion stood out as a foreigner. "See, now you're the one being singled out!" I told him, laughing.

Baba rebuked the kids, *"Imshi,"* (go away), he shouted. But Robbie took up the challenge when he saw a bunch of them trying to throw a ball into a rudimentary metal ring attached to a wall, supposedly a basket ball game. Being tall, it was easy for him to throw the ball into the ring, so the children cheered and clapped. Baba led us to one of the houses, and we stepped inside to a different world; spotlessly clean concrete floor covered with colourful striped rugs, a vase of flowers and a bowl overflowing with fruit of every kind. His mother, my grandmother, wore the typical Palestinian dress with her hair tied into a headscarf. She greeted us with hugs and Mum was enthusiastically kissed on both cheeks. Then she disappeared into the kitchen.

"*Ahlan Wa Sahlan*," said Baba. "That means you are very welcome. It is not a palace, but it is our family home."

"Thank you. You have a lovely home," said Mum, looking at the colourful embroidered cushions.

Baba picked up one of the cushions and gave it to her. "My mother does all the embroidery. You can keep that one."

"Oh no!" said Mum.

"I insist. She can do more cushions." (I later learned not to admire anything too much as in the Palestinian culture, they give it to you!)

"Is this a refugee camp? I thought camps were people living in tents?" Robbie asked. Robbie was really beginning to take an interest in the political scene, I noticed.

"We did live in tents in the early days when my father was a small boy. He came with his parents in 1948. They were turned out of their home in Lydda, that's near the Tel Aviv airport. They had to walk for three days across the hills to Ramallah. It's a long story,"

Baba sighed. "And now they build settlements on our land. Ramallah is surrounded by Jewish settlements." He illustrated with a broad sweep of his arms.

"We saw one of the settlements in the distance yesterday."

"Yes, Robbie, they always build them on top of the hills, looking down on the Arabs. They have pointy red roofs and every modern facility, even swimming pools, whereas we barely have enough water for our everyday life."

"Wow, that's so unfair." said Robbie as he went over to the small window to view the hills around.

At this point, Baba's mother and sister appeared carrying dishes of steaming food. I think it dawned on me for the first time that I have another big family, grandmother, auntie and uncles, which I have yet to meet. There wasn't a table big enough to sit round so we were all given individual small tables. Roast stuffed chickens, courgettes and grape leaves stuffed with rice and meat, potatoes with meat balls in a sesame sauce and salads of every kind. It was like nothing we had ever tasted and all scrumptious.

"Why don't you ask your mother to come and sit with us to chat? I'm sure Mum would love to talk with her," I said.

"Mother doesn't understand English. I think she is shy, but I will call her in and I will translate." He called my grandmother in from the kitchen and his younger sister, my Aunt Sumer, who was not much older than me. The older woman was dressed in the long traditional Palestinian dress, white with black and red embroidered panels down the front. My Aunt was dressed in jeans and a plain blue shirt, contrasting sharply with her mother. They were discussing food and recipes and seemed quite happy to share.

"My mother is telling you they stuff everything here: courgettes, vine leaves, carrots, potatoes, tomatoes, even they stuff people!" He laughed as he was translating how they core out the middle of vegetables and stuff them with rice, meat and spices. His sister spoke a little English. She was working in a clothing factory sewing jeans, as far as I could gather. We continued to chat for some time, then after the coffee we made moves to leave.

Baba went with us as far as the checkpoint. There was so much more I wanted to know. He whispered to me as we left, that next time alone he would tell me about prison.

CHAPTER TWENTY FIVE

My Mum had to fly back to England, naturally worrying about leaving me behind.

"Nothing's going to happen to me now, Mum. I shall be fine," I tried to reassure her, as she boarded the taxi to the airport, tearful to leave me. I gave her letters for Margaret and David and signed a postcard for Jessie 'with my love xxx.'

I stayed on and made several trips to Ramallah on my own. I was beginning to feel more confident, identifying myself as a Palestinian native. On one such visit, Baba took me to the University where he now worked and studied to complete his degree. We sat in the cafeteria, drinking coffee. I watched all the students coming and going, chatting and laughing together. It seemed as normal as any University in England. This was the place where he had met my mother and where he had heard a year later that she was dead.

"Now, my son, I can talk more freely of my time in prison. You see I became so angry after I learned of Amira's death that I joined a group of militants. You see, *yani,* we planned to ambush some Israeli army vehicles with homemade bombs, but of course we were overcome with the firepower of the soldiers. Two of my companions were killed and I was shot in the thigh. I expect you've noticed my limp, Musa?"

"Yes." My hand went to my mouth. I couldn't speak.

"Only one of the soldiers was slightly hurt. For that I was locked up for fifteen years."

I was gob smacked. "Oh Baba, that must have been terrible. You didn't actually kill anyone?"

"No, but the fact that we intended to was enough, I suppose. The first few years were hell. I was in constant pain, not only from my leg, but from the torture."

"My God! You were tortured, too?"

I watched his face and could understand the anger. His hands were constantly moving from rubbing his forehead, to massaging his thigh, to clasping his fists in his lap.

"Yes, but I don't want to think about it anymore. I realise that violence only creates more violence. It's a never ending circle. What's more, my whole family were punished. They demolished our home and they had to live again in a tent until they could build again."

"You mean the house you took us to is new?"

"Yes, my Uncle helped them to build again while I was in prison. Later my father was killed, just shot because he was walking in the town after curfew hours. I've already told you about that."

I could not believe all I was hearing and felt so humbled.

"Oh Baba, I thought six days in prison was an eternity. But fifteen years and tortured too. How have you survived?" I clutched my heart.

"You know they watch your every mood and behaviour. If you had started to scream, kicking at the door or assaulted the guards, it would have been much longer than six days. With me, I learnt to control my anger, otherwise I could still be locked up." He paused to drink his coffee. "Anyway, let's talk about happier things." He smiled and went to fetch me another piece of cake, while I just sat, bewildered, and speechless.

He scanned my face eagerly. "Come on, son, I want to hear all about your life. Tell me about your school. What do you want to do when you graduate?"

"I'm not so good at Science and Maths but I'm top in English and Literature so I hope to study Journalism. Also I play the drum in a band. I adore music, Baba. I

387

guess I like to make a noise! Sometimes it drives my Mum crazy." We laughed.

"You have plenty to write about now and I hope you will make a big noise about all that's going on here," he said, clapping his hands and slapping my thigh.

"Oh, I will, I will! They gave me paper and pen when I was in the prison cell. I can laugh about that now. I wrote down my thoughts every day, just to relieve the boredom. Come to think of it, I never returned to the room after meeting you, so they can read those personal jottings." I put my hand to my mouth. "Oh Hell!... Anyway, they treated me well in comparison with you Baba. You have suffered so much. You are amazing to have adjusted to normal life and be so cheerful."

"It was all worth it now, knowing what a fine son I have. And what a lovely Mum you have." He stared at me, smiling but with trembling lips. "You know you have most of my features, but you have Amira's big sparkling eyes."

"Did you fall in love with her eyes?"

"Yes, but she was altogether beautiful. I just can't believe that this is where we used to sit together, talking about our hopes for the future, but also our fears."

388

"It's all too much to take in." I said.

We just sat, looking at each other. He glanced at his watch. "Musa, I have a lecture to go to in a short while. If I put you in a taxi to Ramallah, will you be able to find your way back to Jerusalem?"

"Sure, I will and I will come again."

"Next time, I shall have time to show you all round the University"

On my return to the hotel, there was a message to say that Avram would pick me up the next morning at 10 am. I was excited and ready for him when he arrived in his car. He took me to his 'studio' which was a small room in an old building. It looked as if it had once been a warehouse.

"This used to be owned by Arabs," he said. "They had some kind of factory here but were turned out in 1948. For once the Israelis left it to go to ruin."

"I am learning so many new things," I said. He ushered me into his dilapidated but clean studio and sat me down in front of an array of drums, a huge timpani supported on a frame, a bowl-like bass drum and two smaller side drums. A piano stood in one corner of the room.

"Now then, Musa, if I play a tune on the piano, can you show me how much you know on the drums?"

I gasped. "I'll try," I uttered nervously, as I took up the sticks.

Avram was patient with me and took me into realms of drumming that I could only dream about. I was utterly thrilled.

The remaining days of my stay in Jerusalem alternated between drum sessions, evening concerts and days spent in Ramallah with my father.

~~~~~~~~~~~~~~~~~~~~~~~~~~~~~~~~~~~~~~~

Robbie and I packed our cases. We were due to fly back to London the following day. I had one last chance to visit Baba. He took me back to the University, about six miles from the city of Ramallah. We sat in the cafeteria, as before. This time we drank hot chocolate and I insisted on paying.

"What have you been doing, Musa?"

"I've been having drum lessons by an Israeli Jew. But he's different, Baba. He is against the Zionist policy and is active with his friends calling for an end to the occupation."

"Good for him! I wish there were more."

"So do I."

The more I sat with Baba, the more I felt a close kinship with him. But I wanted so much more to feel the deep pain that I could sense underlying his cheerfulness.

"You know, Musa, for once we have to thank the Israelis for their detective work in finding you." He gave me a broad smile. "Like your drummer friend not all Israelis are bad people. We are all human beings. Let's live together in peace."

"True, Baba."

We got up from the table and he greeted some of his friends, introducing me as his son. I think they thought he was joking.

"Abdullah, we didn't know you were married. *Mabruk!* Congratulations!" I noticed he winced as they slapped him hard on his shoulders. "Cheers! We can call you Abu Musa now." I didn't understand all the Arabic dialogue but could see that they were teasing him as they walked away, because they obviously didn't really believe him and they totally ignored me.

"Don't worry about them. My family believe me. It doesn't matter what others think. I have my beloved Amira back," he whispered.

He proudly showed me all the modern lecture rooms, theatre, laboratories and other facilities. They were as good as any in England.

"Baba, I wish you could visit me in London."

"I wish so too, but the British will never give me a visa with a prison record."

"Maybe, not now, but when I am eighteen I will work on a visa for you, as we can prove that you are my father. Perhaps I could come back to Palestine when I finish school to do some volunteer work?"

"Musa that would be great. We'll keep in touch by email. I shall want to know everything about your school, your family, everything, everything, do you hear me?"

"Yes, Baba."

"You are a good boy and I'm so proud of you."

Baba came to wave me goodbye at the checkpoint. We both cried openly on each other's shoulders. I felt overwhelmed with emotion as I had no idea when I would be in Jerusalem again.

I stood in line waiting for my turn to check my passport. There was a scuffle at the front and I could see one of the young soldiers knocking over an old man with the butt of his gun. The poor man was struggling to get back on his feet but the soldiers were calling him a stupid donkey in Arabic and cursing and then another soldier kicked him in his bottom and spat on him. Some of the other men tried to intervene, but were pushed back. I was so angry, I couldn't hold back. I have a British passport anyway, so they daren't hit me, I thought as I rushed forward, gently pushing one of the soldiers aside. I tried to grab the hands of the old man whose leg was bleeding and I could see that he was almost blind. There was a little boy by his side, probably his grandson, who was crying and shouting *'Seedy'* (Grandpa). Two of the soldiers approached me and grabbed me, roughly, each one by my arms. Before I could gather my senses, I was held down in the back of a van with rifles pointing at me.

"British, I'm British," I shouted angrily, but without fear.

"You are a Palestinian," came the soldier's retort, pushing me down with his hands on my face. I closed my eyes and had a brief vision of the giant man 'like father, like son' he was mocking.

Then I remembered Avram. His business card was in the inner pocket of my jacket.

Acknowledgments:

I wish to thank my daughters Susan and Hilary for their advice, encouragement and for their help in the editing process.
I also wish to thank Johanna Bertie, my agent in London, for her excellent guidance, patience and suggestions in the writing of this novel.

Patricia Rantisi.

Lightning Source UK Ltd.
Milton Keynes UK
UKOW051237090312

188659UK00001B/3/P